PRAISE FOR TIM PRATT

"Pratt's thoughtful worldbuilding, revealed little by little, continues to impress… This well-imagined universe, populated by original and empathetic characters, has enough energy to power what could become a long-lived series."

Publishers Weekly

"Brilliantly fun space opera that reminds me of Killjoys but with more Weird Alien Cool Shit."

Locus

"The engaging, inclusive, and entertaining Axiom series, may be his best work yet… witty, heartfelt sci-fi romp."

Tor.com

"Fun, funny, pacy, thought-provoking and very clever space opera – a breath of fresh air."

Sean Williams, author of *Twinmaker*

PRAISE FOR [illegible]

"[illegible]"

Publishers Weekly

"[illegible]"

[illegible]

"[illegible]"

[illegible]

"[illegible]"

[illegible]

BY THE SAME AUTHOR

THE AXIOM TRILOGY

The Wrong Stars

The Dreaming Stars

The Forbidden Stars

The Strange Adventures of Rangergirl

Briarpatch

Heirs of Grace

The Deep Woods

Blood Engines

Poison Sleep

Dead Reign

Spell Games

Bone Shop

Broken Mirrors

Grim Tides

Bride of Death

Lady of Misrule

Queen of Nothing

Closing Doors

Tim Pratt

DOORS OF SLEEP

ANGRY ROBOT
An imprint of Watkins Media Ltd

Unit 11, Shepperton House
89-93 Shepperton Road
London N1 3DF
UK

angryrobotbooks.com
twitter.com/angryrobotbooks
What's behind Door Number One?

An Angry Robot paperback original, 2021

Cover by Kieryn Tyler
Edited by Simon Spanton and Paul Simpson
Set in Meridien

ISBN 978 0 85766 874 5
Ebook ISBN 978 0 85766 875 2

Printed and bound in the United Kingdom by TJ Books.

9 8 7 6 5 4 3 2 1

For Liza & Daryl: fellow travelers

A Parting of the Ways • The What, If Not the Why • A Dark Sea • Enter Minna • [Unable to Translate] • Another Loss

I yawned – one of those bone-cracking yawns so immense it hurts your jaw and seems to realign the plates of your skull – and staggered against the bar. I was on the third level of the uppermost dome, where the mist sommelier, clad only in prismatic body glitter, puffed colored, hallucinogenic vapor from the pharmacopeia in their lungs directly into the open mouths of their patrons. I turned my face away before catching the overspill from the latest dose: a stream of brilliant green meant for a diminutive person covered in downy fur the same shade as the smoke. I didn't have much time left; sleep was coming for me, and I wanted to meet it in my right mind.

I stumbled down the ramps that spiraled through the glittering domes of the Dionysius Society, looking for Laini. The glowing bracelet on my wrist flashed different colors when I came into proximity with people I'd partied with during the preceding five days, and I followed the wine-red flash toward a cluster of dancers on a platform under dazzling dappled lights. Other partygoers bumped into me and jostled my battered old backpack, something everyone stared and laughed at here. In a post-scarcity pleasure dome, where anything you desired could be instantiated just by asking your implanted AI to produce it, the sight of someone actually carrying stuff was unprecedented. The locals had all decided I was an eccentric, or someone affecting eccentricity to stand out from the crowd. Standing out from the crowd was almost a competitive sport here.

The locals couldn't even imagine all the ways I *really* stood out. For one thing, I didn't have an implanted AI, something everyone in this world received in their gestation-pods. I didn't have local tech because I wasn't a local. I hadn't been a local any place I'd been for a very long time.

"Laini!" I shouted once I got close, and, though the music was loud, my voice was louder. Before I left home, swept away by forces I still don't understand, I was trained to mediate conflict, and while mostly I did that by speaking calmly, sometimes it helped to be the loudest person in the room. Laini's shoulders, bare in a filmy strapless gown the color of a cartoon sun, tensed up when I shouted – I'm trained to notice things like *that*, too – but she didn't turn around. She was pretending she couldn't hear me.

So. I'd been through this sort of thing before, but it never stopped hurting.

I pushed through the dancers – they were human, but many were altered, with decorative wings or stomping hooves or elaborate braids made of vines. In techno-utopian worlds, those things were as common as pierced ears or tattoos back home... though this place wasn't as utopian as some. In my week here I'd come to realize the aerial domes of the Dionysius Society were home to the perpetual youth of a ruling class floating above a decidedly dystopian world below. It was lucky Laini and I had awakened up here in the clouds. Anyone walking around in the domes was assumed to belong here, since there was no getting in past the guards and security measures from the outside.

Though if we *had* awakened below, with the dirt and the smoke and the depredations of "the Adverse," whatever those were, I probably wouldn't have lost Laini the way I was about to. I'd accidentally brought her to a world that was too good to leave.

I reached out and touched Laini's shoulder, and she turned, scowling at me, green eyes in a pinched face under short black hair. I was the whole reason she was here, and she clearly wished I would go away. I would leave – I had no choice – but I deserved a goodbye, at least, didn't I? I touched my borrowed bracelet and put an exclusion field around us, a bubble of silence and privacy on the dance floor.

"I'm fading." I blinked, and even that was an effort. My eyes were leaden window shades, my breathing deeper with every passing moment, and there was a distant keening sound in my ears. I knew the signs of incipient exhaustion. They had excellent stimulants in that world, but even with my metabolic tweaks, staying awake for five days straight was about my limit.

"Zax… I don't… I'm sorry… I just…" I could have helped her, said what she was thinking so she didn't have to, but I stubbornly made her speak her own mind. "I like it here," she said finally. "I've made friends. I want to stay."

I liked her a little better for being so direct about it, and at least this way there was a sort of closure. My last companion before Laini, Winsome, had gotten lost in the depths of the non-Euclidean mansion where we landed, and I couldn't stay awake long enough to find them again. (Unless, I thought darkly, *they'd* abandoned me deliberately, too, and just wanted to avoid an awkward goodbye.) I couldn't blame Laini for wanting to stay here, either. She'd come from a world of hellish subterranean engines: the whole planet a slave-labor mining operation for insectile aliens, and this playground world of plenty was a heaven she could never have imagined in her old life – the one I rescued her from. We'd been together for forty-three worlds though, the longest I'd kept a companion since the Lector, and it hurt to see her choose this place over me. We didn't even get along that well, honestly; she was suspicious, quick to anger, and secretive – all reasonable traits for someone who'd grown up the way she did – but that didn't matter. For a little while, I'd woken up next to someone I could call a friend, and, in my life, that's the most precious thing there is.

She touched my cheek, which surprised me – we'd been intimate a few times, but only when she came to me in the night, and it was always rough and hot, never afterward discussed or acknowledged. She'd certainly never touched me with that kind of fondness. "I'm sorry, Zax," she said, and that surprised me even more, and then she kissed me, gently, which stunned me completely. Maybe a week in a place of peace and plenty, with its devotion to pleasure as a pillar of life, had softened her.

Or maybe she was just feeling the all-encompassing love-field brought on by some rather advanced club drugs.

"OK." I turned away so she wouldn't see the tears shining in my eyes and made my way across the dance floor, stumbling a little as lethargy further overtook me. I glanced back, once, and Laini was dancing again, having already forgotten me, no doubt. I tried to be happy for her, but it was hard to feel anything good for someone else in the midst of being sad for myself.

I opened up a cushioned rest pod and crawled inside. At least I'd fall asleep in a pleasant place. I curled myself around my backpack – stuffed with as many good drugs as I'd been able to discreetly pocket – and succumbed to the inevitable.

Here's the situation. Every time I fall asleep, I wake up in another universe. That started happening nearly three years and a thousand worlds ago, and I still don't know why, or what happens during the transition, while I'm asleep. Do I spend eight hours in slumber in some nowhere-place between realities, or do I transition instantaneously, and just *feel* like I got a good night's sleep? I wake up feeling rested, unless I took heavy drugs to knock myself out, and if I fall asleep injured, the wounds are always better than they should be when I wake up, if not fully healed. I inevitably sleep through the mechanism of a miracle, and that's just as frustrating as you might imagine.

I never have dreams anymore, but, sometimes, waking up is a lot like a nightmare.

After leaving Laini, I woke to flashing red lights and the sound of howling alarms. I automatically pressed the sound-dampening button on my bracelet, but it was just an inert loop of metal and plastic now that the network of the Dionysius Society was in another branch of the multiverse, so the shriek was unceasing.

I sat up, looking around for obvious threats – always a priority upon waking. I was in some kind of factory or industrial space, on a metal catwalk, near a ladder leading up, and a set of stairs leading down. I stood and looked over the metal railing to see gouts of steam, ranks of silvery cylinders stretching off in all directions, and humans (humanoids, anyway) racing around and waving their arms and shouting. One of the workers, if that's what they were, stumbled into contact with a steam cloud, and screamed as their arm melted away.

I'd be going up the ladder instead of down the stairs, then. I tightened my pack on my shoulders and scrambled up the rungs. Fortunately the hatch at the top was unlocked so I didn't have to use one of my dwindling supply of plasma keys. I climbed up onto the roof, and the hatch sealed shut after me.

I stood atop a mining or drilling platform, several hundred meters above a vast, dark ocean. The sun was either rising or setting, and everything was hazed in red. The air was smoky and vile, but breathable. I've never woken up in a world where the air was purely toxic, though sometimes I find myself in artificial habitats in otherwise uninhabitable places. My second companion, the Lector, theorized that I projected myself into numerous potential realities before coalescing in a branch of the multiverse where my consciousness could persist… but I've always been more interested in the practice of my affliction than the theory, and was just happy I'd survived this long.

The water far below was dark and wild, more viscous than most seas I've seen, as if thickened by sludge, and the waves slammed hard against the platform from all directions. Occasionally dark shapes broke the surface – giant eels, I thought at first, with stegosaurus spines, but then I glimpsed some greater form in the depths below, and realized the "serpents" were the appendages of a single creature.

The thing in the water wrapped a limb around one of the cranes that festooned the platform and pulled it down into the water with a terrific shriek of metal and a greasy splash, and the whole rig lurched in that direction. The creature grabbed more cranes at their bases and began to pull, trying to rip the whole platform down.

I'd seen enough. I try to save people when I can – I was trained, on the world of my birth, to solve conflicts and promote harmony – but there are limits. If anyone had burst through the hatch after me I'd have given them the option to escape this world, but there was no time to rescue anyone without losing myself. I fumbled in my pack and pulled out a stoppered test tube (my second-to-last) and a handkerchief. I was still bitter about the limitations of the pharmacopeia in the Dionysius Society. They had uppers, and dissociatives, and euphorics, and entheogens, and entactogens, but they didn't have any fast-acting sedatives. Who wanted to fall asleep and miss the party?

I yanked out the cork and poured the carefully measured tablespoon of liquid into the handkerchief, strapped my pack back onto my chest, and then lay down on the metal of the deck. The rig was already sloping noticeably toward the water, but not so much that I'd slide into the sea before I passed out. I hoped.

I pressed the soaked handkerchief to my nose and breathed deeply. A strong, sickly-sweet odor filled my nostrils, my head spun, everything got gray and fuzzy, and then that terrible world went away.

I woke sprawled underneath a tree, its branches heavy with unfamiliar apple-shaped fruit in an unlikely shade of blue. My head thudded like it always did when I woke after resorting to such anesthetic measures. I sat up against the trunk and did my threat assessment.

I was in an orchard of blue-apple trees, orderly rows stretching as far as I could see, and there were no sea monsters (or tree monsters) in evidence. The air smelled fresh and highly oxygenated, and the skies were a paler blue than the fruit, and cloudless.

I leaned back against the trunk and exhaled. My breath still smelled sweet from the anesthetic. There are sedatives that don't give me skull-shattering hangovers, but they also work more slowly. Sometimes I need to spin the wheel of worlds again fast, and in those cases, I resort to the hard stuff.

"Where did you come from?" a voice above me said. So much for my operational security. I looked up at a human perched on a large branch, looking down at me – apparently female, around my age, with big dark surprised eyes, skin a shade browner than the trees, and hair in a thousand braids.

"The ocean," I said, and the language I spoke was strange and harsh. Back home we had a simple, logical, constructed language, but these haphazard, organically developed languages are far more common in the multiverse. (That informality has infiltrated even my thoughts, and the way I write now would horrify my tutors.) Still, it was good to know the linguistic virus the Lector injected into me way back on World 85 still worked. For the first few months after the onset of my condition, before I met the Lector, I had only once visited a world where people spoke a language I remotely recognized. It's harrowing, waking up every day or three in an entirely alien place, where even if you find people, you can't understand them. (Not that my days now were much better. Laini had been grim company for most of our time together, but she had, at least, been a brief constant in my ever-changing world: someone who knew me for more than a day or two and then vanished into my past forever.)

"The sea-stead?" she asked. "The seaweed beds?"

"It was more a sort of… factory."

"I have never seen even once an ocean," she said, with a note of wistfulness. "I have never been off the farm." (Maybe that should be "The Farm.")

"It wasn't a very nice ocean. Are these fruit good to eat?" I was starving, and while I had some food in my pack, I tried to avoid depleting my rations whenever possible. I never knew when I'd hit a streak of barren or unpopulated worlds and have to dip into my supply.

"Of course! I can share some of my fraction with you. I am Minna. Senior grafter here, but this is my free half-day. What are you called?"

"Zax." Zaxony Dyad Euphony Delatree – given name, family name, earned name, sphere name, but none of that had meaning except in the Realm of Spheres and Harmonies, and I hadn't been there since I was twenty-two. I thought about the family, friends, and lovers I'd unwillingly left behind as seldom as possible, for the same reason I don't shove pointy sticks into any wounds I sustain. "I'm a… traveler."

"I did not know that was the name of a job." Minna looked at me very seriously. "Do the [unable to translate] send you to the different biomes to make sure all is right and well?"

I didn't hear the words "unable to translate," just slippery syllables. The Lector's world was techno-utopian, and occasionally there were concepts the linguistic virus he'd developed had a hard time parsing. Usually those concepts involved horrible nightmarish things. "Something like that."

"Tell me of the places you have seen!" Minna hung on my every word as much as she hung onto the branch.

I looked around the orchard. "Places with no trees at all," I said, "just rocks, but some of the rocks grow, like trees, and they shine. Places with just one big tree, and a city in the branches. Forests where no person had ever walked before me. Beaches with white or golden or black sand, or all three at once, the water warm or chilling or bubbling or even, once, alive. Mountains with air so clear and crisp you can see for hundreds of miles, and mountains where the fog never lifts and the inhabitants are all born blind. Cities so big you could walk all day and never reach the outskirts, full of temples and factories, towers and parks." I tried to focus on the good trips. I could have told Minna about places where the sun was a dying ruby, where people were just vessels for intelligent parasites, where the trees were carnivorous and ambulatory, but why frighten and confuse her?

"Really? So many places, all different? What a life, so full of wonders. You must be a rare lineage from heirloom stock."

"I don't know about that. Traveling is… it's like life, I guess. Sometimes it's wonderful, and sometimes it's terrible, and sometimes it's boring."

"That does not sound like life as I know it." Minna dropped down from the branch and landed beside me. She wore a jumpsuit dyed unevenly blue, and her hands were stained the same color. She'd plucked a fruit on the way down, and began cutting up the blue apple with a pretty silver knife. She handed me a thick wedge of fruit. It was blue all the way through. "Here you go. The fruit in this sector boosts your immunities. We are going to graft them to mood enhancers, to make the eaters feel good and be healthy too, but the [unable to translate] have not yet settled on which strains to use."

I grunted and took a bite. The flesh was crisp and sweet, and I gobbled it up and licked my fingers.

"Golly, you hungered." Minna handed me the rest of the fruit, and I chomped it down.

"Thank you for that. Do you live nearby?" I'd eaten, and now it would be nice to get under a roof. I'd been in too many places where terrible things came from the sky.

"I live on the Farm." Minna sounded confused that I'd even asked. "Did you want to see my room? Is that part of the inspection?"

Before I could answer – I was debating whether it was better to let Minna think I had special status here or not – a horrible buzzing, humming, clattering noise arose, and I shot to my feet and looked around. "What is that?"

"A harvester." Minna smiled. "Is this your first time on a farm? They might be loud and scary, I think, if you are new, but they mean you no harm."

A mechanical spider ten meters high rose up above the trees to my left, its body a silvery sphere, its countless arms whirling and spinning, some tipped with blades, others with jointed claws, plucking fruit and pruning back branches all at once, tossing blue apples and cut branches into a funnel on top of its body. The harvester came closer, its delicate segmented legs stepping over, around, and through the branches, moving fast. I snatched up my pack and backed away.

"Do not be afraid. The harvester has scanners, and it can tell workers from fruit."

I hesitated, but Minna seemed so unworried that I stood beside her as the spider scuttled down the rows toward us. The machine didn't seem to notice me at all, and it was almost past us when one of its lopping pincer arms reached out and severed my left arm just above the elbow.

Under the Tree • Grafting • The Orchard of Worlds • The Debt of Sleep • A Remembrance • The Cullers Come

I fell, and everything went gray, but I bit my own tongue and willed myself to stay awake. If I passed out now, I might well bleed out wherever I woke, unless I happened to open my eyes in a trauma center, which wasn't likely. Here, at least, Minna might be able to do some first aid, make a tourniquet or something – farm people knew about that stuff, didn't they?

That all sounds so logical and deliberate, as I write it down after the fact. Actually I was screaming and bleeding and terrified. Minna said something my virus translated as "Gosh!" and then the pain at my elbow went away, replaced by spreading coolness. I turned my head, heavy as a cannonball, and saw Minna rubbing a cut piece of yellow fruit on my wound. My gaze drifted downward and I watched the bleeding end of my arm close over, new flesh growing across the wound in seconds. I was maimed, but I wouldn't bleed to death. I was dopey and vague, though, and Minna started to push something into my mouth, another piece of fruit. A sedative? I turned my head. "Can't sleep. Have to stay awake."

She paused. "Oh. Then... I can give you something that will take you far away from your body, without making you sleep. OK?"

"But sleeping *does* take me far away. Every time. Always." I was lightheaded from blood loss.

"Eat this, Zax." The slice of fruit she put in my mouth tasted like copper and clouds.

I'd done enough drugs on enough worlds to recognize Minna had given me a strong dissociative, but the thing about dissociatives is, when you're on them, you don't care about anything, so I didn't mind. Minna helped me stand and led me to a tree, then somehow *into* the tree – the trunk yawned open to admit us. We went down a wooden ramp, into a cozy cavern lit by bioluminescent fungus. The furniture seemed like dirt with soft moss growing on it, and Minna eased me onto a raised platform that could have been a bed or table. She muttered and bustled around, and did some stuff to my stump – ha, I was in a *tree* and I had a *stump* – but I was mostly just floating far away, my mind a balloon on a string only tenuously connected to my body.

After some unknowable interval, Minna helped me sit up and gave me a squishy bulb of juice to sip. Lucidity flooded back into me when I swallowed. I looked down at my arm. My *arm*. Hadn't I lost that arm? Oh. This was a different arm. It was brown, and there was a leaf growing on the thumb.

Minna plucked off the leaf, and it felt like having a long hair plucked from my eyebrow. "Move your fingers," she said.

My hand *looked* like my hand, but made of wood. I opened and closed the fingers, and they worked fine. I ran the fingers across the table. There was sensation, but dulled, like I was wearing thick mittens. "I can feel."

"The feeling should get better when the nerves have time to get used to each other." Minna sighed. "I am sorry it looks like an arm made of wood and not an arm made of you. I do not have the right material to make it look better here. You could go get... but no." Minna took a step away from me when I sat up.

"What do you mean?" I said.

Minna shook her head. "You are an impossible thing. You

cannot be here. I inspected you." She rubbed the back of her neck. "You do not have a chit. That is why the harvester lopped you. It scanned you, but there was nothing to scan, so it did not know you were a person."

"What kind of chip?"

"A *chit*. Everyone has a chit, right here, to keep them in their right place and track the outstanding debt owed to [unable to translate]!"

"Everyone? What if you pay off your debt?"

Minna shook her head. "It never goes down, only up, maybe flat if you work fast enough. You incur more debt just by breathing [unable to translate]'s air. My chit has eleven thousand outstanding. I inherited my mother's debt when she died, and my children will inherit mine in their turn."

I shuddered. Indentured servitude. Slavery, really. Then I blinked. "Did you say you have children?" I looked around her small dwelling and saw no sign of them.

She nodded, smiling faintly. "Two. They ripened long ago, and were assigned to a sea-stead. I had hoped they would remain here, but there were losses in an aquatic biome during a volcanic event, and because my line is good at adapting, my sons were repurposed and re-assigned." She fluttered her hands at the side of her neck and I looked at her blankly. "They have gills now. When you said you had come from the ocean, I wondered if you knew them..." She sighed. "It was foolishness."

I radically revised my estimate of Minna's age and experience. Her seeming innocence was due to isolation, I realized, and not youth. I'd been to worlds where centenarians looked like teenagers, where the old could take a pill to restore them to youth and allow them to grow up all over again, where bodies could be changed as easily as shirts, but I still fell prey to my own assumptions. The Lector called it "cultural programming."

"How old are you, Minna?"

"This will be my eighty-third harvest."

"How many harvests in a year?"

"What is a year?" She cocked her head curiously.

"It's... nothing. A measure of time from another place. What about the father?" This cavern definitely looked like singles accommodation to me.

"The paternal contribution came from a rootstock engineer in a frost biome, or so I was told," she said. "We were a good genetic combination."

"Ah. Right. I see."

She put her hand on the back of my neck. "You do not have a chit." Her voice was full of fear and wonder. "*Everyone* has a chit."

"You've never been off the Farm, though, Minna. I come from a place where things are different."

"Not just different. Impossible." Minna shook her head, braids whipping around. "Even if you are some... outsider... there is no way onto the Farm without a chit. The entire perimeter is one big scanner. No one can enter this biome without authorization."

"Maybe I... parachuted in."

"Through the dome?"

Ah. I hadn't realized there was a dome. Invisible dome, or maybe one decorated with the illusion of a sun and sky. "OK. Truth time." Minna had saved my life, so I owed her that much, even if she wouldn't believe me. "When I said I was a traveler, Minna... do you know what a multiverse is?"

"A... song with lots of verses?"

I smiled. "No, it's like... Imagine the universe is a tree. When the universe was born, it just had a single central trunk. But as time went on, the universe grew branches, and those branches grew more branches, and so on, and all those branches bore fruit. Now imagine each fruit at the end of each branch is a whole different world. Not just a different planet, but an entirely separate universe. Some worlds are similar, and some are different, like... aren't there trees that can grow more than one kind of fruit, pears and apples both at once?" I'd seen trees like that before. I didn't know if that was super-science or just agriculture, but in this world, either seemed likely.

Minna nodded, frowning.

"Right. So... I can travel from branch to branch in the tree of worlds, sampling all the different fruit. And... occasionally I jump from the end of one branch to another tree entirely, one with totally different kinds of fruit. Like a squirrel."

"What is a squirrel?"

"My metaphor might be breaking down," I said. "My point is, I don't travel to different, whatever you said, biomes, in this world. I travel between worlds. I never know where I'll end up. This time, I landed here, with you. I don't know what the Farm is, I don't know what the–" here I reproduced the "unable to translate" sound as best I could, "–is or are, and I'm really just passing through."

I've gotten a lot of reactions to my story over my travels, usually disbelief or mockery, but a few reacted like Minna did: with a look of envy and desire. "You mean, you can just... leave? Without permission or cause?"

"I can... but I've never been back to any world I've visited before. Once I go, it's gone forever. I can't choose where I end up, either. I go to new worlds at random, or at least, I haven't found a pattern or any way to steer. Some worlds are nice, some are boring, and some are terrible and dangerous."

"But there is always another world? Another *choice*?"

"Choice might be the wrong word. I travel whenever I fall asleep. Even if I find a place I like, I can't stay there, because I always fall asleep eventually."

"We have fruit that lets us stay up working for four nights in a row, but then we have to sleep for almost two," Minna said. "The debt of sleep must be repaid. If you travel when you sleep... Forgive me, Zax, but are you sure the worlds you visit aren't dreams?"

That had been the Lector's first theory, not definitely disproven for him until I took him with me to another branch. "If they are, this is a dream too."

"I am not a dream." Minna was very solemn. "When you sleep, you will disappear from this place?"

I nodded.

"If this is true, you should sleep soon, before the cullers come."

"Uh. What are the cullers?"

Minna shrugged. "They come for sick trees, or sick workers, or unauthorized offspring. I assume they will come for an intruder, though we have never had one before. The harvester has gone back to the center by now, and they will have your arm in their hopper, and they will not find a match to your genome in the database, if you really are a traveler from branch to branch. They will send a culler for you. And for me, since I helped you." Minna looked down, tears welling in their eyes. "I am not rotten yet, but they will cull me just the same. If I had scanned you first, and seen you had no chit, I would have known I shouldn't heal you, but... I think I would have helped you anyway. Grafters are from the sect of cultivators, after all, and we do not kill what can be made healthy and saved. The cullers are less merciful."

I clenched my new hand into a fist. "You'll die?"

"I will be processed and fed to the trees. This is as it should be. I live for the trees, so I will die for them. Sleep, Zax. Sleep and jump to a new branch in this orchard of worlds, if you can."

"Minna, you can come with me."

"What?" Her eyes widened, shining.

"You can't ever come back, never see your sons again, but if you think they'll kill you anyway... I can't let you die just for helping me. If I hold you in my arms when I fall asleep, you'll come with me. There's a sort of... bubble, or aura, and it envelops me, and anyone I'm touching, and carries them along. Come with me and we'll go somewhere..." I couldn't say "safe," necessarily. "Else."

Soil showered down from the ceiling, accompanied by a grinding, buzzing noise. Minna looked up. "The cullers."

Crap. I fumbled in my bag. I only had one vial of knockout juice left, not enough for two, and I knew that, but I looked deeper in the pack anyway, desperate. "I can't... I can't put us both to sleep fast, Minna."

"I have to sleep, too, Zax? To enter your dream?"

The first time I took someone with me, on World 40, it was an accident. It was a world heartbreakingly similar to my own, the closest I've come to a place that was like mine, so much so that at first I thought I'd made my way home. People spoke a language that was almost the same as mine, at least close enough for me to understand and make myself understood. Like my home, the Realm of Spheres and Harmonies, that world was a place of gleaming spires and plenty, and I landed in a beautiful woman's back yard. She was the first person I'd been able to talk to in over a month, and I spilled out my story to her, and she believed me, because she'd seen me flicker into existence from nothing.

Her name was Ana. She was a creator of kinetic sculptures and a scientist of motion, and we promptly fell in love. I spent two days in her world – two days of bliss and conversation and sex, and I was so thrilled and energized by our connection that it was easy to stay awake that long. We knew our time was limited, but we made the most of every second.

I fell asleep holding Ana in my arms. She stayed awake. She'd *planned* to stay awake, so she could watch me disappear, but instead, she traveled with me.

When we woke, she scratched my face and jumped to her feet, screaming about holes in the sky, and things pushing through – *worms, worms, worms in the world,* she said. She saw something during our transition, but I don't know what. Before I could try to talk to her or calm her down, she ran away, racing into the alleys of a silent gray city that was all towers without any visible windows or doors. I looked for Ana, calling her name until I lost my voice, searching until I passed out from exhaustion and woke up somewhere new.

After that horror, I vowed to never take anyone with me again… until the Lector convinced me to try it with him sleeping. Being unconscious, it seemed, was the secret to making the journey safely.

I nodded. "You need to sleep too, yes, but there's no time."

Minna opened a chest with moss growing on the lid. "I saw the cullers come for my mother, when she got sick. Sometimes I have bad dreams about that. So for my fraction, I always take a few..." Minna lifted out a bag woven of leaves, and shook a handful of small black berries onto her hand. "These kill waking, and swiftly."

The buzzing increased outside, and more soil sifted down on us. "Grab what you need, clothes, tools, anything, and come here." I held out my arms. I hadn't been able to save anyone on the platform in that dark ocean, but I could save Minna from dying for the crime of helping me.

Minna picked up a larger bag and shoved things that looked like twigs and bulbs and seedpods into it, then came to me, climbing up onto the soft platform. "We'll be OK," I said. I took one of the berries in my hand and wrapped my arms around her.

"I have had no one to hold me since my mother died, and no one to hold since my sons ripened," she said. "It will be nice to die being held." She didn't have much confidence in my plan, apparently, but she popped a berry into her mouth, and I bit into mine.

The roof of Minna's room started to fall in, and metal spines poked through, hooked and questing. I thought the berry wouldn't work in time, but then sleep came down like a hammer blow.

Into a Dream • Early Days • Harmonizer • Crypsis • A Thousand Worlds • Apophenia

My eyes sprang open with no pain or disorientation. Those berries were *much* better than the chemicals I'd picked up in the last city I visited. I had Minna in my arms, and we were on a concrete floor in a bare, dim room about six meters square, with arrowslit windows high on the walls offering the only light. My immediate threat assessment didn't detect anything more dangerous than dust bunnies. An arch-shaped door, three meters high, stood in the center of one water-stained wall, and, judging from the dust, it hadn't been opened in ages.

Minna stirred, and I let her go. "What is this place?"

I smiled. That was always the question, wasn't it? "A new world. Beyond that... we'll have to find out."

"You carried me into your dream?" Minna stood up, swaying. She rubbed the back of her neck. "I can not feel the connection to [unable to translate]."

"I would imagine not." I rose. "The Farm is far away now, Minna. Worlds away."

Suddenly Minna launched into my arms and kissed my face. "I did not believe you! I thought you had eaten tainted zootropic berries and broken with reality! But I am here." She pulled away. "In your orchard of worlds. You saved my life."

"It's only fair, since you saved my life, and my arm... and I'm the one who called the cullers down on you in the first place."

Minna shook her head, braids bouncing. "No. You did not just save me from the cullers. You saved me from dying in the same place where I lived, Zax. I never thought I would see the world beyond the Farm. I never thought I would get outside the dome. Almost no one does – my sons were so elated to be chosen, to be able to live in *two* biomes. To see even a portion of what you have seen… Could I stay with you for a while? Travel with you? I can be helpful, I am a good worker, and…"

No matter how many times it's been stomped, burned, and uprooted these past few years, the flower of hope still grows inside me as soon as it's given the least bit of water and sunlight. "Of course you can stay with me, Minna. As long as you want."

Minna picked up her bag of woven leaves and plucked at it until it produced straps, then put it on like a backpack. She pointed. "Is that a door? It's so smooth. I have never seen a door like that before. What is on the other side?"

"I don't know. I've never been here before. It's always a surprise."

Minna took my hand. "Let's go see."

So we did.

As I write this, Minna is napping in a corner of the little structure where we woke up. She seems remarkably adaptable, but then, she said her line is good at that. She didn't even have to grow gills for this journey. She asked me if I would tell her about myself, later, and now she's got me thinking about the past, and trying to organize my thoughts. Since I usually do that here, I'm doing that here.

The outside was disappointing – there was a fire in the forest here a long time ago, and most of what we can see is ash and stumps and abandoned buildings, though we did find a working water pump. Minna was all for setting off along a half-recognizable track leading over a hill, but I convinced her to let me rest here a little while and catch my breath. This was my third world in as many hours (waking hours, anyway), and even if I feel physically rested, my mind gets jumbled and overwhelmed sometimes.

Sitting here with my back against a solid wall, writing in this journal of endless scrolling digital pages the Lector gave me, helps to soothe the storm of panic hormones in my blood. (Though I get a spike every time I glance down at my left arm and see wood grain instead of flesh. I may have to start keeping my sleeves rolled down. Maybe wear gloves.) Minna and I talked for a while, until she started yawning and curled up on the floor and went to sleep. She looks so peaceful. Maybe the berries have a lingering calming effect. Maybe she's just good at coping. I *like* her.

I remember taking naps. I used to do it back home on free days and vacations. We had a wonderful hammock in the yard that all the siblings and niblings used to fight over, until finally my parents drew up a rotation to keep us from arguing, and after that turns in the hammock became a sort of currency we traded for chores and treats. We all enjoyed those periods of blissful swaying and snoozing and reading and viewing beneath the green leaves, but I think I loved it the most.

No more naps for me these days, obviously. One of the Lector's first interventions during our time together was to alter my circadian rhythms and sleep-wake homeostasis, gradually extending my periods of comfortable wakefulness until I can go about twenty-six hours before I get sleepy, even without the intervention of stimulants. He said he couldn't push my system much farther without potentially damaging me, but I'm glad for what I get. Every once in a great while, I get to watch the sun rise on the same world twice, even without snorting or injecting uppers.

I started keeping this journal on the Lector's advice, and, despite how things ended up between us, that was a good idea. He had me write down entries for each world I visited, and, when I can, I fill in details about the eighty-four worlds I saw before I met him.

My memories of those early worlds are hazy. No surprise there. I realize now I was traumatized, and my mind went vague to protect itself. I went to sleep one night in my bed, tired from a particularly challenging day, the white noise generator humming to drown the sounds from the neighbors in the next hedron. I was working as an associate harmonizer in the Delatree sphere then, helping to bring conflicts into accord for the good of the locality, and was frustrated by a particularly vociferous disagreement between two long-term neighbors who'd had a falling out over the disposition of the community garden in their shared degree of the arc. I'd been a harmonizer for two years, after graduating from a thought-leader track (much to the pride of my parents, who'd spent their lives in worthy but unexciting practical-track positions), and had harmonized far more complex disputes before, but those two were stubbornly irrational and unwilling to compromise – and it was all so *petty*. I wondered if I'd have to contact a senior harmonizer for help, and if that failure to handle things myself would impact my future assignments.

In an attempt to feel less useless and to restore my faith in my chosen profession, I signed up for a volunteer shift at my local community center, because showing people how to apply for public aid, or get medical assistance, or even just making sure they got a good meal and a safe place to sleep, was a clear and concrete way of helping people. Unfortunately, I ended up spending the shift failing to help a woman who was suffering some sort of drug-related problem or psychotic break, and who later attempted suicide. She spoke no language any of us, or our artificial intelligences, could recognize, and we thought she must have come from a recently annexed planet, some divergent colony world. I went to check on her and found her gravely injured, veins opened with the sharpened handle of a spoon she'd stolen at mealtime. I ended up covered in her blood, afraid she would die in my arms, and, in fact, she *did* die, briefly, before a medical bot managed to stabilize her. She ultimately pulled through, but only due to heroic medical intervention. Probably all for nothing, though – she vanished from her bed later, even though the staff swore she never left her room.

I cleaned myself up, and went on with my day. Eventually I went home, and prepared myself for sleep that didn't want to come. I did my grounding and meditation exercises, but once I managed to stop thinking about work, I started pondering the two people I'd been seeing who'd expressed interest in romantic escalation. I liked them both, but as they adhered to mutually exclusive relationship-structural frameworks (ethically anarchic vs. closed loop, respectively), I'd have to make a choice if I wanted to escalate with either one. I finally took a huff of sublimated lotus to help me stop thinking and rest, though I usually eschewed sleep aids. (*That's* changed a lot.)

The one thing I didn't worry about that night was whether I'd ever see my home or my family again, but then I woke up in a dark forest, with vast creatures moving unseen through the foliage. I thought I'd been drugged or abducted, until I passed out from exhaustion and fear in a tree and woke up on a small island in a crystal-clear sea under a sky with two suns. World 3, I know now; the place I come from will always be World number 1.

I wanted to believe I was insane, or dreaming, but the needs of the body make themselves known, and I was so thirsty and so hungry. There were strange fish the color of jewels in the water, and they were so unafraid of predators that I could scoop them up with my hands, as many as I wanted. I ate them raw; I'd gone to wilderness camp, and had some basic survival skills, but there was no wood to make fire with, and fish blood doesn't do much to slake thirst. I slept on that beach, and woke on the roof of a building the color of bleached bone, beside a vehicle that looked like a giant beetle. There were people there, who shouted at me in a language I didn't understand, and I ended up locked in a jail cell; I didn't mind, because they gave me water, all I could drink. That was the first world where I saw people, and they were hairier and shorter and thicker-browed than humans I'd seen before. I think they were a different species, though closely related to my own. I fell asleep in that jail cell and… Well. So it went. I stole a bag for supplies as soon as I could, and bottles for water, and, once I hit a world with sufficient tech, I snatched a container of water purification tablets powerful enough that even salt water (or, in a pinch, urine) could be made drinkable. I can only carry so much, though, and the basic needs of survival are never far from my mind.

Some worlds had little to recommend them, and were places I endured more than experienced, and left as soon as possible. Those get short entries, like:

World 14: green glass desert
World 36: forest of tombs
World 45: moldy tunnels

Others get just a few sentences:

World 105: Fishing village with a lighthouse that seems to be made of flesh and bone, with a living eye on top instead of a light. The village looked deserted at first, but at nightfall the people who lived there started walking up out of the water, all wearing diving suits, dragging nets full of things, not just fish, but also shells and pearls and gears and bits of machinery. They thought the Lector and I were "down from the capital" and treated us like honored guests.

Gradually though, since I left the Lector, I've been writing more and more, and the journal has become more subjective. It's less a data set, with the metrics the Lector demanded, and more of a diary. The ongoing story of my ongoing life. Sitting down and writing makes me feel more calm and centered, even when I write about distressing things. Maybe because there's so little continuity in my life, anything I can carry from one day into the next seems precious. I've been going back and fleshing out the earlier entries, too, when I can, but in general, I'm always moving forward.

This is World 997. Maybe I'll have a little party when I hit an even thousand, if it's a world where such things are possible.

World 998: A jungle, hot and damp, full of golden frogs (which I knew better than to touch) and buzzing insects and chattering birds, but no larger wildlife, as far as we could tell. While we walked among the trees, I caught a familiar scent, and stopped, stunned. "That's skyberry pie. How is that possible? I haven't smelled that since I left home!" I hurried toward the source of the smell, but Minna grabbed my arm.

"To me, it smells like elderflower honey," she said. "We should be careful." We made our way slowly forward, and where the scent was strongest, we discovered a plant with an immense fragrant flower in the center, surrounded by a nest of vines. One vine moved, snake-quick, and wrapped around my ankle, but I yanked it loose without much trouble – the plant wasn't used to luring prey as big as us, I think. There were frogs and birds wrapped up in its vines, though, and the scent was so intoxicating I couldn't stop drawing in deep breaths. "That's amazing. It smells so real."

Minna nodded. "On the Farm there are flowers with petals that look like bees, to make bees want to visit them, and there are insects that look like sticks who hide among the twigs, and there are tricks of smell, too, like plants who eat flies, and so they make a smell like what flies want to eat. Tricksy tricks like those, where one thing pretends to be another, are called crypsis."

Crypsis. "Sort of like when I pretended to belong in your world."

"All things do what they must to survive and thrive." Minna patted me on the arm.

We were careful about finding a safe place to settle down for sleep when night fell in that place.

* * *

World 999: On top of a tower with a roof about a hundred meters in diameter, with no discernible way down, but lots of plants, laid out in neat, orderly rows. I don't know if it was a garden exactly, but Minna identified lots of edible things, including melons that were mostly sweet water inside, and we feasted. We could see other towers in the distance, and some held towering trees, others what looked like mountains. Looking over the edge, I saw thick clouds below us. Minna made a crown of vines and declared me king of the tower. She's adorable.

World 1000. Arbitrary, but it seems important: I mark what milestones I can. We opened our eyes beside a small river that ran down to a rock pool at the top of a waterfall, in a forest of deciduous trees, the air a perfect temperature and humidity for stripping down and swimming, after my usual justifiably paranoid check to make sure there weren't any obvious predators in the water. That didn't rule out the possibility of parasites or brain-eating microorganisms, but it was impossible to be truly safe, and the water felt wonderful. Minna was completely unselfconscious about being naked, and I did my best to be the same. I've been to worlds more libertine and more conservative than the one I hailed from, but it's hard not to think of my home as the proper default, where being nude in front of siblings and niblings at the communal pools is unremarkable, but you tend to keep your clothes on around anyone else unless you have a good reason to do otherwise.

"This is my thousandth world." We picnicked beside the stream, using up the vegetables we'd harvested from the previous world while they were still fresh.

"Is it the best world?" she asked.

I laughed. "In the top ten percent, for sure." Nothing had tried to eat me, imprison me, or murder me, after all.

"Maybe they will be better and better and better each time," she said.

I'd begun to wonder if it was going to be all natural paradises from here on out – if Minna's connection to the natural world had somehow altered my destinations – but, as usual, that was just me finding patterns in coincidence. As proven by World 1001.

Finally, a City • Something Wrong with the Moon • Hothouse • Two Psychedelic • A Descent • Minna Gets Dirty

We woke up in a city, which was honestly a relief after our last few bucolic worlds. Those had been peaceful, and good for Minna's and my respective states of mind, but it's hard to resupply in places with no apparent civilization.

I sat up in the alleyway where we'd appeared, kicked some loose trash out of the way, and put my hand against a cool wall of purplish brick. "We can pick up medicine here, Minna, and maybe more water purification tablets, and some fresh clothes–"

"What is that noise? It sounds like a broken harvester, thrashing itself to pieces."

Minna's ears were better than mine, which was no surprise – she was genetically designed by malign intelligences to be a hardy and efficient worker, while I'd been born by more haphazard biological means. I listened hard, and I did recognize the sound, though I wished I didn't. It was a crowd. An angry one.

"That's just people." I kept my voice calm. "Cities are noisy." Minna had told me a bit about her life on the Farm, and I knew she'd never seen more than a dozen people in one place at a time. I didn't think she'd do well with a protest march (best case) or a riot (bad case) or people fleeing some sort of horrible disaster (worst case).

I took her hand and tugged her out of the alleyway, looking left and right. The streets were empty, the buildings all made of the same purple brick, tall and windowless, the ground-level doors closed off with metal gates. There were a few stunted, leafless trees, and street lamps that cast a reddish light, but half of those were burned out. I looked up at the sky, and then looked away. There was something wrong with the moon. Its light faded and brightened, like someone was playing with a cosmic dimmer switch. "This way." I tried to lead her away from the crowd noise, but it seemed the riots were all around us, and after a few blocks we caught a glimpse at an intersection of a crowd of ragged people running and screaming and waving makeshift weapons.

"Oh, Zax, I do not like this."

"It doesn't look good," I agreed. "But maybe if we keep going…"

A group peeled off from the mass and began rushing toward us. There was something wrong with their eyes; they glowed, brightening and dimming in synch with the moon. I'd been to some strange realities over the years, but only a few had ever felt *broken* like this one did.

I didn't have to grab Minna, because she was holding tight to my wrist. I pulled her into the nearest alley and scrabbled in her bag for the remaining soporific berries. She ate hers and faded into my arms. I swallowed mine just as the horde began pouring into our hiding place, and I felt one of their hands grasp my ankle just as I fell asleep. I wondered muzzily if I'd find a severed hand by my foot in the next world, though in my experience, things travel with me whole or not at all.

I opened my eyes to a thudding headache and terrible heat. I put my hand down to steady myself and gasped – we were lying on oven-hot sand in a desert. Minna sat up beside me, took one look around at the endless expanse of golden dunes, without even a bare rock to cast a soothing shadow, and burst into tears.

"Oh, no, don't cry, please." I patted her awkwardly – I'd only had a handful of companions since I began traveling between worlds (and one of them tried to vivisect me), and I'd begun to lose the knack of giving comfort; a terrible failing, in a harmonizer.

I was mostly thinking, *She should save her moisture. We might need it.* I only had two full bottles of water in my bag. Our dwindling supply of water purification tablets wasn't much of a problem here, since there was no water to purify anyway.

"Where are the *trees*?" Minna gazed around, eyes wide and wet. "Even in that awful city place there were *some* trees, but I don't feel even a twitch or tendril of life, how can this be?"

"It's a desert, Minna. A dry place. Sometimes there are oases, places where water comes up out of the ground and plants grow, but–"

"Let's leave, please, let's sleep now." She hugged herself and trembled.

Her skin was taking on the greenish tinge and I was afraid she might throw up. I hoped not. Getting dehydrated in a desert wouldn't be good. "We used your last berries, and I only have enough knockout drops for one." I hadn't mentioned how low our supplies were before, because I hadn't wanted to worry her. I'd hoped to resupply, and the last world had looked promising at first – urban infrastructure usually means drugs – but for now, we had no access to induced unconsciousness.

"I do not think I can sleep the normal way right now. It is so *hot*. You will not fall asleep without me, will you? I cannot be stranded here, Zax. Even that last world was better than this."

I took her hand, which felt cool compared to the burning air around us. "I'm good at falling asleep, but I'm even better at staying awake." I'd learned a million tricks for both over the years – autohypnosis and meditation for sleep, anxiety and pinching myself hard to stay awake, and more. "I'll wait until you're definitely asleep, and then I'll go too, OK?"

She nodded, wide-eyed. I knew she was older than she looked, but she was still young in terms of experience. Not that I'm a grizzled elder myself, but I'd been to a thousand different realities, and she'd been to a handful, so the gap between our levels of experience was vast. She had remarkable resources, but I still felt a responsibility to take care of her. "Let's just walk. That way we'll get tired faster, and we can move on sooner."

She kept hold of my hand and said, "OK, Zax." I welcomed the comfort of her touch. I loved people, but I'd spent most of the last three years alone. I'd been afraid Minna would choose to stay behind in one of the paradise worlds we'd encountered, but she seemed to genuinely like being with me, and saw my affliction as a doorway to adventure. Of course, other companions had felt the same way… for a while.

As we walked on the burning sands, I remembered being young – before, when I had parents and a home – and going to the beach with my family, running barefoot on hot sand toward the waves. The discomfort somehow made contact with the water even more delicious. Here, there was no prospect of water, and the experience was a lot less comfortable.

We trudged up one dune and down another and so on. We took careful sips of water as we went. "I am like a plant in a hothouse." Minna sighed. "Look at me, I have gone all green."

She *was* green, every bit of her exposed skin the color of spring grass. "Is that– are you sick?"

"Sick? No. When I am hungry, and do not have food, I can take energy from the sun, but I have to get greener to do it."

Photosynthesis! That was handy. At least she wouldn't starve. I worried about feeding myself sometimes, let alone a companion. I'd be OK food-wise, too – I still had some Compleat Eat bars I'd acquired on a techno-utopian world, and those could sustain me for days if need be.

Minna held up a hand to the sun, and little tendrils unfurled from under her fingernails, tiny leaves unfolding to drink the sunlight.

I asked something I'd been wondering about. "Minna, are you… some kind of a plant?" Crypsis, I was thinking. Maybe the [unable to translate] had grown her.

"Oh, no. I am an animal, and one a lot like you. I just have many other traits grafted onto me, to make me more useful to the Farm. They make me also more useful here in the orchard of worlds." She sighed. "Though with only sand around me I am not much use to me or you or anyone."

"It shouldn't take us long to get heat stroke and pass out. I'd say we should lie down, but the sand would burn us. Maybe it will get dark soon." The sun hadn't appreciatively moved in the sky. For all I knew we were on a planet that was tidally locked, or a constructed environment that remained daytime indefinitely.

"Zax, there is something alive under the sand." Minna closed her eyes, swayed a little, then turned. "There. That way."

I'd been in a desert, once, where terrible things moved beneath the sand. "Can you tell what it is?"

"Not animals, I don't think, or not many. Plants."

Huh. Well, who knew what we'd find over the next dune?

What we found was the corner of an ancient stone structure, drifted in sand, but with a human-sized opening in the leeward side. The blackness beyond might have been frightening under other circumstances, but here and now it just looked like *shade*. Still, I reached into my bag and unsheathed my glowblade. I tried to use the knife sparingly – I hadn't found a world with anything like the right kind of replacement power cells – but now was the time. I dialed the blade carefully to the brightness of a powerful flashlight.

I ducked into the darkness, and it was like stepping into a pool. I sagged in the shade and sighed at the cessation of heat, then shone the light around. We were in a small foyer at the top of a set of steep stairs. The walls were carved with drawings of human figures wearing robes, wielding tools of some kind, beside oddly bulbous figures. I sniffed, and there was a sort of pungent organic scent–

"Mushrooms," Minna said.

"Oh, you're right. The things in these carvings do look like big mushrooms. Maybe the people are mushroom-harvesters."

She shook her head, then nodded, then shook her head. "No, I mean yes, they do look like mushrooms, but no, I mean that smell is mushrooms, at least four edible varieties, six poisonous, and two psychedelic."

"You can tell all that from smelling?"

"I spent some months in the mycological caverns below the orchard. They were short-staffed because of the chokedamp.

Fungal organisms are not my specialty, but I know a few things."

I licked my lips. "Mushrooms like moisture, don't they?"

"Most, yes, and I do smell water."

I considered the stairs. "You don't sense any people, though?" I was still learning the extent of her abilities, which she mostly took too much for granted to bother mentioning.

She cocked her head. "If there are animals, they are not many and not big."

"Then let's try to find something to drink." I moved down the stairs, knife held before me, illuminating the walls. Here the carvings had been scraped away, scratched and gouged, leaving ugly scars in the stone. We reached the bottom, perhaps thirty meters below the surface, and followed a corridor. The walls were similarly scarred, but there were fist-sized clusters of transparent crystal along the ceiling, and when the light of my glowblade illuminated them, they somehow absorbed and multiplied that light, and carried on glowing behind us. "Those are nice," I murmured. Maybe I could chip some of the crystals off and take them with us... though for all I knew, they'd explode if I tried.

The pungent smell grew stronger as we entered a vast, round chamber. Crystals along the ground illuminated when we approached, outlining seven paths that radiated like spokes in a wheel, from a three-meter-wide stone bowl full of water that smelled strongly of minerals. "Do you think it's safe to drink?"

Minna sniffed. "It smells good to me."

I'd learned enough about Minna's capabilities to know that just because *she* could stomach it didn't mean *I* could. "I may not have as strong a constitution as you do."

"Even without my internal filtration systems, you should be safe. I detect no organic contamination." She dipped in a fingertip, then touched it to her tongue. "No heavy metal contamination. Safe and sweet and clean from deep below the sand."

The stone side of the pool came up to my waist, and I leaned across and stuck my face into the clear water, wetting my hair, then emerged, shook off the drops, and sucked up double handfuls of delicious coolness. I felt like a dried mushroom dropped into a bowl of water to be rehydrated. Minna was more delicate, sipping a bit and then sitting on the lip of the well while I refilled our water containers. She looked up at the cavern's ceiling, then pointed. Clusters of crystals picked up the light of their neighbors, and a glow washed up the curved walls and to the high, domed ceiling. There were more carvings up there, mostly intact, perhaps telling the history of whatever people had once dwelt here. "I like this place, Zax. Can we rest here a while? I was so jangled and disastered, and this place will solve my brains."

"I like that idea." I trailed my fingertips in the water. Traveling alone, I would have worried that monsters were lurking beyond the doorways at the end of the seven radiating paths, but Minna could sense "pests and predators," as she called them. She couldn't sense *every* danger – she had no sense for poison gas or killer robots or malicious intent, apparently – but this place seemed quiet and peaceful. "We'll stay until you get tired, OK?" Minna's rhythms hadn't been manipulated like my own, and she tended to get sleepy some hours before I did, though she could also get by well enough with occasional naps.

"I smell mushrooms that are good for eating, that way. Shall I gather some?"

"Please do!" I was getting spoiled by all the fresh food we'd had lately, but mushrooms were a rare treat. Even if I'd known how to identify edible mushrooms in one world, I wouldn't have trusted myself to do so in another, but when it came to agricultural matters, Minna was infallible.

She took the glowblade and one of our sacks and went humming along one of the paths, illuminated by crystals, and disappeared into the darkness beyond one of the seven archways.

I lay on the lip of the well and trailed my hand in the cold water, looking at the glowing crystals and the figures on the ceiling. My strange life is often composed of hectic terror alternated with tedious discomfort, so being here, cool, with enough water, the promise of a nice meal with a kind companion, and surrounded by unexpected subterranean beauty, was a pleasure I took the time to appreciate.

I sat up when I heard Minna coming, and frowned when I saw she didn't have the knife or the bag with her. Her clothes were all filthy, but she seemed cheerful enough. She'd made a basket from the front of her shirt and filled it with mushrooms of various hues (from white to deep purple) and sizes (from thumbnail to fist), which she dumped out on the edge of the fountain. "Hello! We can take all these with us. But look!" She picked up a handful of strawberry-sized caps in pale pink. "These will make us fall asleep quick fast! We can leave this place and go to the next one. Open up!" She pushed a cap toward my mouth.

I frowned and batted her hand away. "I thought you wanted to stay here and rest for a while?"

She shrugged. "You said stay until I get sleepy, I am sleepy, let's sleep, OK?" Her eyes were wide and wild, and she kept looking over her shoulder.

"Did something happen back there, Minna?" I'd never seen her behave this way before.

"No happenings, just a boring old mushroom garden, this whole place is boring, let's go someplace new, with people."

"Where's the knife, and the bag? The bag we can live without, but I'd hate to lose the glowblade… and why are you all dirty?"

"Dropped it, lost it, I'm dirty because mushrooms grow in dirt. Why so many questions, damn it, we should go now–"

Damn it? She'd never used language harsher than "gosh" as far as my linguistic virus could tell. Something was wrong. "I should at least go look for the knife – it's glowing, so it should be easy to find. We can leave after that, if you still want to."

She hopped up from the fountain. "No, no, I'll go, you stay, you don't need to go!" She ran down the path and through the archway again.

What was wrong with her? Had she eaten some mood-altering mushroom by mistake? I went after her.

A Mushroom Garden • Crypsis Again • Predators and Pests • Tourists • Not the Same as Forever

The room beyond the doorway was long and low and lit by crystals, and that light revealed plots of earth filled with dozens of corpses covered in mushrooms.

I gagged at the fungal stench and shuddered, then looked around for Minna. She'd only been a few steps ahead of me. Where had she gone? I stood on a stone path that went straight up the center of the room, with various side-paths dividing up the space, and the rest of the floor was soft, damp soil – this was a mushroom garden. Most of the bodies were half-submerged in the soil and deeply decayed, only their shapes and the shreds of ragged robes revealing they'd once been human, but a few bodies were fresher, and as a result far more disturbing.

"Minna! Where are you?"

"I got the knife!" She climbed out of a plot deeper in the room, stepping onto one of the side paths and brandishing the glowing blade. "Sorry I lost it, so clumsy, this is a clumsy place, let's leave."

"Why didn't you tell me about the bodies?" I looked around. "What happened here?"

"Maybe just funeral things. The dead return to the soil to feed the next generation, yes?"

I knelt and shook my head, pointing to some of the fresher bodies. "These people were killed; look, you can see the caved-in skulls, the cut throats, the chest wounds. Someone murdered them and put them here."

"It's just their culture, I guess, but I don't like it either, so let's go."

A low moan came from the soil bed behind her, and Minna stiffened, hunched her shoulders, then hurried toward me. "We should go, go, go, now, now, now."

"What is that noise?"

"Something bad, something that should be dead but won't stay dead, something that–"

Something buried in the soil climbed out and hauled itself onto the path. I stared when I realized it was Minna – another Minna, wearing just her underwear, streaked all over with dirt, expression dazed, with mushrooms growing out of wounds along her neck and chest. "Zax?" she croaked. "Run, Zax!"

The Minna with the knife stopped, turned, looked at her double, then turned back to me. "Yes, let's run, run to another world."

Crypsis. Plants that disguised themselves as other things. Why not ambulatory mushrooms that could look like people? Maybe those carvings weren't pictures of humans harvesting person-sized mushrooms, but people *fighting* them.

"Give me the knife, Minna, and we'll kill that... thing." I held out my hand, but the Minna before me wasn't fooled. She fell back a step instead, holding the knife out.

"You know." She sighed. "You know I took her clothes."

I angled myself so I could block any knife strikes with my left arm – Minna said the living wood was less vulnerable to injury than flesh, and my sensations were still duller in that limb, so being slashed there would hurt less. I still wasn't eager to experience the sensation. "Why did you attack her?"

"Better question: why didn't she *die*? These others die when you stab and stab and stab them."

"There is life all around me." My Minna wobbled along the path toward the predator. "I borrowed some of their life to fill the gaps you left in mine. Why did you attack me? Why not talk to me?"

"I couldn't talk to you until I fed on you, thing." The creature turned sideways, looking from me to Minna and back again. "I had to taste your thoughts to steal your voice. And in your thoughts I saw worlds full of wet things and soft things and flesh things, and that boy over there is the door. I have been here alone for so long in the dark. I have wandered these caverns and stood and looked at the light above where I cannot go, because the light is poisonous to me. I want to pass through the door of sleep and wake in another world."

"No one should be trapped alone in the dark," Minna said. "But why are you alone? Who killed all these people?"

"I did," the creature said. "I am the last of my kind. The meatlings thought they'd wiped us out, but I crept in and fed on their chief, and took her place, and killed them all while I wore her face." She pointed the knife at Minna, but looked at me. "Take me through the door of sleep, or I will kill her."

I held up my hands. "I'll take you, sure, but you have to fall asleep first."

"You want to trick me."

"You tasted my thoughts." The true Minna was still approaching, slowly but steadily. "You know it is true. When he sleeps, he travels."

"I saw that you travel in his arms, meat-thing, but I can travel in his arms while I'm awake."

I shook my head. "One person tried that. I don't know what she saw – I don't know what it's like, the place I go in my sleep, between worlds – but when I woke she was screaming and her mind was broken and she fled."

The creature spat. "I am not weak like meat."

"We can try it your way." I wanted to keep the mushroom-thing's attention, but she must have seen something in my eyes, because she turned and hissed just as Minna leapt on her. They tumbled off the side of the path and into the soft soil.

I raced forward, watching them roll and thrash. The creature lost some of her human definition, becoming grayish and vegetal in patches as she wrestled with Minna. My friend was valiant, but she wasn't made for fighting – she was a gardener pit against a predator. The knife came loose, though, and spun away, stuck blade first in the dirt. I snatched it up, plunged it into the back of the creature's neck, and yanked it out again.

She laughed, shoved my Minna's face deep into the soil, and then climbed up onto the path. "Stupid fleshrag. Blades do not hurt me–"

"Minna, close your eyes!" I shouted, and pushed the emergency button on the knife.

Even with my eyes closed and my head turned away, the light was searing, and the creature screamed and howled. The glowblade has an emergency signal flare function, a full-spectrum burst as bright as the sunlight this creature shunned.

The brightness vanished – the flare drains the power cells, and now my wonderful glowblade was just a knife – and I opened my eyes. The creature sprawled on her back on the path, arms deforming into tendrils, face a blasted blank. She hissed and began dragging herself toward the nearest patch of dirt.

I grabbed Minna's arm and pulled her out of the soil bed. She spat out dirt, then followed me to the central chamber and the fountain. The lights of the crystals grew dimmer with every passing second. "Minna, are you all right?"

"I will heal. I bear with me useful spores, too. Thank you for recognizing me, Zax, for knowing me from the predators and pests."

We hurriedly washed ourselves off in the fountain – Minna just immersed herself completely – and then I showed her the mushrooms the creature had brought me. "These are mostly death and hallucinations or both, Zax, but yes, these little ones, they should make us sleep. Now would be best." She looked up at the fading crystals on the ceiling, already so dim the carvings around them were invisible. "It will be dark soon."

She popped a mushroom, chewed it, and leaned against me, peaceful and cool.

I took a mushroom too, and stepped once more through the door of sleep, and into, I hoped, a brighter world.

World 1003: Another desert, but this time we woke near a river delta, and sat on the shore and watched boats made to look like water birds sail on the current, carrying parties of laughing people. Most were human, but about one in ten had the head of an animal – jackals, eagles, crocodiles, cats. There were pyramids, black and gleaming, made of square panels, some of them lit up to reveal apartments inside. Some of the humans were dressed differently – less often bare-chested for one thing, with fewer golden necklaces – and often held small devices in front of their faces, taking photographs or videos, I think.

We walked until we found an open-air market, full of booths with various delicacies and wares, except apparently it was all free. I ate spiced locusts and skewers of meat, while Minna, who didn't eat flesh, supped on the delicious petals of white flowers.

We sat on a bench and looked up at the night sky, and I saw satellites twinkling. "I think this is an amusement park," I said. "Though I can't be sure. I think everything's free because the guests here bought tickets, and now it's all paid for. The people with animal heads are robots, maybe. Or maybe not. I did visit a place once where everyone had the head of a dog, and they were all very frightened of me for having the kind of head we do. This place is certainly full of tourists, though."

"Tourists." Minna's world had no such concept, and she tested the word thoughtfully. "Is that what we are? Tourists?"

"We certainly never have time to become residents, so in a way, yes. We're on the grandest possible grand tour."

"I am glad you took me with you," Minna said. "Even though some places are scary, it is better than the Farm, and the scary places make the nice places feel better."

"I like traveling with you. I hope you stay with me for a while."

"You have had other friends, yes? Who came with you times and times? Why did they go away?"

I hesitated at the thought of returning to those sad memories, which I shy away from even in this diary. I finally said, "There have been a few, though some only stayed with me for two or three worlds. There was a woman I loved, who got lost and left behind. A scientist who helped me a lot, but who betrayed me in the end, and I had to run away. A little boy I saved from a bad place, and took to a better one – I was glad to find him a home, because it was hard, traveling with someone who needed me to take care of him so much. An android named Winsome – a machine, but they looked like a person, and could think like one – who powered down to sleep and powered up to wake... They were a wonderful companion, but after a couple of weeks we got separated, and I lost consciousness before we could find each other. Right before you, I traveled with a person named Laini for a while, but we didn't get along that well. She just wanted to find a place where she'd never have to work or feel pain again. She came from a terrible world, so I understood, but I still felt bad about our parting. She didn't even look back when she sent me on my way without her."

"I am sorry, Zax." She put her head on my shoulder. "I want to travel with you for as long as I can see ahead."

That wasn't the same as "forever," but maybe she just knew better than to promise such things. Even with the best of intentions, we might get separated someday, through no decision of our own, and then the river of my life would carry me farther away from her with every sleep.

No use thinking about sad possibilities when there are happy certainties, though. I sat with her in silence for a while, then said, "I smell like the inside of an old boot."

"I smell like the bottom of a compost pile."

"I haven't had a hot shower since I left the Dionysius Society."

"What's a hot shower?" she asked.

It was two more worlds before I had a chance to show her, and it's a shame the experience was so horribly marred by what happened right afterward.

Gardens • A City That's Not Visibly on Fire • Shopping Trip • Partners • New Skin • A Foreboding

World 1004: Minna and I went to sleep inside the bud of an immense flower during a torrential rainstorm on a garden world. (Not a jungle world. It was clearly cultivated, though the cultivators were nowhere in evidence.) We were traversing an ornamental pond as big as an inland sea when the rain began falling, torrential and stinging. Minna somehow coaxed the vast yellow flower, which bloomed from a lily pad the size of a ballroom dance floor, into opening, and once we climbed inside, it closed around us, watertight and translucent and as roomy as a vacation cabin.

We nestled in the soft, deliciously scented interior and watched lightning flash beyond the golden walls while we shared out the last of some sweet red bean cakes we'd picked up in the previous world. There was nectar inside the flower, but Minna sampled it and said it was too potent for us to drink without ill effects. I imagined what sort of bees or birds might sup from flowers this size, and wondered how they would even fly if they were of commensurate size, as the atmosphere didn't seem unusually dense or oxygen-rich. But if the garden was home to immense fauna as well as flora, the rain kept the creatures away… though occasionally we heard splashes, and once the lily pad rocked like something had bumped it from underneath, and I thought of goldfish the size of submarines, and frogs the size of houses.

Minna yawned and leaned against me. I'd wondered when we began traveling together if romance, or even merely sex, would blossom between us – they had in the past, a couple of times, intervals of sweetness before things went sour – but Minna had evinced no interest beyond deepening friendship, and my own feelings toward her were more brotherly than anything else. (I'd kissed her once, on the lips, with tongue, in the first new world we visited together, but that was just to share my linguistic virus with her, and it had been no more intimate than any medical procedure.) She dozed off with her head in my lap, and when I could tell she was down deep, I let myself fall asleep, too.

I opened my eyes to a brisk pink dawn and sat up, looking for threats. We were in another garden now, though one more human-scale. Sometimes the transitions between worlds seem strangely linked that way. I fall asleep in a palace and wake up in a temple; fall asleep in a meadow and wake up on a sports field; fall asleep on a rooftop and wake up in a spire. But other times I fall asleep in a war zone and wake up on a peaceful beach, or in the midst of a city and wake in the forest. There may be a pattern to my transitions, but my observations haven't uncovered any yet.

I jostled Minna awake – she yawned and blinked and smiled at me and the sky – and stood up. We were in a park, I realized, not a garden, and beyond the trees towered graceful gleaming skyscrapers, with bulbous slow-moving aerial vehicles drifting among them. Unlike the last city we'd visited, this one didn't appear to be metaphorically or literally on fire. "Civilization." We'd been to so many desolate or rural or simply strange worlds, I'd wondered when we'd find a developed one.

Then again, there could have been thriving cities just over the horizon in almost any of the places we'd visited. It's not as if we woke in monocultural realities that were all desert or garden, necessarily. I assume the various realities I visit are as rich and diverse and varied as the world of spheres and harmonies I was born into, but I never get to see much beyond the area where I open my eyes – how far can you travel, in a day or two, usually on foot? Sometimes it staggers me to think that every place I visit is just one region of one planet (or moon, or construct) in a whole universe of other possible places. Perhaps I even return to the same branch of the multiverse on occasion, and just wake in different sections, or even different galaxies. How would I ever know?

"Civilization? There are lots of trees at least." Minna stretched and breathed deep.

"Trees, yes, and also people, and shops. We can finally resupply properly. Come on." She took my hand and we walked out of the little dell where we'd awakened onto a curving smooth path. People jogged or strolled by or pushed babies in carriages, and they seemed to be the same species we were. Even our clothes weren't *too* different from the local norm, though they were dirtier. One couple standing by a pond, wearing black coats with voluminous hoods, might have been staring at us – it was hard to tell with their faces shadowed – but I wasn't bothered. We probably looked like vagrants, if this world had vagrants. To be fair, that's what we were.

I thought at first this might be a techno-utopia – post-scarcity societies were the easiest to resupply in – but when we left the park there were people handing out fliers on street corners, and a busker playing a thirteen-stringed instrument while people tossed occasional coins, so I knew this was some variety of consumer culture, complete with income inequality. I could cope with that, too.

Minna was understandably drawn to the shiniest towers, the tiered plazas full of shimmering crystal fountains and abstract sculptures that shaped and reshaped themselves as we watched, but I'd been doing this a lot longer than she had, so I tugged her along to the outskirts instead, where the buildings were lower and graffiti stained the walls and trash blew in the streets. There were signs over the shops in a spiky script, but I couldn't read them. The linguistic virus allowed me comprehend spoken languages and make myself understood, but it didn't do anything for the printed word. I could look in windows, though, and I found the one I wanted: dusty, with a display of various objects in a profuse jumble, including musical instruments, gaudy jewelry, and small appliances. "Do you want to come in?" I asked.

Minna looked at the dank shop doubtfully. "If I have to."

I looked at the buildings along the empty street – I hadn't seen any ground vehicles here – and pointed. "Is that a plant nursery?"

Her head whipped around. There was a lot down on the corner, with makeshift shelves of stone blocks and wooden boards set up behind a fence, displaying a profusion of sad-looking plants in pots. "Oooh. Plants from civilization."

"Why don't you go look around?" I said. "I'll do my business here and then meet you. Remember, this is a world where you can't just take things, OK? Look round, and if there's something you want, I'll see if we can buy it when I get there."

"I hate being apart from you," she said, but her gaze never wavered from the drooping plants. "What if you fall asleep while we are separated?"

"We just woke up. We've got all day, and it's only half a block. I'll watch my head and try to avoid getting knocked out." She wasn't being ridiculous – it was indeed a risk for us to be apart – but if something rendered me unconscious while she was awake, she wouldn't be able to travel with me anyway.

"All right. Come soon." She went over to the nursery, almost skipping.

I pushed through the door to the shop, a chime sounding over my head. The lights were dim, better to hide the poor condition of most of the wares on display. There would be valuable things here, but I knew they'd be behind the counter, or locked up in the back. The shopkeeper was white-bearded and thin, and wore a black suit and a complex set of glasses, with lenses of different shapes and sizes and colors arrayed on articulating arms. The lenses moved aside by themselves so he could peer at me with naked eyes. "Are you here to sell, or buy?"

Someone in a nicer shop would have looked at my grass-stained, damp clothes and thrown me out, but a place like this, in my experience, took a more relaxed approach to potential clientele. "Sell, certainly, and buy, possibly." I put my battered bag on the counter and reached inside.

Coins, even coins of the most precious metals, usually brought too many questions – where is this from, what country, what period – that I couldn't answer, or came with answers that were meaningless in a world beyond their origin. Rings and chains and bracelets, however, were recognizable in most worlds inhabited by humanoids, and I always picked those up in places where riches were cheap. I put rings of gold, platinum, silver, and palladium on the counter. "Do any of these interest you?"

The lenses moved into place, and one began to emit a soft blue glow, as he peered close to the jewelry. He grunted. "Pretty varied mix here. A couple of decent pieces."

"They're more valuable as a set, too," I said.

He grunted, which wasn't a yes or a no. "I can offer you eighty scrilla for the lot."

I had no idea if that was a lot or a little, but I snorted derisively and started to sweep the rings back into my bag. Shops like this never gave you a decent offer at first.

The lenses spun. "Wait, wait. I could go as high as a hundred."

"These were hand-forged, not machined," I said.

"All right, A hundred-and-ten."

"One-fifty."

Now it was his turn to scoff. "One-twenty-five, or you can take them anywhere else you like – you won't get a better offer."

"It's a deal."

He nodded, then gestured to a small black rectangle on the counter. A gleaming needle rose from the pad. "Just prick your thumb and the funds will transfer."

Ah. This world had some sort of biometric banking system – take a drop of blood, find the associated account, transfer funds electronically. That was no help.

"Could we do… cash?" I hoped they had something of the sort

in this society, and that my linguistic virus would translate the term appropriately.

"Clotting issues?" he said, then gave a small smile. "Or something you'd like to keep out of a joint account?"

"Something like that," I said.

He reached under the counter, manipulated some sort of terminal, and then handed me a small card, greasy-looking and black. "Universal gift card," he said. "Should work just about everywhere."

I tapped the card on the counter and thanked him. "Could you point me toward a good sporting goods store? And a pharmacy?"

I found Minna deep in conversation with the woman who owned the nursery, the latter wide-eyed and nodding. I noticed that all the plants looked more lush, robust, and vibrant – instead of drooping, they blossomed and reached for the sky. Minna had been doing a little work, it seemed. "No, no," Minna said, "just this, really." She had some flakes of white material in a clear plastic bag.

"But that's just some fungus that was growing on an ornamental shrub, I don't even *sell* it," the woman objected. "You have to let me pay you back somehow."

"You could put a little something on this card," I said smoothly.

Minna glanced at me, then nodded. "That would be fine!"

"Are you her..."

"Partner." Minna linked arms with me and beamed.

The woman shrugged, took my card to her kiosk, pricked her thumb on a needle, touched the card to her black pad, then handed it back. Numbers shimmered on the front, jumping from one-twenty-five to one-thirty.

Minna said her farewells, giving some last care-and-feeding-of-plants tips, and then we strolled away. "What's the fungus for?" I asked.

"You will see. We just need water and I will show you."

We returned to a shinier part of town and found a park with

lots of sparkling fountains and cobbled walkways and surprisingly comfortable benches. Minna scooped a little water from a fountain into the bag, then stirred her finger inside. The fungus dissolved at her touch and the water formed a paste. "Perfect. Now your arm?"

I looked around. The plaza was mostly empty, just two people on a bench some distance away, wearing dark hoods and scattering seeds to feed some of the local flying lizards. I wondered if they were the same hooded people who'd been looking at us in the park, but if so, they weren't paying any attention to us now.

I took the glove off my right hand and pushed my sleeve up, revealing my wooden limb. I'd kept it covered because worlds with fully functional biological prosthetics were few and far between, and I didn't like to draw attention. Minna smeared some of the fungal paste on the arm… and the paste began to spread, flowing all over the wood, forming a membrane, pale and slick. The fungus reached the part of my arm that was still original flesh, and it tingled… and then a wave of color and texture moved across the paste, perfectly matching the shade of my own skin.

I held up my hand in wonder as the substance spiraled up my fingers and covered them with something indistinguishable from my flesh. I flexed the hand, and brushed my fingertips on the stone of the bench where we sat. I could *feel*. I'd had sensation in the wooden hand before, but it was faintly dulled, and this… this was just like the hand I'd been born with. "Minna, that's amazing."

"I am sorry it took me this long to find a suitable substrate. It is just like your real skin, except it will not tan in the sun – it will convert sunlight into energy, though, like my skin does."

I grabbed her in a hug. "I can live with having one pale arm and one tanned one. Thank you, Minna. You're amazing."

"You are the one who shows me a new world every day. I am happy to help." She rubbed a little of the paste on the back of her hand, where she'd gotten a deep scratch in a prior world, and I watched it cover the injury, shimmer, and blend in with her flesh. She was such a remarkable woman. I was lucky to have her. "What now, Zax?"

"A hot meal," I said, "and then we go shopping." She took my hand and we set off into the city.

If I'd looked back, I might have seen the couple in their dark hoods following us.

Good Drugs • A Hot Shower • An Intrusion • Some of Your Blood • An Old Friend • Enter Polly

We found a café where the clientele didn't seem excessively fancy, and ordered by pointing at what other people were having, since we couldn't read the menus. We got soup, bread, and salad, though even Minna didn't recognize all the greens, and the soup was a discordant blend of sweet and spicy I'd never encountered before. The broker had paid me decently for the rings, it seemed, or else food was very cheap here, based on the small dent the meals put in my credit. Afterward, we stopped into a pharmacy – really a housewares shop with an apothecary in the back – next door. I inquired after sedatives, claiming chronic insomnia, and was pleased with what they had available over the counter.

Then we asked directions until I found the district with the sporting goods store the pawnbroker had recommended. The shop was an absolute palace of the recreational arts, and I looked longingly at collapsible canoes and luxurious self-erecting camping pavilions, but they were rather more than we could carry on our backs. I did pick up a newer backpack: waterproof, engineered for comfort even when full of weight, and with countless little pockets. I gave Minna my old pack to carry, and set about filling the new one with dehydrated food packets, a hand-cranked lantern, water purification tablets, a little fishing kit, a camp stove with fuel, and other useful items. We both got new shoes and better socks, and a new set of all-weather clothes each, plus hooded ponchos of some smart material that would keep us warm and dry. The purchase depleted my credit by two-thirds, and I mused about how best to spend the rest, since the money wouldn't be any good to us in the next world.

"Minna," I said. "Remember what I said about a hot shower?"

"It is like a warm rain, but… warmer?"

"Oh, Minna. I have such things to show you."

The hotel was initially reluctant to accept the universal gift card, but when I said, "Clotting disorder," they became apologetic and accommodating. It took my card down to single digits, but we booked a garden suite with a balcony that overlooked the hotel's lush interior courtyard. "We'll fall asleep in an actual bed tonight, Minna. Maybe passing out in luxury will make us wake up in the same."

I let her take a shower first, after showing her how to work the controls (which took some effort on my part; it's amazing all the different approaches to basic plumbing various humanoid civilizations create). She emerged after a while, wearing her new overalls, shimmering and smiling, with small white flowers in her hair. They looked like decoration, but I was fairly sure they'd grown that way. I went into the bathroom, stripped off my grimy clothes, and ran the shower as hot as it would go. The stall was beautifully tiled and the showerhead had ten different settings. I played with all of them. I marveled at the seamlessness of my new arm's new flesh, poking and prodding the totally skin-like skin. I tried all the different soaps and shampoos and conditioners. Being in a world with this level of comfort was rare enough that I always made a point of enjoying it.

Eventually I emerged from the stall, feeling better in my body than I had in weeks. Everything was clean and nothing hurt. I toweled off and dressed in some of the new clothes we'd bought at the camping store, then stepped out of the bathroom. "I think there's enough on the card left for room service–"

"No thank you. I already ate." A figure in a black coat with a deep hood – one of the people I'd seen twice that day, I realized – sat in a chair by the doors to the balcony. The other figure was on the bed, also hooded, holding a knife with a chipped-stone blade to Minna's throat. Minna stared at me, wide-eyed.

"We don't have much money, but you're welcome to it." I had the card in my pocket, and I tossed it onto the bed. "Take it and leave."

"I don't want that," the one in the chair said. Something about his voice was familiar, but I'd been to so many worlds, and heard so many voices, that I was used to false senses of recognition. I couldn't actually *know* him – I'd never been to this reality before. "I want some of your blood."

I shook my head. "Clotting disorder. I don't have an account you can access with my blood."

"You misunderstand. We're not local thugs. We're not locals at all. Have you forgotten me already?" He pushed back his hood and smiled.

I didn't smile back. I stared. He was the Lector. Dark hair going gray at the temples, brushed back from a high forehead, round silver-rimmed glasses that weren't for correcting vision – he was from a techno-utopia – but for scanning his environment, noble features like the face of an emperor on an old coin. He looked friendly and capable and benevolent, but I knew he was only sometimes the first, always the second, and never the third, though he'd fooled me for a long time. "How… How did you get here?"

I'd traveled to scores of worlds with the Lector. He'd studied my ability (or affliction), theorized about its origins, gifted me with the linguistic virus and other tools that had saved me more than once, convinced me to keep a journal to catalogue the worlds I visited, and acted as a father figure and a mentor… until the day he tied me up and tried to vivisect me in an abandoned hospital in a post-apocalyptic world. I'd escaped, stunned and broken by his betrayal, and ferociously, spitefully glad he was left behind, trapped forever in a horrible place devoid of human life.

But he was here. He'd followed me somehow.

"Your blood, Zaxony." I recognized that affable, lecturing tone. "I took your blood, back in that charming hospital where you abandoned me, and I synthesized a sort of… potion, I suppose you'd call it, with your primitive understanding of science. A *magical* potion. I drink it, or rather take a drop onto my tongue, and for a while, I'm like you. When I wake up in the same world twice I know it's time for another dose." He stood up. "You tried to strand me in a dead world. Some people might want revenge for that." He picked up a rectangular metal object – his "traveling case," a miniature laboratory and manufactory, a bit of techno-utopia made portable – and opened it on the bed, revealing gleaming glass cylinders, plastic tubing, needles, and small scientific devices I couldn't identify. "But for now, just more of your blood will do. I'm running quite low on my serum. I've isolated the active compound in your blood, but haven't been able to synthesize it."

So it was something in my blood that made me travel? That was more than I'd known before, but it wasn't the issue I focused on. "You've been following me, all this time?"

"Often several worlds behind. I was stuck in that hospital you abandoned me in for a while, perfecting the serum. I wasn't even sure at first I was visiting the same worlds you did, or in the same order, but occasionally people remember you. I seem to appear in the same place you do, too, within centimeters. I've seen the remains of your campsites, once or twice. It finally occurred to me that I might try to get ahead of you, and lay in wait. So that's what I did, quite recently. You spent a full day in that place with the river and the people with animal heads, didn't you? It seemed the sort of place to attract you. I took a sedative moments after I got there, and did the same in the world with the lily pads. I've been here nearly two days."

"Who's your… friend?"

He glanced over. "Do you think you're the only one who can take on companions, Zaxony? Show your face, dear."

The other figure pushed her hood down, and I groaned. She

looked just like Minna, but when she smiled, her teeth were sharp triangles. The fungal shapeshifter from the desert world.

"I call her Polly," the Lector said. "Because she's so polymorphous." He giggled. I'd forgotten about that incongruous high-pitched laugh of his – to think, I'd once found it endearingly childlike. "I met her not long after you did. That's when I realized how close I was to catching up. I told her to keep that form, because it might prove useful."

"She's dangerous, Lector. She's an infiltrator, an assassin. Her kind killed a whole culture."

"She is a deft infiltrator," he said fondly. "She went to the front desk and pretended to be Minna and said she'd lost her key. That's how we got into your room. As far as being an assassin, well. Not if you cooperate. Sit there." He nodded to the chair he'd departed, and I sat, keeping my eyes on Polly and Minna. "There's still so much work to be done, Zaxony." He began setting up a jar, tube, and needle array on the table by my chair. "I'm convinced there must be a way to control where you travel, or at least influence it. There is some kind of steering mechanism happening in your subconscious – otherwise you'd be dead by now, waking up in a pool of lava or an endless sea of carnivorous creatures or falling from a great height. Something in you *must* reach out to make sure the place you're going is safe, and since not all places are safe, it must be able to choose alternate destinations. I will find out how to control that mechanism consciously."

"Are you trying to find your way back home, Lector?" I said.

"Oh, no. I was respected there, and life was pleasant, but I have greater goals now."

"We will create an empire that spans the multiverse," Polly said. "We will open routes of trade and conquest between worlds."

The Lector chuckled. "I may have shared some of my more ambitious ideas with Polly. Forgive her. She finds thoughts of conquest exciting. Though once I can synthesize the active ingredient in your blood, such ambitions are not outside the scope of possibility."

"I will lead his army, to quell the unruly," Polly said.

I shook my head. "Lector, that's... You come from a world of peace and plenty, how can you want... what she wants?"

He waved that away. "I come from a world of stagnation and complacency. I've never felt more alive than I have since I met you, Zaxony. Each day is a new adventure. I am dizzied by the possibilities. Once I unlock the secrets hidden in your body, I'll begin to narrow down those possibilities, and chart my ascendance. Your arm, please."

I rolled up the sleeve on my left arm. The Lector swabbed the crook of my elbow with something cold, then stuck a needle in. The sensation was familiar. I'd let him take my blood before, when I thought he was my friend, and trying to help me instead of himself. I watched as my bodily fluids began to drip into the glass jar.

"Let Minna go," I said. "You don't need her."

"I need her as leverage, Zaxony. Normally, if I needed blood from an unwilling donor, I'd sedate them, but here we are."

"At least have Polly take the knife from her throat. I'm cooperating."

He glanced over. "I think you can be a bit less vigilant, Polly. From what you told me, the girl is some sort of farmhand. Hardly a threat."

Polly bared her teeth at me, but she did lower the knife. She kept an arm around Minna's chest, though.

"We could work together again, Zaxony," the Lector said.

"You tried to kill me."

"I was studying you! I theorized that your ability came from an unknown substance in your blood, but is that substance secreted by a gland, or produced in your marrow, or caused by a virus, or is it some kind of bizarre antibody? I learned all I could non-invasively, and sadly, more extreme explorations became necessary... but you fled before I got very far."

"We were friends, Lector. Then you tied me down to a table and came at me with knives."

"Knives! So dramatic. They were scalpels."

"So what if it was my marrow, or my glands? How does knowing that help you, if I'm dead? It's like the story about the hen who lays diamond eggs, and the farmer kills her to get all the diamonds inside at once, but then–"

"Please spare me the folktales of your primitive homeworld, Zaxony. I didn't plan to kill you. I was just going to do a little exploratory surgery and take some samples for further study. It's unfortunate that I couldn't sedate you. In truth, I planned to give you stimulants to keep you from passing out and traveling due to the shock of the procedures. I would have used local anesthetic where appropriate, though, of course. I'm not a monster."

"I'm a person, Lector. Not an experimental subject. Don't you have any sort of... of scientific ethics?"

He chuckled again. "Oh, Zaxony. We've visited all those worlds, all those different cultures, places where murder is sport, where they've conquered death and commit elaborate suicides as art... Haven't you realized that ethics, morality, all those ideas, are entirely arbitrary? They're just local norms. We transcend such things, my boy. At least, I will. You lack the imagination. I–"

The Lector stopped short when the point of a stone knife poked into the side of his neck. "Let Zax go," Minna said.

I tore the needle out of my arm and jumped out of the chair. Polly was on the bed, writhing, and she fell off the far side with a thump. "What did you do to her?" the Lector said.

"This." Minna put her hand against his cheek, and her flesh began to crawl – literally, to crawl off her hand, and onto his face. It was the fungus paste, I realized, the new skin she'd made to cover my wooden arm and her injury; she could control the material, and I watched as it crawled across the Lector's mouth and sealed his lips shut with a seamless sheet of skin. The Lector's eyes went wide. Minna withdrew the knife, and the Lector scrabbled backward on the floor, making incomprehensible noises and trying to tear at the new skin, without success.

The flesh began to climb up to his nostrils, and I put a hand on

Minna's shoulder. "No, Minna, we... we don't kill, not if we can help it."

"He is a weed," she said. "He is a predator. A pest."

"I know, but he's a person. We can get away, and leave him behind, without killing him."

Minna sniffed. She stepped toward the Lector, and he cowered, but she just brushed his face with a fingertip, and the new flesh stopped moving.

"What now?" she said.

"We take our things and go. He said he's almost out of his serum, so we can escape–"

The Lector leapt up, grabbed the jar of my blood, and rushed for the balcony. He vaulted over the railing, and Minna gasped. We both ran out, and watched him drop eight floors to the inner courtyard. He hit the ground and rolled, clutching the jar to his chest to protect it from breaking, then ran off toward the lobby. "He has reinforced muscles and bones," I said. "It's something they do on his world. He can take a lot of punishment."

"Zax, he got your blood, he will make *more* of the serum, he'll–"

I held up my arm. "He put the needle in my wooden arm, Minna. Right in the crook of my wooden elbow. Did he really get my blood?"

She looked at me, then laughed, a bright tinkle. "No, it looks like blood, but it is really a kind of sap. The wooden arm doesn't connect to your circulatory system, just your nerves. What he collected in that jar... it would probably taste good poured over pancakes, but I do not think it can help him travel. We–"

"Kill you both."

We spun, and Polly rose up from the far side of the bed. Since Minna had sealed her mouth and nostrils, she'd opened a new mouth and nose on her forehead, giving her face a strange, upside-down look.

I looked longingly at my new backpack full of wonderful gear, but it was all the way across the room, too close to Polly. My old, battered sack was on the floor near my feet, so I grabbed that, pulled Minna into the bathroom, and slammed the door just in time for Polly to thump hard against the other side. She began pounding on the door and screeching in an entirely inhuman way.

I opened my bag, glad I hadn't emptied its contents into my new pack. The little sack from the pharmacy was there, and I popped a pair of fast-acting sleeping pills from a blister pack. "You first." Minna obligingly swallowed, and curled up beside me. I waited a few moments for her breathing to deepen.

A tendril slipped beneath the crack under the door, like a curling vine. Polly, reaching in. "Just leave us alone," I said. "There's a whole world out there for you to prey on."

"All the worlds," she hissed. "I will feast on all the worlds." The tendril quested blindly toward me.

I pulled Minna into the shower and shut the glass door for a little more protection. Then I took a pill of my own, swallowing it dry. The edges of my vision got hazy right away, and my head nodded.

"All the worlds," Polly said, over and over. "All the worlds."

As I drifted off to sleep and whatever world came next, I was grateful for the first time in a long time that I couldn't dream, because I know that voice would have followed me into my nightmares.

Traps • Poor Butterflies • Cages and Pits • Summoning Circle • Last Ones • Here to Help

In World 1006 I woke to a cloud of white butterflies. I rose, and they spun and whirled into the air like a snowfall in reverse. The butterflies were settled all over Minna's sleeping body, attracted I think by the little flowers that had bloomed on her head like a crown. I shook her, and she smiled up at me before she even opened her eyes.

I felt OK, too. The transition is good for panic: my heart was no longer pounding, my body no longer humming with the chemical accelerants that drive fight and flight. I looked around, and it seemed like a nice world: long grasses bobbing in a breeze, butterflies and flowers everywhere, the air perfumed. The sky was a delicate pale blue, and there were things like kites crossed with hang gliders in a profusion of colors, swooping among the clouds. Vehicles, toys, who knew? I couldn't quite tell if they were small and close or large and far away. "It smells good here," Minna said. "Life, life, so much life." She held out her hands and butterflies landed on them as little flowers opened up on her knuckles.

I nodded. "We have to keep going, though. The Lector said he was running low on his serum, but I don't know what that means, exactly. I'd like to put a few morc worlds between us."

Minna nodded. "He said he appears in a world where you do, yes? I think I can help to slow them down." She drew out her pouch and shook a handful of seeds into her hand, sorting them and plucking out three black ones. "The [unable to translate] used these against some of the workers during a…" She hesitated. "Disagreement. I plucked a few of the seeds because I was interested to see if I could graft their fast-growing properties onto nicer sorts of plants."

"What do they do?"

"We call them strangler vines, but they do not really *strangle*. I know you said we cannot uproot those weeds and kill them, and you are my friend so I will do what you wish. If I plant these and give them a little spit of my mouth and blood of my body they will grow faster than fast into a little nest of vines. They will settle and be still until someone touches them, and then they will *grab*." She swiped out both her arms like she was snatching an invisible bird from the air. "They will not hurt, but they will hold long and strong."

"Let's do it. Anything to widen the gap between us and the Lector." The one good thing about my situation was that I could walk away from anything, leap free of any danger, step away from any consequences. The thought of an enemy pursuing me across worlds was a new and distressing one. Before now, I could escape any problem as long as I had a sleeping pill handy… not that I acted with impunity anyway. Just because my presence in those worlds was ephemeral didn't mean that the lives of the people who lived there were unimportant. As a harmonizer, I'd been taught that every person is part of a whole, and every act has consequences, often unintended ones. While the worlds I visited were, as far as I could tell, hermetically sealed from one another, they *could* affect each other… through the medium of me. I had a responsibility not to ruin any lives I touched. I stole things, sometimes, when I had no choice, and I fought, when my life was at risk, but I always strove to minimize the damage I did. If I *acted* with the impunity I truly possessed, I would be a monster, like the Lector or Polly.

Minna dug a little hole in the spot where we'd appeared, put seeds in the hole, spat on top of them, then produced a thorn from her fingertip and cut the back of her hand, letting a few drops of blood fall in. She pushed dirt over the seeds and said, "Stand back, my Zax." We both withdrew. The long grasses around the spot where she'd planted the seeds turned dry and brittle before our eyes, her seeds somehow sapping them of their vitality to feed themselves. Finger-thick vines of slimy green burst up from the ground and curled into a circle like a rolled-up garden hose. Minna looked around, picked up a stone, and tossed it into the circle. Vines rose quicker than I could see and snatched the stone out of the air, wrapping it completely in filaments. I whistled. "That's fantastic, Minna."

She beamed. We moved some distance from the vines and I plucked out more sleeping pills. We settled onto the ground, butterflies landing on us when we stopped moving, and took more pills.

We woke in a cobblestoned square beside a fountain that bubbled with something viscous and black. My mouth was dry and my head was fuzzy. Too many sedatives, too close together. I groaned, and Minna patted my cheek. "I worry: these pills, putting you under, putting you out... I can control my body and things that go inside in lots of ways, but you..."

I sat up, nice and slow. "I'll be OK. The Lector didn't just give me the linguistic virus. He used technology to improve the function of my liver and kidneys, increase the resilience of my stomach lining, allow me to go longer without food or water, and various other things. All so he could keep feeding me uppers and study me for longer, of course, but it means I can live the way I do without lasting side effects. My head will clear soon."

"Still," Minna said, "I will think about better ways for you than drugs."

"I'm never opposed to self-improvement."

We considered the new world in which we'd arrived. The

square was enclosed by a black wrought iron fence that curved overhead and became a dome, so it was like we were inside a large birdcage. A thin gray fog attenuated the light, making everything hazy, but there were buildings of gray stone rising up nearby. A handful of butterflies spiraled up from me and flew about in wild, erratic loops – they must have been carried along in the transition. I wondered if the journey had driven them mad – could butterflies go insane?

I sometimes worried that I was carrying spores, viruses, or other invisible bits of detritus from one world to another, and in my darker moments I had nightmarish visions of leaving worlds devastated by alien pathogens in my wake. I'd never ended up in a world that killed *me*, though, and I had to hope I wasn't poisoning the multiverse; surely the Lector would have gloated about my causing that kind of destruction, if he'd seen it in my wake. Though the Lector and Polly were a kind of poison in themselves.

"Poor butterflies," Minna said. "I sense some other life in this place, but not nearby." She watched as the butterflies flew between the bars of the cage and vanished into the fog. "Should we stay a while or go farther? Even if the Lector and Polly follow, the vines should hold them for a while."

There was a gate in the cage that we could leave through, but I had worries. For one thing, this was a place where the fountains bubbled black ichor, which didn't bode well in terms of us fitting in with the inhabitants. For another... we were in a cage. *Why* were we in a cage? Maybe it was just an architectural whim, but maybe not. I'd been on an archipelago once where the locals lowered tourists with water-breathing apparatuses into cages, then lowered those cages into the sea, so the tourists could see the terrifying toothed sea monsters that teemed around them without being eaten. Were there creatures here, in this fog? Were there cages scattered all over this city, meant to protect inhabitants in the event of an attack? I still had plenty of sleeping pills. "Let's move on."

* * *

World 1008 was a pit full of bones, some old and yellowed, some fresh and white with bits of meat clinging to them. Something roared out beyond the rim of the pit, and then human-sounding voices laughed uproariously and applauded. Minna whimpered. I felt the familiar yearning to help, to harmonize, to bring balance… but I could sense we were in a place where harmony was not welcome. We quickly took more pills, and as I drifted off, I thought, *I wish I could do some good.*

On the 1009th world, we appeared in a circle of seven standing stones. I stared up at a full moon, straight above me, perfectly centered above the circle, and the moon had a halo of ice crystals in a perfect circle around *it.* When I sat up, Minna's head in my lap, I looked into the eyes of a figure standing outside the circle. The moon was so bright and everything else so dark that I could see her clearly. She was tall, with dark skin and long black hair cascading down across bare breasts. Halfway down her stomach her skin gradually changed to gleaming black scales, and her legs were scaled until they reached taloned birdlike feet. Wings, membranous and batlike, rose from her shoulders, and small pointed horns protruded from her forehead.

I raised my hand and offered a tentative wave. Humanoids didn't tend to develop bat wings naturally, and the scales were very strange too, but I had been on worlds before where science had created strange new variations on the human form for reasons of religion, art, or commerce. This didn't seem like a technologically advanced world, though – the stars were clear and bright, and there were no sources of light pollution glowing beyond the perimeter of the stones. The air, too, smelled incredibly clean; there's a special quality to the atmosphere that's unique to pre-industrial worlds.

Or, perhaps, post-industrial ones. I had been to a few fallen worlds in my time, places that had once been home to technologically advanced civilizations, but collapsed into ruin and disarray, the marvels of the prior age passed into myth and legend. In such fallen worlds, I sometimes found people who seemed unlikely to have evolved naturally – uplifted animals, intelligent machines, hybrids and chimeras, ignorant of their own origins.

The local's eyes literally flashed red as she gazed at us, and her tongue was forked when it flickered out as she spoke. "The summoning is complete! Finally the Last Ones have answered our call." She knelt, lowering her head. "Please, Last One, heed my plea: my people need your help."

Oh, dear. We had, it seemed, appeared in some kind of summoning circle, and this person thought we were the answer to her prayers.

Minna stirred and blinked up at me. "Mmm, Zax, it smells nice here." She sat up and saw the woman watching us. "Hello, friend!" she said cheerfully. Even after all she'd been through, she was still ready to think the best of people. "What's your name?"

"I am called Drywanu."

"I'm Minna, and this is Zax." She walked across the circle, and the woman leapt to her feet and stepped back, eyes flashing red, as Minna stepped through the stones. She cocked her head. "Huh. That felt sort of funny."

I followed her, and there *was* a sort of buzz or shift as I stepped out of the stones, as if I'd come through a charged field of some kind.

"Impossible," Drywanu said. "The Last Ones were known to appear inside the circle, but they never step through!"

I looked back into the circle. There were small, shiny spots on some of the stones, that could have been the lenses of cameras… or projectors. Maybe the Last Ones had projected holograms of themselves into the circle in response to "summonings" in the past, and that buzzing field was part of some old machinery meant to keep whatever Drywanu was from passing through. "When did you last see a Last One in this circle?" I asked.

She crossed her arms and shivered. "A thousand full moons or more, the old ones say. Most have given up coming for counsel, but things are so dire, I came these past ten nights, praying for a reply. My elders say the Last Ones have left this world entirely, but you… you look as they did, and you *step through*. How can this be?"

"The world is full of mysteries," I said. Always a true statement. "We're here, now. How can we help?"

"Will you come and see, Minna and Zax?"

"We will."

Starving • Cornucopia • A Descent • Six Hundred Cycles Late • A Favor • The New Ones

The stones stood at the highest point in the surrounding countryside, and Drywanu led us down. "I will take you to our village, Morgenrothross, named for the Last One who founded this place and kindled the life within us." She glanced at us, almost shyly. "Do you… know him?"

"I'm afraid we haven't had the pleasure," I said.

The land was rolling hills, topped by stands of trees, the slopes covered in lush grass. We followed a well-worn path, leading us through wooden gates in low stone walls. There should have been animals grazing in a place like this, but there weren't. Maybe they were sleeping. I hadn't grown up around agriculture, and wasn't quite sure how it all worked. Eventually we reached a sort of dip in the ground, filled with a handful of low houses, some built partly into the ground, and others made of wood and earth, all with roofs of living grass. There were small chimneys poking out of some structures, but the night was warm, and no smoke rose. The village was organized around a central structure that looked a bit like a gazebo, strikingly different from the rest of the construction because it was made of shining bright metal.

"The Last Ones have heard our pleas!" Drywanu shouted. Figures emerged from the houses, watching us, some pointing, some gasping, some falling to their knees. The people here were variously winged, horned, spined, and scaled, a variety and profusion of shapes that reminded me of the fantasies and fairy tales of my youth… but these beings were not frightening: they were frightened.

"Zax, they are starving." Minna shivered. "I can feel their life flickering. These are the strongest. The old and the young are too weak to come outside. They are dying."

"We mean you no harm!" I called "We're here to help, if we can." They all just stared.

"The cornucopia." Drywanu gestured to the gazebo. "It has failed. We were forced to eat our animals, not just a few, but all, and when we request more, none appear. We have tried to eat the grass and the bark from the trees, but they do not sustain us. Some of us set out on a journey to find more animals, more food, but beyond the valley there is a shimmering wall of hard light, beyond which none may pass, and it does not break, or even crack, no matter how great the blows turned upon it."

Was this place some kind of terrarium? Were these people created as toys or entertainment?

Drywanu went on. "When we approach the cornucopia, it does not give us plenty any more, but only shouts at us, in unfamiliar words. Some of the more superstitious folk think the cornucopia is a god, and that it is angry, as it never spoke before. They try to appease it with blood or milk or liquor, to no avail. I do not believe it to be a god itself, but rather a tool of the gods – a miracle wrought by the Last Ones." She looked at me, her eyes damp. "Isn't it?"

"It is not a god," I said. I had never yet been to a world where there were gods, though there were some with creatures powerful enough and vain enough to claim they were. "May Minna and I approach the cornucopia?"

"You are the Last Ones. This world was made by your hands. It is all your domain, and the permission is not mine to give."

Minna and I went to the gazebo-thing. The structure was five meters high, made of gleaming vertical struts of metal that seemed not to be welded or bolted together but somehow grown into their current shape. The roof above was a graceful dome, and on the ground, in the center, there was something like a well, a circle two meters across, made not of stones but metal. The circle was full of some liquid that glimmered like quicksilver.

We approached the well, and it did indeed shout at us, a mechanical voice in a language different from the one spoken by Drywanu. The linguistic virus managed to translate it, though: "ERROR! SERVICE NEEDED. HUMAN AUTHORIZATION REQUIRED."

I cleared my throat and said, "I'm human. How do I give authorization?"

"INSERT APPENDAGE INTO APERTURE FOR VERIFICATION."

The humanoids all gasped. "It has never shouted *those* sounds before," Drywanu said, standing outside the gazebo. "And those words you said... Are you speaking with the cornucopia in the tongue of the gods, Last One Zax?"

"I'm trying." I looked at the shimmering liquid, thinking of mercury poisoning, and of other dangerous outcomes... but in a pinch Minna could always grow me a new arm, couldn't she? I extended my right forefinger and touched the liquid. It was icy cold and buzzed against my flesh.

"HUMAN STATUS CONFIRMED. SERVICE ENTRANCE UNLOCKED. PROCEED TO PLATFORM AND DESCEND."

I pulled my finger out, and the liquid withdrew, disappearing down invisible drains and revealing a platform, flush with the level of the ground. "I think we're supposed to stand there." I offered Minna my hand, and helped her step over the lip of the well, then followed her. Drywanu and the others had all fallen to their knees and bowed their heads, and they were making various murmurations. "No, no, none of that," I said, embarrassed. "We're just here to help. Please. You can stand."

One or two of them did, Drywanu among them, but the rest, if anything, only groveled more.

The platform began to descend slowly, and I wished we'd asked for a lantern or something. Minna's body began to glow faintly, which helped, illuminating a smooth shaft of metal around us. I wondered what we'd find at the bottom.

After two full minutes of descent, we stopped before double doors, which slid open. The large room beyond was dusty, with tubes in the ceiling flickering to provide life, but half of them didn't come on at all, and half the remainder were dim. The walls were covered with dark screens and blinking lights, mostly red.

When we stepped out of the elevator, one of the walls sort of... unfolded, reshaping itself into a large screen and tilting a control panel covered in dials and buttons toward us. A map flashed on the screen, showing some kind of floor plan, and then a row of the tiles beneath our feet illuminated, blinking on and off in series down the length of a passageway. "PROCEED TO POWER STATION B AND REPLACE DAMAGED COUPLER."

I looked at Minna, shrugged, and followed the illuminated floor. The hallway was lined with doors, some with round portholes of glass in their centers. Minna peeked into one, and then another, and then a third, gasping each time. "Zax, look, they are full of animals and plants!"

She was right. One porthole showed an aquarium inside, full of flickering fish, from the size of my hand to the size of myself. Another had birds fluttering beneath an artificial sun. There were things like sheep in another, in an underground meadow, and one with something resembling cows in a field, and another with short-eared rabbits hopping around in the grass. The habitats were narrow, but seemed to extend endlessly back, farther than we could see.

We finally reached a door without a porthole, marked with unfamiliar symbols, and it slid open to reveal a wall of... well, fuses, probably, or circuit breakers, or something – there were fist-sized cylinders slotted into holes in the wall, gleaming with glass threads and silver wires. One of them, about eye level, was melted and black, the silver threads dark. "Just pull this out?" I asked the air. "Where are the replacements?"

A drawer slid open to one side, revealing a neat row of fresh components. It took me a minute to figure out how to remove the old coupler – there was a little tab to push to make it pop out – but it came free easily enough once I did, and a new device slotted into its place easily. A new hum began, and the lights in the hallway flickered as some dying system came online. "SERVICE COMPLETE. SUSTENANCE DISPENSER NOW ACTIVE."

"Let's go back up and see if the cornucopia works!" Minna said.

"Soon. We should check on a few other things first." I raised my voice. "Are there any other components in need or service? Or that will need service soon?"

"SEVERAL," the mechanical voice replied. "SCHEDULED MAINTENANCE HAS NOT BEEN PERFORMED FOR OVER SIX HUNDRED CYCLES."

"I'm impressed this stuff still works at all," I said. "The Last Ones built to last. Tell us what needs to be done."

Minna and I spent the next hour pulling open panels, re-securing wires, tightening bolts, resetting switches, replacing lights, and generally doing what felt like a century's worth of maintenance all at once. When everything was running as optimally as possible, we dusted off our hands and returned to the elevator.

Then I paused. Things here would run smoothly for a long time, probably, given how well it had worked so far, but what if something else broke after we left? Drywanu's people wouldn't be able to do anything about it, and the summoning circle didn't seem to be much help if we were the only assistance it had produced in all those scores of full moons. "Is there a way to allow non-humans to access this place?" I said. "To let the… locals come down?"

"ALLOWING CHIMERAS ACCESS TO THE CONTROL CENTER IS NOT ADVISED. THEY MAY ALTER THEIR BIOME AND THEMSELVES IN UNANTICIPATED WAYS."

I considered. It probably wouldn't be good to let just *anyone* come down here, especially since the locals were totally unfamiliar with the technology – they might break open the rooms where the animals were bred to get them all at once, for instance, upsetting the artificial ecosystems that kept their populations stable and made them available for requisition from the cornucopia. But we could show Drywanu, and she could show any others she thought were trustworthy – or even tell everyone, if she thought that was the best decision. Giving one person such power was dangerous, but Drywanu was clearly devoted to her people, and part of being a harmonizer is judging how someone might best contribute to society. I thought Drywanu would be a capable caretaker. "Can we create a password that allows access, instead of a biometric test?"

"YES. SPEAK DESIRED PASS PHRASE."

Before I could think of something, Minna said, "Thank you, Zax" in the language of the chimeras.

"REPEAT PASS PHRASE."

"Thank you, Zax," she said again.

"PASS PHRASE ACCEPTED."

I looked at her curiously. "Why did you make that the phrase, Minna?"

"You do good every chance you get, Zax, and never get much in the way of thanks. I like that these people will thank you forever."

I shook my head, but I couldn't help smiling. Her gesture embarrassed me, but it was also sweet. We stepped back into the elevator and rode two minutes back to the surface. When we emerged, there were dozens of chimera standing around the cornucopia. We stepped out, and the liquid silver flowed back over the platform. "How do you usually request things?" I asked Drywanu.

She stepped forward hesitantly, then said, "One slowgrazer, please."

The fluid in the pool shimmered, and then, slowly, something like a lamb rose up through the liquid, shaking off droplets as it came, then making a small *lowing* sound. Drywanu gasped, and another chimera – this one covered in fur and taller than me

– rushed in and picked the animal up, hugging it, and making sounds it took me a moment to recognize as sobs. "We're saved!" he said.

Others crowded around the cornucopia, requesting grain, and fruit, and other things, and Minna and I drew back, Drywanu with us. "Once this settles down, we want to show you something," I murmured.

"The Last Ones made us." Drywanu looked through a porthole in the underground corridor. "This is known. But they made these creatures, too? They made all this?"

"They started with living things that occurred naturally," I said. "Then they..."

"Grafted," Minna said. "Combined things in different ways. Probably at first they made their creations just a little different – healthier, hardier, faster to grow, less needful of food. Once they did all that, they changed themselves, or changed other things, and became more creative, and made you."

"The Last Ones used to live among us, the stories say. Then they left, to live in the sky, but they would still visit us sometimes. Then even that stopped. They created this place here, to sustain us. They made provisions for our wellbeing, even beyond their time on this world. They wanted to take care of us."

Like pets, I thought, but didn't say that. I wasn't sure she would even understand. People really did love their pets, anyway, even if I was opposed to the idea of intelligent creatures being treated that way.

"Thank you, Zax," Drywanu said. She chuckled. "That phrase will become the mantra and the prayer of my people."

"Minna did a lot too," I said. She'd planted some of her store of seeds in the fields to grow into vegetables, because she didn't want these people to be entirely dependent on the cornucopia, just in case; it turned out the fruits and vegetables produced by the system were seedless, probably to prevent the rise of agriculture among the chimera, but their time as pets was over now. They could develop more freely after we were gone.

"Minna will be revered as a saint as well. For the fields to produce food for us, instead of only grass to feed the animals? That is a true miracle, and one I cannot wait to see." Drywanu took Minna's hand and smiled at her, then looked into my eyes with her disconcertingly direct ones. They flashed red. "Is there anything *we* can do for you, Last Ones? We owe our lives and futures to you."

"Oh, no, we don't need–" I said, but Minna interrupted.

"Someone may appear in the summoning circle," she said. "He looks like a Last One, but he is a… Do you have people here who hurt other people?"

"Sometimes, someone is too angry, or goes mad," Drywanu said.

"He is like that, he hurts and he might kill, and if he comes with a companion, she is even worse," Minna said. "You must not trust them, no matter how sweet their words. They will not stay long… but they may ask about us. They mean us harm. It is better if they do not find you at all, but if they do, please do not tell them we came before?"

Drywanu frowned. "We have heard stories of evil Last Ones. I heed your words. But, forgive my impertinence… would it not be better to seal the circle?"

"What do you mean?" I asked.

"When the Last Ones did not wish to be petitioned, in the days gone by, they would seal the summoning circle, enclose it with an impenetrable dome that let neither light nor sound inside or out. Can you not seal it thus?"

I looked at the ceiling. "Can we seal the circle of stones?"

"PASS PHRASE REQUIRED."

"Thank you, Zax," Drywanu said.

"EXTERNAL INTERFACE CLOSED," the voice said.

That wouldn't stop the Lector and Polly from sleeping their way to the next world, but at least it would protect Drywanu's people from their malicious impulses.

"I leave it closed until we have need to call on the Last Ones again." She cocked her head. "But you… you are not exactly the Last Ones, are you? There are many stories about them – their sport, the tribute they demanded, the ways they liked us to… entertain them. Most of us did not like taking part in those entertainments. You have only helped us, and given us the means to help ourselves, and that is not what the Last Ones did. Their assistance always had a price. They never offered us freedom. Who are you?"

"We're just travelers," I said.

"We are helpers," Minna said. "We go where we go, and we help where we can."

"You are the New Ones, then. I am glad you came. If you ever return here, we will welcome you. All my people will."

I wished we could return, but at least when we left this place, we would leave with good memories.

Farewells • The Lighthouse • Vast and Cool • Implications • A Gem • Minna the Jeweler

Drywanu took us see the gleaming mirrored dome sealing off the circle of stones, and I was pleased the Lector and Polly wouldn't be able to harm this place even if they did make it here. Afterward, the villagers made us a feast, and there was dancing, and music, and strange flutes and drums.

After I'd had my fill of revels, I found Minna, and we took a bath in a spring Drywanu showed us as the sun rose. I took the opportunity to refill our water bottles, too. We returned to find the village all aslumber. The chimera were nocturnal, it seemed. Drywanu yawned, and gave us supplies – fresh food, mostly – that we added to our bags. She thanked us about a thousand more times, then bid us farewell and went into a low house to sleep. We were given a room of our own, and we talked a bit, and I updated my journal, and then we settled into a blissful natural sleep, and moved on.

We woke to dawn on an island, perhaps a mile across, with an abandoned, lichen-encrusted lighthouse perched at one end. We decided it was safe to linger here on World 1010. With luck the Lector was stuck in vines or trapped in a summoning circle and all out of serum and gone from our lives forever. There were fruit trees Minna said were compatible with our body chemistries, and we found several nests full of eggs. And once I forced the door and explored the lighthouse we found a lot of dust and decay, but also fish hooks, and Minna was able to produce filament-thin vines to use as line. There was a little protected lagoon full of fish, swimming in clear water (not salty, which was strange; perhaps it wasn't a proper ocean, but some kind of immense lake), and we bathed and swam and splashed and relaxed. Soon we had a fire going and fresh fish to eat (well, Minna ate kelp and fruit), and we rested with full bellies and watched the waves roll in and out in peace and silence. It was one of the loveliest days I'd had in months.

"This is nice," Minna said as night fell and unfamiliar stars – always unfamiliar stars – filled the vault of the sky. We were on the beach, by the lighthouse, where we'd sat to watch the sun set. "I wish we could stay longer."

"I have some stimulants left. Not very potent, but we could do another day. We could both use–"

A bright red light suddenly shot down from the lighthouse, illuminating us in a circle of blood-colored brilliance. "Identify yourselves." The voice was booming and amplified and came from the lighthouse.

Minna and I scrambled upright. We'd gone into the lighthouse, all the way to the top, and there hadn't been anyone there, just panels full of mysterious knobs and dials and dark readouts and broken screens, and where the light should have been, a fist-sized gem faceted like a cut diamond. Certainly nothing that looked like it could talk or make demands or hear responses. Maybe it was an automated system?

"I'm Zax. This is Minna."

"Why are you here?"

"We were… marooned, I guess. We didn't know the island was inhabited."

The light pulsed, the color shifting toward purple, then back.

"Designate Zax is an unknown variety of augmented human.

Designate Minna is a humanoid of unknown origin." The light pulsed again, flickering, then abruptly turned white, and spread out, less sharp-edged spotlight and more all-encompassing illumination. "You are unknown variants, but both fall within acceptable tolerances. You are allies. It has been 63,041 days since I received a status update on the state of the war. Do you have any news?"

"We don't know anything about a war, I'm sorry," I said.

A moment of silence, then: "It had occurred to me that in the past century and a half the war might have ended. My posting was always a remote one, guarding against an unlikely attack. I feared that all the humans and allied intelligences had been destroyed. I am pleased that some have survived."

"Are you some sort of machine intelligence?" I said.

"I am a vastcool-class crystal intellect grown on the last surviving substrate harvested from the mind-fall of Year One. As far as I know I am the only remaining one of my kind, as the last of my cohort-mates went offline, as I said, more than 63,000 days ago. There may be others, beyond communication range. Do *you* know if any of us survive?"

"We aren't from this world," Zax said.

"That seems impossible. I scanned you and detected no extra-planetary taint. Unless the void infection has been cleansed? But who would have cleansed it, if the allies fell?"

"We aren't from a different planet," I said. "Or, not exactly. Do you know the word 'multiverse'?"

"A hypothetical universe of universes. Yes. But if they exist, these other worlds cannot be contacted."

I shrugged. "And yet, I contact them. We're travelers, sort of. Sort of explorers. And sort of refugees."

"If this is true, the implications are immense."

"The implications also are very small and also personal," Minna said.

"Would you two come to the top of the lighthouse?" the voice said. "I recall that humans and allied forms do not generally enjoy being shouted at from above, and I am amplified and on high."

"We will," Zax said. "Do you have a name?"

"Vastcool Class Crystal Intellect Three Three Three. Those stationed here sometimes called me Victory-Three, or simply Vicki. I do not object."

"Pleased to meet you, Vicki," I said, and meant it. I'd never met a crystal intelligence before, and if I couldn't appreciate new experiences, my life would have almost no pleasures at all.

We returned to the lighthouse, and made our way up the spiraling metal stairs. The gem we'd noticed before was glowing, now, and must have been the source of the light – presumably it was the body of Vicki itself.

"Please tell me the mechanism of your travel." The voice was pleasant, here, less booming and mechanical, though I couldn't tell where it came from, exactly – it emanated from the gem itself, somehow, was my best guess. Minna gazed at the immense gemstone inside its glass cage.

"I don't really understand the mechanism myself, Vicki. It's a... medical condition, is the best way to put it. Whenever I fall asleep, I wake up in a different world. If someone falls asleep in my arms, they travel with me."

"Can you only transport living biological matter?"

I shook my head. "My clothes go with me, my bag, the contents of my pockets... anything relatively small that's touching me directly. I don't take chunks of the floor with me, or a building I'm leaning against, or anything like that."

The gem brightened, then dimmed. "It must be a very difficult life. But I think going somewhere new every day... that would be preferable to never going anywhere at all, ever. Am I a small enough object for you to carry with you, Zax?"

I don't take on companions lightly. They can never return home, and it's important for them to understand that. "There's no coming back if you go with me. I've never seen the same world twice, and I can't control my destination. If we take you with us, you'll never see this place again, and you could end up someplace much worse."

Another pulse of light. "I have fully inventoried everything within the reach of my senses. I admit I am curious about what happened in the wider world, regarding the war and the infestation, but it seems unlikely that curiosity will ever be satisfied, even if I remain. I can intuit certain things – the enemies from the tainted void intended to turn this planet into a zone of infection too, but the birds still come to and from this island, and the fish thrive. I suspect the forces fought each other to a draw, or else to mutual annihilation.

"I am alone, Zax and Minna. I have grown very weary of being alone. I was once a protector, but now I am a prisoner. I would like to join you, if you will permit it. I believe you will find me a congenial companion, and if not, you can at least take me to a place where I might find new data to examine."

"Give us a moment?" I said.

"I will shut off my sensors until you tap on the glass." The glass suddenly darkened, turning black, hiding the diamond inside.

I went to the railing of the circular walk that looped around the tower, and Minna stood beside me, the ocean breeze rustling my hair. "What do you think?"

"You are the traveler, Zax, and may travel with anyone you wish."

I shook my head. "You're my companion. Your voice matters. I've never taken two people with me at once before, because holding two people is too much – I can't transport them both. But Vicki is a kind of person who's more portable, so it's an option. If you don't think it's a good idea, though, we can move on alone."

"I feel strange," Minna confessed. "I have a sense for life, as you have seen, but Victory-Three is not a kind of life that I can sense. He, she, they, it reminds me of the cullers and the other machines from the Farm, but they were not thinkers on their own, just the teeth and claws of the [unable to translate]. I am unsettled in the company of life that does not *feel* alive, but is feeling strange a reason to leave someone alone forever? Such a creature, made of crystal, could live forever, don't you think?"

"It seems possible."

Minna nodded. "No one should be alone forever. Living things live in systems. A thing alone is a thing that dies, and a thing alone that cannot die is a tragic thing. I say let them join us, and if they are not nice or good or do not fit, we can put them down on another beach."

I smiled. "I'm really lucky I found you, Minna." Her view of the world reminded me of my own training to be a harmonizer. Being hurled through the multiverse with no control over my destination meant being torn free of such systems of interconnection and interdependency, and that was painful for someone raised to think of himself in the context of a whole. Perhaps I could build a little ecosystem of my own, though.

We went back inside and Minna tapped on the glass. The panes lightened to transparency again. "We would be pleased to have you join us, friend Victory-Three," Minna said.

"Oh, thank the unpoisoned core," Vicki said. "I was terrified you'd decide to leave me. I am positively *starved* for new data, and that sounds like something we'll have no shortage of on our journeys."

"I don't know how your senses work," I said. "Practically speaking, you're a fist-sized gem – will you be all right wrapped in cloth at the bottom of a bag, or will that blind or deafen you?"

"I interact with the world via light and air," Vicki said. "If there's some way I could be out in the open, at least most of the time..."

I considered. "I could try to hang you from some kind of string, to wear you like a necklace, but you look like you'd be a bit heavy..."

"Oh, if size is a problem, wait. Mind your ears." A humming began, first low, then shifting up, becoming a whine, and finally a high-pitched sound right on the edge of my perception. The sound made my teeth hurt and my eyes water and my bones vibrate, and I winced and shuddered. Minna seemed unaffected, which was curious... until I realized that her level of bodily control probably allowed her to seal off her ears at will.

The diamond suddenly shattered, breaking into a hundred twinkling fragments. "There," Vicki said, voice now a multi-part harmonic chorus with itself. "Each of these shards contains the entirety of my knowledge and self. Take any one, and it is the same as taking the whole of me."

"Some of these pieces are small enough that we could set them in a ring," I said.

"Let me." Minna held out her hand, closed into a fist, and a small vine quested out between her knuckles, looping around to form a circle. She picked up a twinkling oval of Vicki's body and pressed it to the top of the vine ring, and the chip sank into place, impossibly hair-thin tendrils wrapping around the gem chip to form a setting. Minna slid the ring off her finger and offered it to me. "Safer on your body than mine," she said, "for purposes of traveling."

I slid on the ring, which fit perfectly, of course; the vine probably adjusted as necessary. "How's this, Vicki?"

"Oh, exquisite." Just one voice now, from my finger, and I noticed the other shards had turned black. "When do we depart?"

I laughed. "Minna and I had planned to stay another day, but…" I looked at her and raised my eyebrow.

"Victory-Three is eager to begin exploring," Minna said. "They have waited long enough, yes?"

Do You Sleep? • A Crystal World • An Interesting Hypothesis • A Voracious Reader • Weeds and Perennials • Unwelcome Arrivals

"There's one thing that concerns me, Vicki." We sat on the sand, packing the last of the useful things into our bags – cooked fish wrapped in broad leaves, some seeds Minna had harvested, the fishhooks we'd found. "Do you sleep?"

"I am capable of shutting down my systems for a predetermined time, or until a given stimulus occurs. I thrive on data, and it's useful to shut down my consciousness during times when no new data is forthcoming. If I hadn't been charting fish and bird populations and astronomical events, I would have been dormant when you arrived. That state is my closest analogue to sleep. Why?"

"I took a person with me to another world once, when I was asleep, and they were awake. Something about the experience destroyed her mind. When we landed in the new world she ran away, screaming. I don't know what she saw, or felt, or what happened to her during the transition... I couldn't find her before I fell asleep again. I don't know if that kind of damage is something that would happen to everyone, or if it would even affect a crystal consciousness like yours, but I've never risked taking anyone with me again while they were awake."

"I see. I can go dormant if you wish, though I am curious about what the transition entails... May I suggest a compromise?"

"We're always open to compromise here."

"I am capable of partitioning my consciousness, temporarily. I can create an isolated kernel of myself that will remain conscious and recording data, while the remainder of myself 'sleeps.' I can then run a diagnostic on that kernel when we reach our destination, and determine whether it is in good working order, without actually accessing its data in the process. If there is some madness-inducing stimulus present during the transition, at least we'll know for sure, and I will purge the kernel rather than let it infect my consciousness. If not, or if the harmful information doesn't prove detrimental to my non-biological consciousness, I can examine the data and perhaps even share it."

"If you think it's safe, it's worth a try." I didn't want Vicki to go mad, but I trusted them to know their own capabilities. In the worst-case scenario, an insane chip of diamond was unlikely to cause harm to others at least, and, best case, perhaps I'd finally get some answers.

We settled down on the beach. Minna took her sedative, and Vicki shut most of their consciousness down. I swallowed my pill too, and just before I fell asleep, I heard Vicki's conscious kernel say, quietly, "I am so happy."

We awoke in a crystal world, number 1011. The sun was bright, but not so bright we couldn't look upon it, with an intensity like that of a powerful overhead lamp. The star was surrounded by a sphere of faceted crystal. We were in the heart of a city, but one where all the buildings had been encased in a glittering armor of translucent glass, in shades of green and blue and pink and yellow. Tiny crystals crunched under our feet, like sand.

"Nothing lives here, Zax." Minna took deep, slow breaths, and her fingers interlaced with mine, gripping hard. I knew worlds without life were hard for her, but she was getting better at coping.

"Can you stand it here for a little while? We could look for supplies."

Minna nodded, but she was chewing on her lip. I decided to be swift. I began walking, to put some distance between us and our point of origin, just in case we were still being followed. We'd have to tell Vicki about the Lector and Polly before long, but I wanted to let them get settled into this new life a little before I told them we had enemies.

"Are you all right, Vicki?" I kept one eye on the crystals at my feet, to make sure they wouldn't start climbing up my boots and onto my body. I couldn't tell if this crystalline strangeness was the aftermath of a weapon or some kind of pollution or even an alien life form, but it was better to take care.

"I am. I apologize for not speaking. There is a cascade of new data here, and I am still doing a first-level sort."

"How's your, what did you call it, your other kernel? Can you access whatever that part of you experienced when we traveled?"

"I... Hmm. The partitioned portion shut itself down, and purged itself. I can't access the data, because there's nothing to access. How peculiar."

"I would have said 'ominous.'"

"That as well. It is at least another data point, duly recorded. I am more interested in the data available in this world. As far as I can tell, these crystals are not conscious, or, at least, they do not communicate in any way that I can recognize. Still, I find it an interesting coincidence that we should appear in a world full of crystals immediately after I joined you."

I nodded. "It's strange. Sometimes there are... not patterns, but sort of, affinities? If I think of gardens just before I fall asleep, sometimes I appear on a garden world, and if I think of cities, sometimes there are cities... but it doesn't always work. It doesn't even usually work. Sometimes I concentrate ferociously and it doesn't make any difference. I've imagined home with great vividness and fervor hundreds of times and never returned there, that's for sure. I can't tell if the phenomenon is real, if some part of my mind is helping me choose the next world, or if it's just confirmation bias. Sometimes I try anyway, because it can't hurt, but it's frustrating, not knowing how any of this works, and the occasional sense that I *can* control my destination to some extent makes my total failure to control it even more disheartening."

"Maybe you are just in the wrong part of the garden sometimes," Minna said.

I frowned. "What do you mean?"

"Yes, explicate," Vicki said.

Minna got that thinking-hard line that appeared sometimes on her forehead and gestured vaguely with her hands. "Let us say you are in the garden, and you are hungry. You are hungry for many things and must decide which to pick. There is nothing in the part of the garden where you stand but blackberries and... tomatoes. If you say, 'I want a bunch of blackberries,' and reach out, you can pluck them and you are happy and have what you want. If instead you want tomatoes, you can have those, too. But let us say you want an apple. The apple trees are in another part of the garden. You can say, 'I want an apple,' and reach out all you want, but you cannot pluck one then and there. There are no apples there to be picked, only blackberries and tomatoes. You would have to walk down a long path and take many turnings to reach the apples. Do you see?"

"You are saying that each world may be, in some sense, adjacent to or coterminous with a number of other worlds," Vicki said. "That there could be choice, but not *infinite* choice."

"Is that what I am saying?" Minna asked.

Vicki went on. "Perhaps from here we could reach a desert world, or an ocean world, but not a city world – the nearest city world is, as Minna says, in another part of the garden. If Zax wants to go to an ocean or a desert, his wish will be granted. If he wishes for a city, though, the multiverse is unable to oblige, so instead he travels to a world at random, or the one that's 'closest' to his desire, in some multiversal sense, perhaps. The same random process happens if he expresses no desire at all when he travels. Hmm. I will have to gather more data, but that *is* an interesting hypothesis."

"Huh," I said. "I never thought of that. It's no more provable than any other idea I've come up with, but it does make me feel a little better about my various failures." I kept walking, toward a building that looked like a shop of some kind. The door hung open, but the opening was covered by a crystal shell. I gave the crystal a kick, and it shattered into tiny coin-sized prisms. I ducked inside, sighing. "I had such wonderful lanterns a while back, and a glowing blade, but I lost them. Minna can glow, a little, but keep your eyes open for something brighter."

"Let me be light." Vicki glowed, shining out pure white light from their place on my hand. "I can widen or tighten the beam as desired."

"You're a useful gem to have along." We were in a shop or a warehouse, with lots of shelves, sadly most empty. Whoever once lived here had done some panic-shopping or looting as their world changed to crystal.

Minna came in after us, glowing with bioluminescence herself, and moved off among the shelves to look for things worth salvaging. I investigated, too, moving carefully and quietly. I kept expecting to see dead bodies cocooned in crystals, but there were none, and while there was disarray, the place wasn't a disaster. It had been some sort of general store, and I found bottles that seemed to be rubbing alcohol, and bandages, and needle and thread, and strong thin rope. There were cans with pictures of unfamiliar vegetables on them, and I took a couple of those as well.

I met up with Minna in the back, and she was wearing something different from before, a loose-fitting dress of pale blue she'd pulled on top of her overalls, and a lacy emerald-green scarf wrapped around her neck. "There are such colors!" she said, and led me to the back corner of the store, where a small section of clothes hung on racks and rested on shelves. The only thing in my size was a T-shirt with a picture of a grinning, pig-like creature on the front, beneath a few words in an alien script. I wished again that the linguistic virus worked with written language, though I supposed I was unlikely to encounter anyone else who could read the text, either. I did find some thick wool socks – they came in trios instead of pairs – and happily put those in my bag as well. "Do you see anything you want, Vicki?" I said. "Do you... eat, or anything?"

"I absorb solar energy. If I wish to grow in size, I must take in additional physical matter, usually liquid with silica in suspension, though other feedstocks are usable. Mostly I hunger for information, and you are already providing a feast. I wonder if the entire planet – based on the gravity, this seems to be a planet – is crystal. The shell around the local star certainly suggests it is a more than purely local phenomenon."

"There's no way to tell for sure," I said. "I can never explore more of a given world than I can see in a day or two or three. Still, we can sit down for a while, eat our fish before it goes bad, and I can update my journal–"

"You keep a *journal*?" Vicki said.

We dragged a table and two chairs outside so we could enjoy the sparkling sunlight while we ate... though I didn't eat anything myself until I'd taught Vicki enough of my language to begin devouring my data; it would have been cruel to make them wait when they were so excited. I began by reading aloud from the journal. Speaking deliberately in my own tongue, instead of letting the linguistic virus do its work for me, required a conscious effort. Then I translated what I'd read into Vicki's native language, as best I could; fortunately, their tongue is a logical and constructed one, too, with many structural commonalities. It turns out Vicki's computational capabilities are almost as effective as the linguistic virus at processing speech, and since that processing power can also be turned toward comprehending written language, it's superior in some ways. If I'd had someone who spoke my native language to converse with, Vicki said they would be able to learn it rapidly, just by listening to us and analyzing the patterns. "Language acquisition is akin to code-breaking, and that was one of my functions."

I wrote down all thirty-four characters of the Realm's alphabet and noted the sounds each letter corresponds to, though of course some of them make different sounds in different contexts. Vicki scanned the first few pages of my journal as I read them aloud and pointed at each word to indicate in which direction I was reading. Vicki queried various words and phrases and idioms as I read, but the questions diminished as they began picking things up from context: "I am an extrapolation engine," they said, which seems like a useful thing to be.

After a couple of hours, Vicki said, "I have enough working knowledge to continue on my own."

I'd expected this to be a multi-step process, perhaps taking weeks or months, so I just blinked down at the ring on my hand. "You learned to read that quickly?"

"I process information the way that you breathe, Zax," Vicki said. "Data and patterns and systems are like air. May I read the rest of your journal?"

I resigned myself to swiping the digital screen a thousand times to turn the pages, but it turns out Vicki can run all sorts of machine peripherals – something to keep in mind if we reach a sufficiently advanced world, I suppose. Vicki figured out how to interface with the digital journal and send signals that would swipe the pages on their own. "I can't just download all the data in a gulp," Vicki said, "because you're essentially *drawing pictures* of your alphabet on the screen. I could create an interface with a keyboard–"

"I like writing with a stylus," I said. "Back on my world, I used ink on paper when I wrote. For some reason it helps me think better than typing on a keyboard does. I feel closer to the language, somehow."

"There's no use arguing with someone's subjective experience," Vicki said. Who knew crystal intelligences could sigh? "I might put together a character-recognition program to copy your journals to a more easily machine-readable format, if you don't object?"

"As long as I get to keep scribbling," I said.

Minna extended tendrils from her arm, and one of them held

Vicki's ring up to see the journal. (That freed up my hands to finally eat something.) The process didn't seem to require much in the way of conscious attention from Minna, as she sat and basked with her eyes closed. She was very green, soaking in sunlight.

"Minna, what do you call the beings who ruled your world?" Vicki asked at one point.

She made the "[unable to translate]" sound again, and Vicki said, "Hmm. Zax, my language acquisition method differs from yours, and I have an interpretation to offer. I think you might render the word as 'those who judge and guide from on high,' though 'those who bring death on those who displease them' fits too, along with a range of meanings in between. Something seemingly self-contradictory like 'Nurturer-Butchers' might be closest. Do you agree, Minna?"

"You said what I said, in different words," she replied.

"I don't know if I feel better knowing that or not," I said.

"It is *always* better to know," Vicki admonished before returning to my account.

I scooped bits of cold fish into my mouth, wondering how worried we should be. We'd put a handful of worlds between us and the Lector, but was it enough? He'd pursued me for hundreds of worlds, so when he said he was "running low" on serum, I had no idea what that meant.

"This Lector is an interesting figure," Vicki commented after a while. "He demonstrates a very methodical approach to understanding your condition. You didn't write about meeting him, though."

"I didn't start the journal until after we met, and was kind of haphazard about catching up my prior history. I probably should document the story of how we got together, but honestly, I don't much enjoy thinking about it."

"Ah. An unhappy parting of ways, then. I suppose as I keep reading I'll find out what became of him."

"The Lector is a *weed*," Minna said. "And a perennial. He goes away and reappears."

"Whatever do you mean?"

"He stole my blood and made a serum that lets him travel to other worlds the same way I do," I said. "He's pursuing me even now, trying to get more of my blood, and to keep studying me. Minna and I encountered him not long ago – he changed tactics, and traveled to a world before me instead of just following, to lie in wait. Which, now that I think of it, disproves the hypothesis that I – and he – can somehow control where we go, or even narrow down the choices. We must be traveling a pre-set path of worlds, or else how could he get ahead of me?" That idea depressed me.

"That's not necessarily true," Vicki said. "If the Lector only got ahead of you once, it could be luck or coincidence that you ended up in the same world as he did."

"Sure, but he followed me successfully across hundreds of worlds."

"Indeed, but what do you think the Lector was hoping for, desiring, desperately wishing to find, every time he closed his eyes and transitioned?"

Oh. "Me."

"Yes. He was probably thinking, 'Take me to Zax.'"

"Ugh." I pushed the last bits of fish away from me. "He's obsessed."

"Invasive plant," Minna muttered. "Thief of resources."

"I didn't realize we had *foes*," Vicki said.

"I'm so sorry. We should have told you what you were getting into before we brought you with us. Maybe it won't be an issue. We hope we're left the Lector behind forever by now, that he's out of serum, but we can't be sure."

"I always appreciate more information, Zax, but having an enemy doesn't frighten me. That is a paradigm I understand well. You do realize I am, in part, a tactical and strategic engine? I thrive in the face of a conflict. What is your current plan to deal with this threat?"

"Just... put space between us. The Lector failed to get more of my blood last time we met, and we're hoping to keep jumping through worlds until he runs out of serum and gets stranded. In fact, we should probably move on pretty soon, just to be safe."

"Why retreat? Why not set a trap, if you know where he's going to appear?"

"Yes," Minna said. "This is a question I also have asked."

"I don't want to kill the Lector, or anyone," I said. "I want him to leave me alone, but I'm not a murderer."

"I am still reading about him, but it seems clear he will not hesitate to kill you in order to further his own ends. If he is not stranded, and continues his pursuit, you may be forced to kill him in order to save yourself, and to spare the multiverse his depredations."

"I'm… We're not at that point yet, Vicki. My purpose, all my training, is to help people live in harmony – not to stop people from living entirely. It's always better to run away from a fight if you can."

"Your rules of engagement are noted," Vicki said. "Will you accept non-lethal measures?"

"Yes. In fact, Minna set a trap just a few worlds back that should slow him and his companion down–"

Minna bolted to her feet, eyes wide. "*Zax*! There is other life in this world now! Suddenly and from nowhere like poof!"

That could only mean the Lector and Polly had caught up to us.

Run or Hide or Something Else • The Pit • Wildlife Preserve • A Temptation • Negotiations • Bad Faith

Luckily we were streets away from our point of arrival, so we weren't in imminent danger of discovery, but who knew what resources the Lector and his psychotic sidekick had to track us down? If nothing else, we'd probably left a discernible trail in the crystals we'd walked through – they didn't take tracks as clearly as fresh snow or even damp earth, but you could see the traces if you looked closely, and the Lector was excellent at observation.

"What do we do?" Minna said. "Sleep again?"

I considered. We only had so many instant sedatives, and I liked to save them for situations when escape was the *only* option, not just the most attractive one. "We could try to hide, wait them out, hope they move on?" That left us open to potential ambush if we ended up in the same world after them, though. I wished Vicki was right: I wanted to be able to *steer*. Being buffeted by the randomness of the multiverse had been terrifying at first, and later become exciting (at least sometimes), but most of all it was just frustrating.

"There is an option besides running or hiding," Vicki said.

"I told you, I don't want to kill anyone."

"It doesn't have to come to killing. I've done a passive scan of the environment, and I have an idea, if the two of you are willing to provide the manual dexterity I lack..."

"I know you're here, Zaxony!" the Lector shouted. "I used your blood to make more than just the travel serum. I also made... call it a compass. I have a device that detects your presence. It's leading me right to you."

"Oh no," Minna whispered.

"He may be lying." I spoke softly into her ear. We were crouched in a dark and dirty storage room on the ground floor of a building that might have been apartments before the world crystallized. Heaped boxes formed a barricade in front of us, with enough gaps in the pile for us to see the door. We'd chosen this position carefully, at Vicki's instructions, and prepared as well as we could. "He does that a lot. He probably yells 'I know you're here' in every world, just on the off chance he's right."

"Given the level of technological prowess you described, we can't rule out a tracking device, though," Vicki said. "We'll know soon enough."

We waited, and it wasn't long before I heard the crunch of feet approaching through the crystals. We'd left a trail on purpose this time, detectable but not *too* obvious. The Lector had underestimated me for a long time, but it was possible, after getting the better of him in our last meeting, that he was more cautious now.

A figure appeared in the doorway: the Lector, wearing a white coat, all dirty and smeared. He cocked his head, considering the scene: a small room, the floor covered with a messy spread of flattened cardboard, with boxes stacked messily at the far end. He held some kind of gleaming metal pistol in his left hand. "There you are, Zaxony. I *smell* you." The Lector rushed into the room, eager to capture us – and then howled as the floor dropped out from underneath him. I waited a moment to see if Polly was going to race in to his aid, then, when there was no sign of her, rose and went with Minna to the edge of the pit.

Many of the buildings here were in decay and disarray, with assorted structural damage. Vicki had scanned the surroundings and found the perfect site for a trap. A room with a hole in the floor about three meters across that dropped the same distance down into some sort of basement room. The exits down *there* were blocked by rubble, Vicki assured us. We'd trapped the Lector. Which didn't stop him from shooting – there was a *thwap* and something blurred out of the pit, past my head, and embedded itself into one of the cardboard boxes. Minna went to investigate. "A little dart."

"Some sort of tranquilizer?" Vicki said. "That doesn't make much sense. Knocking you unconscious would only allow you to escape. Perhaps... Minna, would you pluck that dart free? I'd like to take a look at it later. But be wary of the tip."

She carefully worked the dart – it was small, half the length of my pinky finger – out of the box, then fished in her bag and came out with a bit of cloth, bundling up the dart and stowing it away.

"You filthy meat-thing!" the Lector howled, and then... his face changed, the flesh melting and shifting, and soon it wasn't the Lector down there at all, but a vaguely humanoid fungal creature. "I will *eat* you!"

Oh, no. Polly. Which meant the Lector was–

"I thought it best to send a scout ahead," a voice said. I looked up, and the Lector was there, leaning in the doorway, arms crossed, looking casual and comfortable. Polly howled wordlessly from the pit. "I don't recognize that other voice. You've made new friends, Zaxony, but I don't see them. Don't you want to introduce me?"

We said nothing.

The Lector shrugged. "Your new companions are cowardly trap-setters, it seems. Those *vines* a few worlds back! Very interesting specimens. It took me forever to hack them away – they kept growing almost as fast as I could slice them. I wonder, in that world with the standing stones, and the peculiar dome that surrounded us, preventing us from venturing out – did you have something to do with that, too?"

"I don't want to fight you," I said. "I don't want to hurt you, either. I just want to live in peace."

The Lector shook his head sadly. "This has become an existential matter for me, Zaxony. I *must* get more of your blood, or I might find myself stranded in some horrible place like this, where my talents would be wasted."

Minna began creeping around one side of the hole, and I began to move around the other side. I knew what she was thinking, because I was thinking it, too: there were two of us, and only one of him. He didn't have a confederate holding a knife to Minna's throat this time. "Oh, are you planning to rush me?" he said. "Drop me in a hole with my pet? Adorable. I urge you to try."

I lifted the hand with the ring on it and said, "Blind him." Vicki obligingly lanced a searing blast of light, narrow and focused, directly into his face, and Minna leapt at him.

She passed right through his body, landing with a squawk in the corridor beyond.

The Lector grinned, not in the least discomfited by the light or anything else. "I broke apart the stones in that world with the dome – nothing much else to do there – and found the most interesting technology, projectors that create very realistic illusions. It was a small thing to integrate those projectors with some of the microdrone technology I brought from my home world. Zaxony, this would all be easier if you would just accept that I am much smarter and more capable than you are."

"Minna, you can sense life, yes?" Vicki said. She stood behind the image of the Lector, nodding. "How precisely can you locate that life?"

"Who *is* that talking?" the Lector said. "Are they broadcasting from some other location? If so, they're a brave companion, to be more than an arm's length away from you. What if you get sleepy and strand them here?"

We ignored him as Minna shook her head. "Maybe... a direction, and near or far, strong or faint, but it is not a map in my head with a dot flash flash flashing. There is something alive..." She gestured toward the pit, then gestured out the door behind her. "Somewhere over there. I thought the man of light was real because he was close enough."

"I can scan for structural details, but finding living things is beyond my abilities," Vicki said. "Perhaps if Minna and I combine our powers, we can track him."

"Let's do it." I'd had enough of this. My life was hard enough without being pursued. It was time to do the pursuing.

"You really shouldn't ignore me like this," the Lector said.

"Let me *out*!" Polly howled.

None of us responded to either of them, or looked back when we walked past the projection of the Lector. I wondered if it was murder to leave Polly in this world, but I thought not. She would be able to extend tendrils to the top of the pit, given time, and crawl out. I hoped it wouldn't happen until my friends and I, and the Lector, were all long gone. Let this crystal world be Polly's prison. A lifetime of solitary confinement was arguably cruel, but it was mild punishment for the gleeful killer of a whole civilization. I wasn't comfortable sitting in judgment, but I supposed Vicki and Minna and I could be a sort of tribunal of last resort, and I knew *they* would have advocated for a harsher sentence than banishment.

The illusion of the Lector walked along with us as we navigated a series of narrow halls. "Zaxony, I believe we can reach an accommodation. While I would personally undergo a minor surgery without anesthetic to further the cause of science, I understand your reluctance to do the same. My impatience and frustration led me to act... precipitously. I apologize."

"Apology not accepted."

"I have seen the error of my ways. I implore you to work with me, rather than against me. Travel with me again, and eventually we'll find a world with sufficiently advanced biotech to allow me to clone you, or pursue other avenues of study to discover the source of your power. In the meantime, all I'll need is the occasional blood sample to replenish my supply of serum–"

"Why would I want you to have that power?"

"Because in exchange, I'll find a way to cure you."

I stumbled at that, but kept going.

"Think of it," he said. "Once I've unlocked your secrets, I can remove this curse from you. You can travel with *me*, then, until you find a nice world where you can settle down and become a... guidance counselor, or whatever it was you wanted to be back home. Then I'll head out into the vastness of the multiverse to make my mark, and you can have a nice, small life, no longer forced into a nomadic existence that doesn't suit you. I'll even solemnly swear, connected to any lie detector you like, to leave your new home world out of my plans for conquest once I learn to control where I travel. That world can be a sort of wildlife preserve. You'll never see or hear from me again. You and Minna and your... talking jewelry, it appears... can be very happy together, I'm sure. What do you say?"

I want to say I wasn't tempted, but the idea of being able to stay somewhere quiet, without danger or fear, was naturally appealing. They say you always want what you can't have. When I lived at home in the Realm of Spheres and Harmonies, all I wanted was to venture out to places of danger and conflict, so I could help them achieve peace and accord. The center of the Realm where I lived was settled, and only ever required minor adjustments to keep everyone within the acceptable parameters of satisfaction, but I always gravitated to the bigger problems – the ones that required more inventive and dramatic decisions. There were precious few of those problems in Central, but in outlying regions of Realm space, and in newly annexed regions, there were plenty of serious conflicts – clashes of cultures, struggles for resources, sometimes even acts of violence. Those were territories where the "Harmonies" part of the name of our Realm was still purely aspirational, and I aspired to help achieve that aspiration. I had plans to continue my career in those dangerous places once I'd attained a higher level of seniority and proven myself, fueled with the zeal to make the Realm a better place.

Now, though, that my life is a succession of dangerous places, often with problems that even the most highly trained harmonizer would find insurmountable without completely rebuilding the structure of a given society, I desperately crave peace, and comfort, and quiet.

Even if I did trust the Lector to do as he promised, rather than jumping on me again, scalpels drawn, at the first opportunity, there was a problem: the infinity of worlds the Lector would poison with that kind of power, the lives he would trample without even noticing them, and the people he would toy with and spoil for amusement and spite. I couldn't doom people, *worlds*, to that kind of fate. "No. You don't get to win."

"That's a very childish response, Zaxony. I thought you believed in fostering scenarios where *all* parties involved get to win–"

Minna slapped her palms together, and the Lector abruptly vanished. "Got it." She opened her hands, and a little sprinkle of sparkling glass and metal sifted down.

"That drone was so small or well-shielded I couldn't even detect it," Vicki said. "Well done, Minna."

She shrugged. "Sometimes you have to kill pests to save the crop." She pointed. "There is life still in this direction."

We made it to the lobby of the building, and opted not to leave by the door we'd broken our way through. That was too obvious a point of egress, and the Lector might be watching. Soon we found a side door, covered in crystals like the rest, but unlocked. We'd make noise smashing through it, but if we moved fast, we could get out of sight quickly. Of course, the Lector could have drones flying around watching us, but I doubted he had very many of those left. I knew from my time in his world that they were expensive and prone to malfunction.

"Let's take a moment to plan our next moves," Vicki said, and we hunkered down by the door for a few minutes, talking about possibilities. Vicki made some interesting suggestions, and Minna and I talked about the best way to put their ideas into action. The main approach Vicki had in mind was worryingly direct, but we were short of options.

"I hope this works," I said.

"I estimate a sixty-five-percent chance of success," Vicki said.

"Don't be discouraged by that. My analytical engine built in a lot of doubt because you and Minna aren't professional operatives, but I am confident in your abilities."

"That's reassuring," I muttered. I kicked the crystal covering the door, making it rain down jewels, and strode out into the waning light of the crystalline sun. "Lector!" I shouted. "Come out, and let's finish this!"

"How do you propose we do that, Zaxony?" The voice came from a nearby building, the same one where Minna and Vicki had agreed the Lector was most likely located. I imagined a sniper rifle, pointed at my head, but I knew he wouldn't want to kill me – not as long as he needed an unlimited supply of my blood.

"I've considered your proposal," I called. "I don't like it, but you're right – my whole purpose is to bring people into accord. We might be able to reach a compromise. But I'll need assurances, and safeguards, and you have to treat this as a *negotiation*, not an opportunity to make threats."

"You dropped my friend into a *pit*, Zaxony, and now you want to be polite and courteous?"

As if the Lector had friends. I'd believed *I* was his friend, once. "You threatened to murder *my* friend not so long ago. I'll let the past go if you will."

A pause. "Fair enough! I'm coming out."

The Lector approached me from the base of the building, smiling faintly, and stopped two meters away. We stood together in a bare square of crystal-covered earth, the buildings around us casting long shadows. "No more ambushes planned?"

"We used up all our cleverness already," I said.

"If you hadn't snagged me with those vines, I might have underestimated you and blundered into your pit, so perhaps you've been *too* clever, hmm?"

I took a deep breath and adopted the soothing, attentive tone I'd learned to use in my training. "Lector. We're here to negotiate an end to our hostilities, and find a way forward that will satisfy us both." I stepped toward him and held out my hand.

He looked at my outstretched hand and frowned. "You want me to touch you now?"

I kept my hand out and my eyes on his. "It's traditional in the Realm of Spheres and Harmonies to begin such negotiations with a handshake."

"A primitive act, but if it makes you happy." He grinned. "Remove the ring, though. Once upon a time, handshakes were a way to tell if the other party had a dagger hidden up their sleeve, but the effectiveness of that tactic ended once rings with hidden needles were invented."

I twisted Vicki off my finger and passed them to Minna, who stood solemnly behind me.

The Lector reached out and clasped my right hand. Then I reached out with my left hand, enfolding his hand in both of mine.

Minna had hollowed out a hole in the center of my left palm, which was, after all, living wood underneath, not flesh. She'd concealed the dart Polly fired at us in the hole, so only the very tip of the needle protruded. The Lector had been closer to correct than he realized.

I squeezed the Lector's hand as hard as I could, and watched his eyes widen.

Smashing Things • You Go On Ahead • A Pink Bubble • A Gentleperson Naturalist • Slugs • How Interesting

The Lector grimaced, and then his face froze. *Everything* froze, his muscles locking in place so firmly that I had to struggle to wrench my hand from his grip. He began to fall over, like a toppling statue of himself, but Minna caught him and eased him onto the ground.

"You were right," I said to Vicki. "The dart is a nerve agent or something, locking up his voluntary muscles but leaving him awake. A good way to trap me for an involuntary blood donation." We stood over the Lector, his eyes shooting back and forth, the only motion in his rictus features. "Minna, will you stay with him?"

I went into the building where he'd been watching us, and found his bags. One looked like a battered canvas duffel, but I knew it was a waterproof, tear-resistant smart material. The other was his "traveling case," repository of his home world's technological prowess in miniature. I lugged the bags outside and dropped them next to the Lector, then took his hand and pressed it against the side of his suitcase. With his biometrics engaged, I was able to open the case and consider the bounty inside.

I lifted out a small ampoule with perhaps an ounce of liquid inside and held it up to the sunlight. The serum. He didn't have much left, but then, I didn't know how much was required to activate his power, or how long it stayed in his system – maybe this was enough to keep him going for months.

I dropped the vial on the ground and crushed it with my heel. The rest of the contents included a mishmash of technological wonders and practical supplies. A case full of microdrones, also stomped to dust. Some protein bars, which I handed to Minna. Mysterious devices, all gleaming silver and copper dials, that I considered and then smashed on general principle. I found his blood extraction equipment, jars and tubes and needles.

I enjoyed breaking those a lot.

I discovered more darts, and jammed them point-first into the ground, discharging their poisons, then stomped them, too. He had rope and tape, probably intended to bind me, but I moved them to my bag.

The case itself was a wondrous device, a portable computer and laboratory capable of synthesizing chemicals and creating mechanical components from raw materials, but I had no idea how to use it, so I bashed it as best I could with a rock.

Then I used the Lector's biometrics to open the duffel, and while it was mostly clothes and food, there were other things that interested me more: drugs. Bottles of stimulants and sedatives I remembered from our time together. There were even a handful of the instant-sedative patches we'd used together. Stick one of those on your skin, and you're out in half a second.

Once I stashed what I wanted in my own bag, I crouched next to the Lector. "I thought you were my friend. I trusted you. My *real* friends think I should kill you for that betrayal… but that would make me almost as bad as you. Where I'm from, when all attempts at harmonization fail, and we're faced with someone who simply cannot be reconciled with their society… we banish them. We send them into exile, where they can do no harm to others. I could leave you here, in this lifeless place, but for all I know, you still travel when you sleep, and you might rescue your pet monster and arm yourself and follow me. Instead, I'm going to send you into the next world now, without your weapons and your drugs and your serums." I sighed. "You might have a few more worlds in you, but I think we can avoid each other in the time it takes you to run out of power. I hope you end up in a nice world... but one where no one else lives for you to harm."

His eyes had stopped moving, and were fixed on me, wet and unblinking.

I tucked a couple of protein bars and a bottle of water into his pockets, then slapped a sedative patch onto his cheek and stepped back.

I'd never seen anyone else travel, of course. I halfway expected something like a dreamy dissolve, his form turning to fog and then blowing away, but it was far more abrupt than that; he was simply gone, all at once, and a small wind stirred in the space where his body had been.

"Well done, Zax," Vicki said. "We should travel ourselves, before he has time to prepare a trap, in case we end up in the same world he does, and the paralytic wears off. Though this is a great opportunity for you to try to steer – do your best to go to a world where the Lector *isn't.*"

"I'll try."

We gathered ourselves together, and shook out a couple of the Lector's fast-acting sedatives. Minna curled into my arms, snoring, and Vicki shut themself down. I sat for a moment, listening to the distant sound of Polly's howling. No matter what happened with the Lector, at least we'd be leaving *that* homicidal vegetable behind forever.

I took my pill and held it in my mouth. *Not the Lector, Not the Lector, Not the Lector,* I thought, but it was just as I'd feared. His image was fixed in my mind as I fell asleep, and I feared we hadn't seen the last of him.

I woke up rolling, going fast enough that when I tried to stop I just got tangled in my own limbs and scraped my elbows and ended up face-down at the bottom of the hill. I sat up, groaning, just in time for Minna to crash into me and knock me down again. We both lay there for a minute, staring up at a dark sky full of luminous opaque bubbles in shades of red and blue and green. After a moment we both started laughing. We hadn't landed on top of the Lector, but that didn't necessarily mean he wasn't lurking off somewhere in the dark nearby. "Minna, do you sense any life?"

"Lots and lots," she said. "Many living things in this place, all around and up in the sky also."

"Those things above us are ships of some sort, I think," Vicki said.

One of the bubbles, glowing pink, was descending toward us, getting larger and larger. "Oh, good. Then it probably won't try to eat us." I got to my feet and helped Minna up. "Let's not get crushed by it, though." We hurried through the dry grass, but the bubble adjusted its course to follow us, moving like it was being blown on the wind, but *fast*. Did it *want* to land on us? We started running, and then my hair stood on end, like I'd passed through an electric field, and Minna, a step behind me, shouted in alarm. I turned to see if she was OK and the bubble – the size of a house, up close – struck her, and then me.

That tingling hair-on-end sensation enveloped my whole body, but there was no sense of impact, and a moment later I found myself on a level floor, while Minna stood nearby, hands covering her mouth, eyes wide. The floor was silvery and solid, but the walls were curved and faintly pink and translucent, and we watched the ground drop away. I saw tiny figures below – animals, people, maybe even the Lector? – but then we were too high for me to see anything but the outlines of the landscape, fields and stands of trees.

A voice spoke, and we turned to see a figure wearing a black outfit with lots of buckles and straps descend a set of stairs that extended itself downward as he approached, each riser somehow sliding down from the one above just in time for the stranger's boot to land. He had long white hair but a youthful face, and wore transparent goggles that showed off eyes of an alarmingly bright shade of blue, made even more striking by contrast with his dark skin. He spoke, and after a few words, the linguistic virus caught up, and he started to make sense. "... level of technology absolutely unprecedented among the groundlings. Did you crash your ship?"

"We got lost," I said. That statement was always true, and often a good opening. "Thank you for helping us. I'm Zax, and this is Minna." I decided not to mention Vicki for now. In some worlds, talking rings would be too much of a novelty.

"I am Gladius Mundanius Miraculus," he said, and bowed. "This is the *Good Ship Codswallop*." The stairs withdrew into the ceiling as soon as Gladius stepped onto the floor beside us. "I'm happy to be of service, of course, but tell me about your *ring*."

I waited to see if Vicki would speak up, but they didn't. Tactics, probably. Don't reveal too much of yourself to an unknown individual. "It's, ah, an environmental scanner. And it makes light."

Gladius leaned forward, gazing at the diamond. "Truly an impressive degree of miniaturization. My passive scanners clocked its processing power and swooped down to save you before the groundlings could take you to pieces and sell the parts. You must never believe the stories about their hospitality – their culture of welcome stops as soon as they think you have something they can use. That's how I knew you weren't tourists. *They* know better than to descend with any tech more advanced than a lighter."

"We appreciate the help." So, no high tech on the ground. If the Lector *was* down there, at least he wouldn't be able to commandeer a bubble-ship full of responsive matter.

Gladius waved that away. "Where were you headed before your accident?"

"No particular destination in mind," I said. "We were just wandering, when we got lost."

"Deciding what to do with one's time *is* the hardest problem, isn't it?" Gladius said. "I choose to occupy myself as a gentleperson naturalist. I was just on my way to gather specimens from the Carcosan Plateau. Have you ever been there?"

"We haven't."

Gladius clapped his hands. "It's simply *grotesque*. Would you like to join me? I'd take you to the cloud-hub so you could secure another ship straightaway, but it's rather a distance from here, and in the wrong direction. I was going back there after my little sojourn anyway, so if you don't mind a small delay… It's always more fun to explore with company."

"We're happy to go with you," I said.

"Excellent! We'll be there in about two hours. In the meantime, I'll have the ship show you to the guest suites, so you can get cleaned up. I find the touch of the ground simply *intolerable*, and always enjoy a good sonic scouring afterward."

Vicki figured out how the showers worked. (Vicki loves reading about themself in this journal, too, after so thoroughly absorbing the earlier chapters; they say the experience is like reading a wonderful novel and then finding yourself in the world of the book. Apparently I am writing a "bildungsroman," whatever that is.) Gladius gave us two adjoining rooms, separated by a wall that became opaque or transparent on request. Minna is absolutely unselfconscious, but I am still a product of my upbringing, and enjoyed the privacy – I thought the chance of being rendered unconscious while she was in the other room was fairly low.

I have used sonic showers of various sorts before, and honestly I never find them very satisfying. Something about the physicality of water running down my body just makes me feel cleaner, no matter how efficiently sound waves can vibrate the dirt and oils from my skin to be whisked away by currents of air. A sonic shower makes my hairs stand on end and my teeth vibrate too, or at least, I imagine so. Still, it was a welcome chance to freshen up.

I emerged to find whitish-pink glistening slugs the size of my feet crawling over my clothing, and couldn't help but whimper. "Vicki, what are those?"

Vicki rested on the low table next to the bed, which was really a lozenge-shaped pod full of squishy cushions. They said, "They are cleaning machines… or bio-machines, it's unclear… they apparently slurp out sweat, dirt, proteins, and other things from your clothes, and use them as sustenance."

"How do you know that?" The slugs moved slowly, writhing and wriggling, and Vicki's explanation did nothing to offset my instinctive revulsion.

"I queried the ship," Vicki said. "I don't think this vehicle is intelligent, exactly, but it's capable of answering simple questions."

Something about the way Vicki said that gave me pause. "Did you ask the ship anything else?"

"Oh, a couple of things." Vicki's voice was airy and nonchalant, but I could detect some strain underneath. Since Vicki could control its vocalization down to the tiniest arc of a frequency curve, I knew I was meant to detect just that. I assumed we were being listened to, and our conversation monitored or recorded. A ship that could answer your questions could listen to anything else you said, too, after all. "I asked about this Carcosan Plateau, and our host's expedition."

"Collecting specimens," I said. "What kind of specimens? Plants, animals?"

"The Carcosan Plateau is a groundling community," Vicki said. "Gladius is going to acquire a few of the inhabitants."

Groundlings. I wasn't sure, but from context I got the sense those were just people without access to high technology, and that Gladius didn't think much of them. "What does he do with these... specimens?" I tried to match Vicki's carefree tone.

"As he said, he's an amateur naturalist. He has a sort of zoo, at the hub. He studies the groundlings, breeds them, trades interesting specimens with fellow enthusiasts – apparently there are various teratogenic chemicals in the soil that sometimes leads to unusual physical qualities. Extra limbs, or strangely formed ones, and various peculiarities of size and coloration... The naturalists tend to dissect the more interesting specimens. Or vivisect them."

I flashed back to the day I first escaped the Lector, strapped down to a table, about to be emptied of my blood. "Oh." Gladius had helped us, but only because he thought we were the sort of people who counted as people, not filthy groundling specimens. If I hadn't had Vicki on my finger, Gladius would have ignored us… or taken us for his collection. "How interesting."

"I certainly thought so," Vicki said. "The very same word. *Interesting*."

Well. I'd hoped for a restful day, but now, it turned out, I had to crash a mad scientist's evil airship.

A Moment of Privacy • Soil Remediation • Hopeful, Not Haphazard • Cousins • A Bit Earthy • Plan B

I rescued my clothes from the slugs, which crawled off unbothered by the interruption. I expected them to be slimy, but they weren't: they felt squishily firm, like the cushions on the bed. I shoved those clothes into my bag and put on some of the fresh things we'd looted in the crystal world instead. (I could have put the same clothes back on, but knowing the slugs cleaned things didn't make them *seem* any less gross.)

I slipped Vicki back onto my finger and knocked on Minna's door. "Come in!" she trilled. When I entered, she was sitting naked on the edge of her pod, humming and tightening her braids, and she turned her happy smile to me. I tried to focus on looking at her from just the neck up. "Zax and Victory-Three!" she called out. "Look at the squishies!" She pointed at the slugs moving across her own clothing. "Can we keep one?"

I shuddered. "I, ah…"

"I don't think they sleep, Minna," Vicki said. "The transition would be too dangerous for them."

"That is a reason that is reasonable." She looked at me, wrinkling her nose. "Something bothers you, my Zax. What is the bother?"

"Ah…"

Vicki flashed a pulse of light. The slugs instantly stopped moving, their color shifting to a redder pink, and the ambient illumination in the room dimmed. "I've disrupted the ship's computer access to this room – I sent an error message, and the system is in diagnostic mode, but I don't know how long it will take. We can speak freely for a moment, though, without being monitored."

Minna sighed and bent to recover her clothes from the slugs and began getting dressed. "Oh no. What is the secret bad thing?"

"Gladius wants to kidnap the people who live on the ground so he can do experiments on them," I said. "The groundlings are poor and sick, and Gladius and the other people in these airships prey on them. Just for fun, as far as I can tell."

"Even the Nurturer-Butchers only did terrible things to us on the Farm in order to increase yield and productivity," Minna said. "That is bad but to do such things for fun is worse. Hmm. I know we cannot save all the ground people but we can save the ones we can save here and now, yes?"

"I love you two." I swept Minna into a hug. "You're both, just, so…"

"We care about you, and the things you care about," Vicki said. "You care about people being good to each other. I admit, my personal worldview is a bit more pragmatic, but cruelty for cruelty's sake is as appalling to me as it is to anyone of sound character."

"If the ground is poison, you remediate. You don't laugh at the sick things that grow. You don't harvest them and show them to your friends so they can laugh too." Minna shook her head. "Ugly bad ways. We have to tear those ways down. We pass through, we are the *ones* who pass through, and we should leave the places we pass through no worse than they were before we came, and always better if we can."

My very own ethos, presented in her usual adorably roundabout way.

"Yes," Vicki said. "Let us review our options. If we disable the ship now, we'll plummet, and even if we can sleep our way out of imminent death, I know you wouldn't want to directly contribute to Gladius's demise, Zax, however directly he might have contributed to the demise of others. Presumably he'll have to draw close to the ground to collect his specimens, though. I think with Minna's assistance and some of the Lector's little treasures we took as spoils, we can make sure the ship lands safely, if a bit bumpily, but never takes off again."

I shook my head. "I have to talk to Gladius first. I can try to make him understand that what he's doing is wrong. If I can change his mind, he might go on to change the minds of his people… Don't look at me like that." Minna was expressionless, and Vicki couldn't look at me at all, but I could feel their doubt. "I know that must sound hopelessly naïve, but sometimes talking to people works, and it's always worthwhile to try. We can leave this world with one act of sabotage, or with an act of education. The first ends with one big bang, but the second could leave echoes and reverberations long after we leave."

Minna shook her head. "Not naïve, Zax. You are not a spring shoot, or a leaf still wet with dew. You are hopeful, and even hard frosts and rootworm cannot kill your hope." She stood on tiptoes and kissed my cheek. "You are a beautiful perennial."

"As she says, of course," Vicki said. "But do you mind if we prepare an alternate plan, in case you fail to win over our host?"

"Backup plans are good. I'm hopeful, not haphazard. Of course. I…" The lights flickered and then came back strong, and the slugs began to crawl away.

"I'm so very sorry about that, we suffered a glitch in the system." Gladius's voice came over some sort of hidden speaker, full of good humor. "Is everyone all right?"

"We're fine!" I called. "Do you have time for a chat, though? After my time on the ground, some civilized conversation sounds like just the thing, and my companion is too sleepy to talk now."

Minna yawned widely and ostentatiously.

"Of course! Join me on the bridge. The ship will show you the way."

I slipped Vicki off my finger and onto Minna's – if something *did* happen, and I ended up swept from this world, they'd be able to take care of each other here. I followed the pulsing lights on the walls out of the room and down a corridor that hadn't even been there before. This ship was remarkably configurable, but I'd seen such technology before, and only had to fake being jaded and unimpressed a little bit. I went up a ramp and onto a semi-circular platform that must have been in the top of the bubble. The walls were transparent here, only a few green floating markers and symbols seemingly hanging in the air.

Gladius stood near the front of the platform, behind a smooth white podium that projected an illuminated control panel beneath his hands. He manipulated the elements on the screen deftly, making fine adjustments to sliders and dials that had no effect I could discern. "Zax! Have you ever been on a collecting expedition before?"

"I haven't." I stepped up beside him and looked into the onrushing night. I had to approach this subject the right way, or he'd get defensive or outraged and shut me down right away. I wished I knew him better, or knew more about this world – it's hard to change someone's mind when you don't know how their mind got that way in the first place – but I'd have to trust my intuition, luck, and general principles. "The ship said you have a zoo, of sorts?"

A humble nod. "Not one of the *grand* menageries like the Prefect has, of course. But I keep a few specimens, some breeding pairs from different regions that might yield interesting hybrids, a genuine living howler because sometimes it's enjoyable to scandalize one's country relations, and of course a handful of fighting groundlings for the odd summer exhibition. I know some people find the fights distasteful, but it's obvious that you have to help the poor creatures channel their natural aggression somehow."

I nodded, keeping my face bland. "Impressive. What do you make of those who say the groundlings could be civilized if their conditions were improved?" Assuming *anyone* he knew said such things was a gamble, but even the most depraved societies usually had malcontents and idealists.

Gladius raised an eyebrow at me. "You know, I was struggling with your accent, but let me guess: you're from the Keret Peninsula?"

"Guilty." I gave a sheepish smile.

"You aren't *involved* with the model towns, are you?"

I shook my head. "No, no. I have a cousin, she's young, head full of ideas and no practicalities, you know, and she's interested in... all that."

"Ah, well, cousins. Orbs preserve us from the younger generation." Gladius shook his head, elegantly doleful. "Of course, it's inarguable that the groundlings can be *trained*, but so can rats and hounds. We know the groundlings can learn language, at least well enough to follow commands – I've seen that myself – but there's no reason to believe they have the light of consciousness inside them. They're just... stimulus-response machines."

"Do you think so? Surely they feel, and have love for their kin, and other qualities we possess ourselves."

Gladius shrugged. "Bats, I'm told, are quite loyal to their family groups. I wouldn't invite one to dinner. The people who chose to stay on the ground instead of retreating to orbit during the Late Unpleasantness – " (I could hear the proper name-ness of those words) " – were obviously congenitally mentally deficient *anyway*, and all the subsequent years spent on that rotten land hasn't made them any better. Wiser men than we have explained how the groundlings and those of us who live above have diverged into separate species, due to the changes wrought here and there respectively. Do we have a common ancestry? Of course, and that's why so many charitable societies from your softhearted peninsula still drop care packages on the groundlings to improve their lot, much as my mother looks out for the prospects of my most idiot cousin. I say softhearted, and not soft*headed*, because I am a kind and generous soul. Unlike my late father, who thought your whole peninsula should be cast down to the soil, if you identify with the groundlings so much." He looked at me to see if I was insulted, I think.

"I've heard worse." I was all equanimity.

"The Keret Peninsula." Gladius shook his head. "I can't imagine what it must be like, to grow up with *dirt* under your feet, even if that dirt is cleansed and raised up three elevations above the ground itself. No wonder you feel sympathy for the groundlings. Those model towns, though... trying to make groundlings into *people*? It's a waste of everyone's time. You might as well put a chicken in a ball gown and expect it to dance."

"The groundlings are people, though." I kept my voice light. "Or so my cousin says. Whatever mistakes their ancestors may have made, they were just like us, once. She says they're sick, and they labor under difficulties we can't even imagine, but if you scour off the dirt, and treat the injuries and illnesses, the differences disappear."

"I've never met a groundling who was *anything* like me." Gladius shuddered. "Your cousin can waste her life however she wishes – finding ways to pass the time is the hardest thing, I always say – but I do find those missionary types tedious. Fortunately they hold no sway in the cloud cities, just in the lower settlements, like your home province. I swear, I think sometimes being closer to the ground spoils the brain, no matter what the scientists say about how low the radiation levels are these days." He coughed. "No, ah, offense."

"None taken." I know enough to recognize a lost cause. Gladius's snobbery was his armor, and his need to feel superior was probably his greatest driving force. He even had to look down on his country cousins and those soft wretches from the Keret Peninsula in order to feel secure in his own importance. "I'm just as alarmed as you are by the ideas espoused by my more radical acquaintances – I just can't show it quite as openly without risking war with my cousins, and who wants to be frozen out or served the worst portion of the feast at a family gathering?"

"Ha, yes, we have to coddle the delicate ones sometimes if we want a proper meal, don't we?" Gladius slapped me on the shoulder, and we were friends again. "Is that Minna one of your cousins? I ask, because she strikes me as a bit..."

"Earthy?" I said.

Gladius's eyes widened. "I would never be so harsh as *that*! But, as you're the one who said it..."

"She's a darling girl," I said. "She just doesn't see things as clearly as you and I do. I try my best to protect her, of course."

"It's our duty as gentlepersons," Gladius said. "Thank you for the stimulating conversation, Zax. I can't remember the last time I had a talk with any teeth in it. We stand on ceremony and politeness more in the cloud cities than you lot in the peninsulas. How invigorating."

"I feel the same way." The thing was, on a certain level, I *liked* Gladius. He'd been kind and generous to us, and he wasn't even stupid, exactly. He'd been shaped by his world and his upbringing, as everyone is, but they had shaped him into something vile and reprehensible. Some people could grow beyond such conditioning, with the right guidance. I feared Gladius wasn't flexible enough to change easily, and I certainly wouldn't be around long enough to take him by the hand and guide him to a better worldview.

That left Vicki and Minna's Plan B. "I'd better go check on Minna, and make sure she hasn't gotten into any trouble."

"Quite, quite. The ship tells me she requested a tour. I believe she's down in the propulsion room now. The lights there *are* quite pleasing. So sparkly. Sometimes I look into them and imagine I'm one of our ground-dwelling ancestors, staring into a fire and seeing gods and portents and monsters."

"I'll go down and join them." I paused. "Thank you, Gladius, for picking us up. You didn't have to do that."

"Of course I did. I am a *gentleperson*." He gave me a jaunty wave and returned to his board.

I followed the lovely ship's light downward, imagined the contents smashed to bits on the ground, and started trying to come up with Plans C, D, and E.

Engine Room • Metal Rain • Gladius Touches Down • A Rescue • A Common Language

The engine room *was* beautiful. Minna stood on a shining silver balcony bordered by delicate fluted railings, looking into a sphere of white light six meters in diameter, with a coruscating spiral of purple, blue, red, and indigo ribbons of energy in the center, spiraling upward, except sometimes they seemed to be spiraling downward instead. "It's a closed timelike curve," Vicki said. "See how the spiral vanishes up at the top of the sphere and reappears again at the bottom? It's remarkable, a continuous closed flow of energy. I have no idea how this engine sustains itself, but it does, and, moreover, it supplies all the ship's power and propulsion. Our friend Gladius has remarkably advanced technology, beyond anything I ever saw in my world, despite his moral simplicity. How did your talk go?"

"Gladius is very... set in his ways. I don't think I made much of an impact, unfortunately."

"It was good of you to try," Vicki said, and to their credit, sounded sincere.

Minna pointed at the spiral of ribboned light. "Victory-Three thinks if we throw a chair or something into that spinny thing, we can probably break it and crash the ship."

I winced. Vicki must have noticed, because it said, "Don't worry, there's no surveillance in here. The very nature of this engine makes electronic observation impossible. We're not even really observing the engine directly ourselves, because just our attention would cause the spiral to collapse into de-coherence, so what we're seeing is a projection of one possible set of…" Vicki trailed off. "Well, just trust me. We can talk freely."

"Surely the engine is protected from that kind of direct sabotage?" I said.

"You'd think so," Vicki said. "But apparently not. I suppose Gladius and his people never considered the possibility that anyone with ill intent would make it this close. I queried the ship, and while its defensive and offensive capabilities are formidable, they're all firmly directed outward, and down. The engine is very delicate, and any amount of disruption should ground the ship." Vicki paused. "Throwing a chair into it *would* be very bad for the chair, though. What do you think? Should we cripple the ship, when we can do so without risking our own lives in the process?"

"I think we have to," I said.

A huge magenta slug came wriggling into the chamber, and Gladius's voice emerged from it, slightly fuzzed with distortion – the impact of the engine on its workings, I supposed. "We're just dipping down toward the plateau now. Looks like there are a few specimens in one of their fields, doing something agricultural with wooden sticks or what have you. They'll do for our first pass. Here, I'll transluce the hull so you can see the collection process."

The white around us went clear, and I clutched instinctively at the railing while Minna gave a little wail. We were close to the bottom of the ship, apparently, and it looked like one misstep would send us plummeting down through the clouds. Then we dropped further, and the land rushed up at us, frighteningly fast. What first looked like the slope of a mountain revealed itself to be a field on the edge of a cliff when the ship shifted its orientation and began to drop straight down. There were humanoid figures in a field of waving grass or wheat or something, hacking at the soil with hand tools, and they took no notice of the ship, even as we drew near; it must have been cloaked or camouflaged in some way, and I knew from experience how silently it could fly. We skimmed over the ground, low, and Gladius said from the slug, "I'm going to send out the manipulator beams and scoop up that one with the funny woven hat."

"Now, Minna," Vicki said.

She bent, scooped up the wriggling slug up in her arms, and hurled it directly into the heart of the engine.

The slug *sizzled* when it struck the ribbons, and flashed away to vapor that stank of salt and oil, but it did some damage in the process. The ribbons, which had flowed together so smoothly, came disentwined and lashed around wildly like whips. One hit a section of the railing just a meter away from us and sliced right through the metal, leaving a molten smear on the balcony floor before it snapped away. I grabbed Minna and hauled her back toward the exit as the ribbons spat bright flashes of energy and then went suddenly dull. The hull flickered to an opaque, metallic gray, and we stumbled and fell into each other as the ship struck the ground at an angle, probably digging a furrow into the field as it lost its momentum. Once it rumbled its way to a stop, we struggled upright. I hoped we hadn't struck any of the people working there. Killing them in the process of trying to save them was not a desirable result.

"Are you OK?" I asked.

Minna said "I think so," and then the ship's hull vanished – was it some sort of field, and not real material at all? We were sitting in the churned dirt now, crushed plants beneath us. Suddenly objects began to rain down around us – more slugs, now gray or black, and a chair shaped like an egg, and small unidentifiable metal objects, and boxes and bottles and bits of cloth… and Gladius, who floated down gently, with some sort of golden glowing harness strapped around his chest and waist.

"The engine failed, and the force field couldn't hold out for long under auxiliary power!" he called out as he settled. "Are you all right? The medical suite is offline, but there's a first aid kit, erm, somewhere." He hovered with the soles of his boots just above the dirt, looking at the contents of his ship, scattered across the field. "I don't mind telling you, friends, we're in a bad way. I've never heard of a total catastrophic failure like that. I didn't even have time to send out a distress signal, which means we'll have to make our way to the nearest camouflaged hermetic node…" He turned, his goggles glowing. "Oh, dear. The locals are coming. I don't see our weapons locker, it's so blasted dark down here even with vision enhancers, but it must be *somewhere*, maybe closer to the edge of the cliff."

A trio of locals – who looked completely human, just dirtier and more ragged and less perfectly symmetrical than Gladius – raced toward us, waving their arms and making a lot of noise. I stepped back, wondering if we'd made a horrible mistake. Maybe the locals would murder us on sight. They certainly had enough reason to attack people who fell from the sky. They shouted as they ran, and after a moment their words became comprehensible to me, even if they didn't quite make sense: "Get away from there!" "Hurry!" and "Stop her!" were a representative sample.

Gladius rose up about three meters into the air for safety.

They reached us… and then ran right past us, parting around us and paying us no mind at all. Were *we* cloaked somehow?

I turned and watched them rush toward the edge of the cliff – closer than I'd realized – and they all begin to wail and peer over the side. "Hold on!" one of them shouted. "We'll get rope!"

Oh, no. We weren't invisible; they just had bigger things to worry about. I set off running, Minna following close behind, and, after a moment, Gladius floated after us, coming closer to ground level but still skimming over the field, not sullying himself with the dirt of the ground. One of the groundlings ran past us back the way he'd come, another peered over the edge of the cliff, and a third wailed. I put together what happened quickly enough from what I overheard. "One of their children was playing near the edge, and when we crashed, she got scared and lost her footing. She went over the edge."

"You *speak* their gibber?" Gladius sounded both impressed and disgusted.

"You're a naturalist. I'm a linguist."

"I didn't even know they *had* a proper language," he said. "I thought it was like… bird cries or dog barks."

I went to the edge, crouching next to the person looking over the edge. The little girl had landed on a small ledge about five meters down. Her tiny dirty face was twisted in pain, and she lay on her side, clutching at her ankle, so she probably couldn't have climbed back anyway. The groundling beside me stared at me for a moment and then said, "Who *are* you?"

"We're here to help," I said firmly. I stood and pointed to Gladius. "I need you to go down and get her."

Gladius drifted, centimeters above the soil, and peered over. "Oh, dear, it's a young one. I haven't seen one so small up close. They're too much trouble in captivity, prone to despair and vulnerable to illness. The ones who make it to adulthood are more robust, naturally, they'd have to be–"

"Gladius! *Help her.*"

His goggles were transparent at the moment, so I could see him blink rapidly at me. "Ah. Yes. Quite."

Gladius stepped over the edge, and the person beside me gasped, but Gladius didn't fall, just fiddled with a control on his harness and slowly descended to the level of the ledge. "It's all right!" I shouted down to the girl in her language. "He's going to help you back up!" Switching tongues, I said, "Be careful of her leg, Gladius, I don't know how badly it's hurt."

The naturalist stepped onto the ledge and knelt, deigning to touch the earth at last. He said something – if it was something offensive, at least the girl wouldn't understand it – and then bent awkwardly and scooped her into his arms. She locked her hands around his neck, and he began to ascend, rising to the plateau and stepping onto the ground. The wailing person stood up and snatched the girl away from Gladius, clutching her and sobbing tears of relief. The other person, bushily-bearded face covered in tears, reached out and grasped Gladius's shoulder. To his credit, the naturalist didn't flinch away. "Thank you. *Thank you*. The sky people have never helped us before."

"He says thanks," I translated. "He's very grateful."

Gladius stared at the hand on his shoulder, then at me. "Ah. Tell him it's no trouble at all, my pleasure, quite."

I passed that on, then returned to Gladius's language. "You said there's a first aid kit somewhere?"

Gladius blinked at me again, then nodded. "Yes, it's in a big white… Ah, it's over there." He pointed to a rectangular trunk, half-embedded in the dirt. I rushed over and pulled the case out of the dirt, found the button that opened it, and looked inside. There were more of the slugs there, in various sizes, these glowing softly pink. I lifted out one about half a meter long. "Will this help her?"

Minna was standing next to Gladius, murmuring something to him, so I had to call again before he looked at me and said, "Ah, yes, yes, it will. Just… apply it to the injured area."

I went to the person I assumed was the girl's mother and said, "This looks strange, I know, but it's medicine. Will you let me help?"

She was nervous, of course, but I'm good at sounding soothing and knowledgeable, so she sat her daughter down on the dirt and pulled up the hem of her ragged dress. I placed the slug on her swollen, possibly broken, ankle, and the biomechanical bandage began to glow a deeper pink. "Does it hurt?" her mother asked anxiously.

The daughter shook her head, eyes wide. "The squishing thing is warm and now it stopped hurting!"

"Just stay there for a little while, until, ah…" I had no idea how to tell when the slug was done doing its work.

Gladius knelt down beside me. "Until its color changes back to pale pink," he said. "Then you'll be just as good as new."

It took me a moment to realize that Gladius was speaking the groundling tongue. "How can you understand them?"

"Your Minna, she gave me a sort of pill, though in truth it seemed more like a seed, and after a few moments, their words just… made sense to me. I had no idea you'd created such things on the Peninsula."

I looked at Minna, who was talking to the bearded man, and marveled. She'd put the linguistic virus into a seed? She was so matter-of-fact I sometimes forgot how remarkable her abilities were.

A common language would go a long way toward enacting Plan C. "Gladius," I said. "Would you be open to a… *different* approach to your studies?"

Cultural Immersion • It Never Ends • We Do What We Can Do • Familiar Stars • A Dream • A Bed of Flowers

"On my world we had a scientist named Jayne Weatherall," Vicki said. "She altered her physiology to become semi-aquatic, and she lived with a pod of oceanic cetaceans for years, emerging only occasionally to have her notes transcribed and transmitted to other researchers. The creatures never mistook her for one of their own, but they did accept her, in time, as a sort of fellow traveler. Her research contributed greatly to the general storehouse of knowledge, and many people credited her work with spurring conservation movements that protected those creatures, bringing them back from the edge of extinction. I saw the animals occasionally during their great migrations, even from my island – they survived the wars better than many other creatures did. Is that the sort of person Gladius is going to be, do you think?"

"I hope so." Minna, Vicki, and I were seated on benches hewn from fallen trees, surrounding a rock-lined firepit. Gladius was off in one of the dwellings – clever things, built half into the ground, with entrances disguised in boulders and heaps of rocks – meeting with this village's elders.

I'd proposed that he study the groundlings *in situ,* a prospect that was much more enticing to him now that he could speak their language. I'd met the chief elder, briefly, and she struck me as a very shrewd individual, who knew more about the "sky people" than the sky people knew about her kind. I had a feeling she was going to squeeze Gladius for every advantage that could help her people. The villagers were already out in the fields, salvaging useful things from the wreckage.

"If Gladius sets himself up as their savior, that's problematic in its own way, of course," Vicki mused. "What if he tries to make himself a god to these people?"

I sighed. "I have to take Gladius at his word, ultimately, that he *wants* to be a naturalist, and study the groundlings as they are, rather than trying to transform them into what he thinks they should be, or to gratify himself. He does seem interested in their society, in his own way – it just never occurred to him to actually come down here and treat them as people, rather than specimens." I reached over and took Minna's hand, and she squeezed it back, smiling. "Giving him the linguistic virus was a great idea. They stopped being animals to him once he could understand them. I *saw* the change in him."

"Being able to talk together does not fix everything, but it is hard to fix anything at all without understanding," Minna said. "I knew giving him the knowledge was not an ending enough on its own, but it is the beginning of a start."

"A common language is a great help in any first-contact situation," Vicki said. "If we'd been able to communicate with the infestation from the void back on my world... well, I doubt they would have had anything to say we cared to hear, and vice versa, but at least the opening of the conflict would have been less *confusing*."

I was glad I hadn't grown up on Vicki's world. "We just have to hope it's enough. I think Gladius might do some good here, and improve the lives of the villagers, on at least a small scale. At the very least, we saved some of these people from being captives in his zoo."

"Gladius might change these people in some ways," Minna said, "but they are going to change him more I think. He is starting to be fond already, and maybe it is the fond of a person for a pet, but it might become more as he knows them longer and better."

"It's hard, trying to do good, and never knowing how things turn out. We can only do what we can do."

"That's all anyone can do, but doing your best consistently takes courage and effort, so don't minimize your actions too much." Vicki made a sound like throat-clearing – they were picking up our mannerisms. "So, Zax, Minna... is this what we do, then? We go to a new world, and if there are people to help there, we help them? Over and over, without a known end, for as long as we're able?"

Oh, no. The disillusionment didn't usually set in quite this quickly, but Vicki thought faster than most of my companions. Once people realized there was no destination, that they would never see the fruits of their efforts, that tomorrow would bring a fresh and unpredictable set of trials – once they really internalized that I was just going to *keep going*, until I died – they started looking at each new world as a potential forever home until they finally settled on one and said their farewells. "That's it," I said, forcing a note of good cheer into my voice. "No end in sight. Every day is a brand new experience."

"That's *wonderful*," Vicki said, and Minna's face lit up. She'd been thinking the same worried thoughts I had, apparently, and I could tell she'd grown attached to our jeweled companion. "It's a functionally infinite stream of new data! It's not even purely self-indulgent, because we have a mission to harmonize, as you'd say, along the way. I was grown with a strong sense of duty, because it's the only way crystals of my class could serve contentedly in a war that could conceivably last until our local star went supernova, and I'd worried, a bit, about abdicating all responsibilities to gluttonously feast on new information. I thought the lack of a greater purpose might create cracks in my consciousness. The war at home was clearly concluded some time ago, but now, we have a new battle to wage, endlessly – a battle against chaos, disharmony, and pain. Yes?"

"We'll keep doing what we can," I said. "I *have* to try to help, not just because it's my inclination or my training. Because otherwise… my life would be nothing but confusion, and fear, and mere survival. I would give in to despair, if I couldn't find a way to make my passage through these worlds meaningful. I'm a skipped stone, but I can leave ripples that make a difference, sometimes." I nodded toward the dwelling, where the laughter of Gladius and the elder occasionally drifted out. They were getting on famously.

Minna snuggled up against me, and Vicki glowed with a mellow light. We sat for a while, then I said, "I'm going to update my journal, and then… it's been a long couple of days. Is anyone else sleepy?"

We opted not to make a big production out of saying goodbye, but one of the slugs recovered from the field was functional, and I figured out how to make it take a voice recording: "Gladius, thank you so much for your help. My companions and I need to make our way back to the Peninsula, so we're heading for the nearest hermetic node." (I had no idea what those were, but apparently they were the first step to getting back to "civilization" from down here, so it seemed a safe enough sort of lie.) "Be good to the locals, and they'll be good to you. I wish you well."

The thought of the slug trundling up to Gladius and speaking in my voice struck me as incredibly hilarious, which told me I was getting tired and punchy. We slipped off into the fields, where Minna settled down in my arms and soon began to snooze. Vicki went into their shutdown-mode. I lay there for a while, gazing up at the stars.

There was a constellation I thought I recognized – the Crane, we called it back home, the shape of a long neck and two long feet. The sky was rarely familiar to me, but sometimes it seemed to be. The Lector (*was he somewhere in this world, looking up at this same sky, trapped here forever now?*) had various theories to explain the intermittently familiar skies, all about parallel or divergent universes as opposed to entirely alien ones, the logical consequences of controversial models of physics, and the occasional recurrence of familiar patterns in an infinite universe. I had never made much headway with figuring such things out, and was usually too busy with the necessities of survival to worry about the bigger issues anyway, but I always felt a little happier when I saw stars I knew.

I slept, and, for the first time since I began my sojourn through the multiverse, I dreamed.

In my dream I was home, and my family was gathered in the great room, beneath the shifting soft glow of the squidlight chandelier mother brought back from the Undersphere. So many familiar faces were there: my aunt Quinlan and uncle Mallory, and my vice-uncle Curtz, and my cousin Gertish and the enby partners in her triad, and my mother and father and side-father, and my sometime paramour Sensilla, beside a person I didn't recognize, holding her hand. They were all older than I remembered, by a few years, and there was a great spice-and-fire cake on the table, the kind I always had on my nameday. I wondered suddenly if it *was* my nameday, and thought it might be, three years since the last one I'd celebrated, probably, though it was so hard to track time the way I traveled, with days of different lengths and no way to tell how long I slept.

"I'm late, I'm sorry I'm late," I said, but they didn't seem to see me at all, or hear me, and my mother was crying and my father was crying and my side-father was trying to comfort them both, but Hall was always clumsy about things like that, and the stranger beside Sensilla seemed embarrassed, and Gertish sighed and stuck her finger into the frosting and sucked it off her fingertip and looked up and into my face and her eyes went wide and she said–

"Zax!" I felt weirdly sluggish and lethargic when I blinked my eyes open. Something smelled sweet, like spun sugar candy. Usually I wake from the transition refreshed and energetic, unless I took heavy sedatives, but everything was foggy now. Minna's face was centimeters from mine, shouting, and her nose and mouth were covered in moss and trailing vinelike tendrils that made her look like some sort of ancient forest deity. The vines waved from the force of her breath when she shouted my name, and I giggled, because it was *funny*, everything was so funny–

Then the tendrils grew down and wriggled into my nose and sinus cavities and I gagged and tried to cough them out, but they were persistent. Moss fuzzed over my mouth, and I sucked in a breath, thinking I was being suffocated, but the air flowed in just fine – it just smelled like greenery now instead of sugar, that was all.

I sat up and looked at the bones and rotting carcasses of dead animals all around me, with hundreds of orange flowers growing through ribcages and eye sockets and sprouting in wild profusion on flesh. The scent of the flowers must have been overpowering, because my head was just a meter from something that looked like a newly dead cow (but with spiraling horns, like an antelope), and I hadn't registered the stink of its carcass all.

"Come, come, these flowers are strong." Minna tugged at me, and I went dazedly along after her, my head still clearing. We made our way to the twisted trunk of a nearby tree, away from the flowers, though I could see other patches of them dotting the forest around us.

"Were you thinking about how tired you were when we traveled, Zax?" Vicki asked. "How much you could use a rest?"

"I… Maybe. What *is* this place?" The tendrils fluttered and tickled my lips and chin when I spoke. "And what's this all over my face?"

"They strain out the bad in the air," Minna said.

"Filtration," Vicki said. "When we arrived here, neither of you woke up, and though I can only take very limited environmental samples without peripherals, I could tell from the dead animals that we were in a dangerous situation. I shouted until Minna woke, but she was very bleary. Somehow she had the presence of mind to create that vegetable gas mask."

"This happens on its own," Minna said. "We never know when the Nurturer-Butchers would assign us to the poison garden, and some of the fungal caves had things that were very bad to breathe too. Mushrooms that try to turn you into mushrooms and such. So this happens." She gestured at her mossy beard. "But I was a little fuzzy at first and did not think to pass the protection on to you right away."

"The flowers emit some sort of soporific gas," Vicki said. "Animals are attracted to the scent, and sleep, until they die, and then their bodies feed the flowers. It's an elegant system, in its way. You have some sealed bottles, don't you, Zax? Perhaps we could take some samples. If Minna can find a way to, mmm, diminish their potency, these flowers could be useful as sedatives, perhaps."

I could see the sense in that, so I went through my bag until I found some airtight containers. Minna plucked some blossoms, some stems, and some roots, and sealed them up firmly. "I will look at these coma-flowers later and see if there is any use to them, but they are a predator and I will take care."

"You saved me. Both of you. If I was still traveling alone..." I shuddered. "I never transition into instantly deadly situations, but sometimes I do appear in dangerous ones. I would have just... kept sleeping here."

"Your eyes were moving," Vicki said. "Did you dream? I thought you couldn't dream anymore."

"I... Yeah, actually. I dreamed."

"Hmm. Perhaps you only travel during the first phase of sleep, sometimes called transitional sleep, before the dreams begin? If you were dreaming here, you might have been in the wrong stage of sleep, but if you moved into another, one without dreams, you might have traveled to another world then – one *without* coma-flowers rendering you unconscious. Your power might have saved you if we hadn't, as automatically as Minna's mossy mask saved her."

Power. Ha. I shrugged. "Maybe. That makes sense, about the stages of sleep, but maybe the flowers stimulate dreaming, to keep the creatures here peaceful and still and occupied while they die, and I would have never moved into another phase."

"The feeling of incomplete data itches, Zax. Still, there's no way to know for sure without experimentation, and the risk hardly seems worth the data it would yield, though I'll keep the hypothesis in mind in case a future opportunit–"

Then the Lector flashed into existence in the middle of the wildflowers, right where I'd been minutes before.

Sleeping Lectors Lie • The Agony of Uncertainty • The Singular and the Collective • Engine of Despair • World 85 • The Needle

The Lector moaned and shifted, but didn't wake. He was dirty and ragged, soil smeared on his clothes and his face and even in his hair.

I sank down by the trunk of the tree and put my head in my hands. Minna sat beside me and took my hand silently. "Well," Vicki said. "Apparently all the serum wasn't out of his system yet. Do you think this disproves my hypothesis that you can steer your destination to some extent, Zax?"

"I don't know." I didn't look up. "I was trying *not* to think of the Lector when we went to that last world, but it was like trying not to think of pink pangolins: the harder you try, the more you think of them."

"I could do it," Minna said. "But I do not know what a pangolin is."

"I could do it, too," Vicki said. "But I can consciously partition my consciousness, so I have an unfair advantage. Your point is taken, though."

"It's hard to control my destination when I can't even control my own mind, I guess." I finally lifted my gaze to the Lector, dozing in the midst of carnage. "What do we do about *him*?"

"We can watch, and see if he changes sleep stages and transitions away," Vicki said. "That would rob him of the ability to direct himself to a world where we're located, if that is indeed something he does. In turn, that might increase our ability to travel along different branches to different destination, and away from him."

I groaned. "He's on my mind now, Vicki. We'll end up wherever he does, if that's the way this process works. We don't even know if he's got more transitions in him after this. He seemed pretty desperate to replenish his supply of serum, and we took away the little bit he had, so he must be using whatever's in his system."

Minna said, "We could leave him here to sleep. It would be a peaceful ending. More peaceful than he would offer you, Zax."

"I can't leave him to certain death, Minna. I *can't*. Even in an infinite universe, life is precious. He could still learn, and change, and become better – Gladius was as bad as the Lector, in his way, and he showed promise at the end. Even if the Lector won't ever become a better person, I won't let him turn *me* into a worse one."

"Do you propose we take him with us?" Vicki said.

I shook my head. "There's behaving ethically, and there's behaving idiotically, and I'm going to try to stay on the right side of that line." I wasn't sure how, though. We could drag the Lector away from the flowers and tie him up – there was rope in my bag. Nothing he couldn't escape from when he woke up, but enough of an impediment to let us put some more worlds between us. There were animals here, so there was life, which meant he could probably survive, if this was his final destination. "I wish we had a way to know if he was going to travel again. It would be good to know if we're just buying time, or if we can finish our involvement with him forever."

"The uncertainty is maddening," Vicki agreed.

"I could maybe make a test," Minna said, and we both stared at her. "It is not my exact specialty, but there were many ways to test for things – good and bad, toxins and medicines – in the therapeutic gardens on the Farm. Moss that changed color in the presence of this and that, vines that flowered one color for this thing and another color for that one. If I could see what's different about Zax's blood, then we could test someone else's blood, and see if it was the same kind of different or not."

A test for the ability to travel between worlds? "How long would it take you to make a test like that?" I said.

"If Vicki can help, then I could maybe before we next fall asleep, I think."

"Let's do it." We still had some of the Lector's medical equipment, so Minna took a small sample of my blood and went off to set up a workbench using rocks and branches. Hardly a sterile environment, but that doesn't seem to bother her.

She's over there now, spitting in dirt and sorting things in her bag and crumbling moss into beakers, and Vicki is helping with some kind of spectrographic analysis.

I updated my journal, and now I'm just sitting here, looking at the Lector.

I didn't start keeping this account until after we met, at his encouragement, and in those early days he was such a constant companion and everything was so crammed with incident that I never wrote about how we first met, as Vicki has noticed. Minna seems like she's going to be at her work for a while, though, and the words are flowing today, so I might as well get it down now, while it's suddenly bright and shining in my mind, as present as the Lector's own presence in the flowers before me.

World 85. A full nine hundred and twenty-eight worlds ago. I'd been traveling for fewer than three months, not even a full season back home, still falling asleep after sixteen or eighteen or at most twenty hours awake. I was dirty, dressed in clothes I'd stolen from a shop on World 83 staffed by artificial beings that looked like moving assemblages of steel rods. The automatons, or mechanical people, pursued me for several blocks after I snatched up the clothes, their voices shrieking at me incomprehensibly, but I was pretty much used to such reactions by then.

I was usually hungry, always terrified, and so, so, so, so, so, so, so, so lonely. In the Realm of Spheres and Harmonies everyone who doesn't intentionally opt for a life of solitude is constantly enmeshed in social structures: intimate groups, family groups, occupational groups, avocational groups, philosophical affinity groups, geographical groups, and more. We largely define ourselves by our relationships to others. Those in opposing systems sometimes called us hive-minded or groupthinkers, but that's not fair; we're individuals in many ways, but we're not individual*ists* – we don't venerate the singular over the collective. The goal is to find satisfaction and autonomy within a set of overlapping systems of mutual support and assistance. In the Realm, everyone helps everyone else become their best selves.

The night I first traveled, I lost that. I was a single cell torn from a body. One musical note excised from a symphony. A grain of sand that had once been part of a beautiful beach. I was traumatized, because in those days, even the worlds that weren't wild or hostile were terribly alien. There was nothing worse than finding myself in a village or town or city, as I did every tenth or twelfth world, meeting people who looked a lot like those I'd known, but speaking in languages that were completely unfamiliar… or, worse, maddeningly close to my own, with the odd sound or string of syllables or false cognate that seemed for a moment to make sense, until the absence of comprehensible context washed away the illusion.

In my old life I occasionally dealt with people from places newly annexed to the Realm of Spheres and Harmonies and who hadn't yet learned our tongue, so being in a crowd of foreign speakers wasn't inherently unbearable. The temporary lack of a common language isn't so bad. It can even be exhilarating, and expand your sense of the limits of your own worldview. The endless and inescapable lack of a common tongue, though, and the knowledge that I would never, ever have time to learn more than a word or two of any given language before sleep snatched me away to another place, was an ongoing engine of despair. I spent a lot of time being yelled at or chased for reasons I still don't understand.

World 84 was peaceful, with a lagoon full of slow fish who'd never learned to fear predatory land-dwelling bipeds, a sky full of whale-sized creatures in pastel colors that looked like immense jellyfish drifting on the wind, and no sounds but the washing of the waves. I still think back on that world fondly: lying on my back, belly full of fish, watching distant creatures undulate among the clouds. Of course, over the horizon, there might have been war, fire, or pandemic. Perhaps people plied the skies in airships and hunted those whale-jellies, and pastel blood rained down, or maybe they were predators that would have stung and consumed me if I'd caught their eye. But my little corner of that world was peace, and I miss it still.

I was in a decent frame of mind when I went to sleep, at least by the standards of those early days. I opened my eyes on World 85 and did my usual scan for immediate threats. I was on the grass of a quad, surrounded by stately buildings of old brick, and there were humans walking around, dressed not so differently than they did in my world, though perhaps in colors and cuts a bit more muted and conservative. They all looked prosperous and healthy, and none of them paid me any mind, so my arrival had gone unnoticed. (Sometimes people screamed and hit me with things. Once I woke up in someone else's *bathtub*, and I can hardly blame them for smacking me.)

Some of the people around me were poking at translucent hand-sized rectangles that I rightly assumed were interface devices for some unseen technological network. I sat up, glad my clothes were relatively fresh, and, with no immediate threats to deal with, observed my surroundings a bit more closely. There was something peculiar about the blue, partly cloudy sky, a strange sort of glimmer or refraction – I kept catching prismatic flashes from the corner of my eye. There was some kind of dome or protective field up there, maybe. I'd seen things like that before.

I walked along some of the winding and well-manicured paths, realizing this was a campus for some kind of educational facility.

(It was one of the "Greater Colloquies," according to the Lector, and he always said it as if I should be impressed.) The place seemed strangely old-fashioned to me – my world had moved beyond such campuses long ago, favoring a decentralized system with meetings held in virtual spaces – but there were flashes of advanced technology here and there, including gleaming multi-limbed robots that scuttled to-and-fro without raising any interest from onlookers, and occasional people gazing into empty space and muttering, suggesting some kind of virtual or augmented reality interface in action.

The campus was a relaxing place, full of fountains and groves, and seemed to stretch for miles. There were sculptures of noble-looking people and various animals here and there, with plaques written in incomprehensible script, and lots of benches and low walls and places clearly meant for restful contemplation and conversation. The place felt, well, *harmonious*. It struck me as an environment created deliberately to give the mind room. I felt very at ease there.

Especially when I found the food stalls. I walked around a stately building and found a gleaming pod of seven oblong silver booths arrayed around a stone square filled with tables and chairs. The booths had windows in the sides, and robots inside, and they were dispensing things in bowls and things in cones of waxed paper and things in cups and things on sticks and things on pieces of bread, and it all smelled amazing: savory and sweet and rich. Fish roasted over a fire was perfectly pleasant, but it had been worlds since I'd eaten food prepared by someone else.

I watched, and as far as I could see, there was nothing involved in the transaction besides speaking to the serving robots or pointing to a list of items. I knew that just because there was no visible exchange of money, that didn't mean money didn't come into the situation – the robots could be passively scanning the ubiquitous translucent tablets and silently debiting people's account – but I'd encountered a couple of true post-scarcity worlds by then, so I was hopeful. I picked the pod with the shortest line, waited patiently, and when I got the front of the queue, pointed to a couple of items on the display board at random.

The robot – a sort of multi-armed teapot of a thing the size of a toddler – spun and whirled and gave me a bowl of noodles and broth and a big sticky ball of rice with little seeds stuck all over it, and a big container of fizzy water. I grabbed a few napkins from a dispenser and found the spoons and picked the last empty table in the square.

I was slurping up the noodles – the broth was rich with whatever the local equivalent of garlic was – when someone spoke to me. I looked up, into the kind brown eyes of a man old enough to be my father (later I found out he was far older than that), with dark hair touched gray at the temples, wearing steel-rimmed spectacles. He was dressed in a pristine white coat over a dark suit, and held a tray of food and drink. He repeated whatever he'd said before, and though I couldn't understand him, I could tell from his body language what he was asking: *May I sit here?*

I gestured magnanimously, using my full mouth as a reason not to vocalize. I enjoyed the opportunity to give something to someone else, even if it was just permission to have a seat. He sat down, ate a bit, and spoke to me, those reasonable, even tones I would come to know so well. I did my best to indicate by body language that I wasn't interested in conversation – of course I was *desperate* for conversation, but being reminded that I couldn't actually have any was eroding my feelings of peace and calm – and answered him with grunts and shrugs.

While I was eating the sticky ball – sweet outside, with a savory red paste in the center, strange but good – he seemed to get the hint and pulled out his tablet, setting it on its edge on the table (it balanced itself, somehow) so he could look at the screen while he ate.

After a few minutes I noticed he was frowning, and he spoke to me again, very slowly and seriously. I shrugged, shook my head, and stood up. A scuttle-bot came over and scooped up my utensils and napkins and bowl and stuffed them into a compartment in its torso. I was contemplating getting seconds – "eat and drink when you can" is still my motto, since I never know when my next meal is coming – but the man stood up and followed me, so I gave him a pleasant wave and walked away. I moved fast, but I didn't quite run. People stare when you run, usually.

I found a beautiful formal garden, laid out in neat curves and straight lines, full of flowers and bowers and pergolas and fruit trees, and settled down on a reclining bench made of some pliable material that shaped itself to my body and supported me so evenly and effortlessly it felt like I was floating. I lay there, gazing at the white flowers bobbing on the vines around me, nowhere close to dozing off but consciously letting my body relax from its state of near-constant vigilance. The stress, the isolation, and the lack of social contact was wearing badly on my mind by that point, and a chance to let my breath and heart rate slow in a place that seemed, in spirit if not aesthetics, similar to my home world was a treat to be savored.

If I hadn't been so relaxed, I would have noticed the man from the food court creeping up behind me with a needle in his hand.

The Linguistic Virus • Holding Forth • Braided Worlds • Scanned • Theories • Answers in the Blood

Something seized my arms, and I struggled upright, but I was pinned in place by unyielding metal claws – a scuttle-bot had crept up on either side of my bench, and they were holding me down. The man in the white coat smiled down at me and made noises that were clearly meant to be soothing. "Let me go!" I shouted.

He held up a finger as if telling me to wait, then moved in, holding a syringe in one hand. I whipped my head around to try to keep him from doing whatever he was planning to do, and the scuttle-bots extruded more arms and gripped the sides of my head. The man made more soothing noises, and then he pushed the needle into the side of my neck and depressed the plunger.

The needle stung going in, and there was a brief rush of cold, but no other immediate effects. He withdrew the syringed, capped it, and dropped it into his pocket. I stared up at him, bewildered, as he babbled away pleasantly for a bit, the words just meaningless sounds, until suddenly they started to make *sense*.

"...should be active any minute now, so just speak up once you can understand me. I could understand *you* all along, of course, because I myself am a carrier of the linguistic virus. I'm intrigued, because your language is utterly unknown to me. I apologize for the drama of holding you down and so forth, but it was clear you couldn't understand me, and injecting you with the virus is the easiest way to open communication. Without the ability to talk, we have nothing... Ah, your eyes went wider there. Does that mean the virus has taken effect?"

"Virus?" I said. "You gave me a disease?"

"No, a virus is not necessarily a disease," he said. "They're very interesting structures, made of proteins and genetic material, and they're capable of self-replication, so they have some qualities of life, but they also have qualities of *non*-life. Viruses *are* excellent at carrying information, however, and altering other organisms. The linguistic virus was created in a lab. It alters those portions of your brain that process language and makes them... more adept, let's say. Almost anyone immersed in a foreign language will pick up a general working knowledge of the vocabulary and grammar given time, but this virus accelerates the process dramatically. They gave me a Golding Prize for developing the technique, you know, though they tried to take the medal back when I admitted the virus could be passed from person-to-person through a basic fluid exchange. I could have spared you the needle, but I thought you'd take even less kindly to a sloppy kiss on the mouth from a stranger. The Golding board called me reckless, as if I hadn't included sufficient safeguards. I made a few calls and had the malcontents on the committee removed, of course, and no more was said about the subject." He cocked his head. "You have no idea what the Golding Prize is, do you? The man who invented the Flensing Beam all those centuries ago, Hierophant Golding, grew remorseful over the damage caused by his inventions and endowed a foundation to celebrate scientific achievements that *don't*... well, flense people at a distance, essentially. The linguistic virus has been instrumental in bringing peace to several war-torn regions in the outer layers of the Core, and its creation earned me my place as the Lector of this Colloquy."

"Oh," I said. That was my first experience with the Lector's tendency to monologue. "Could you let me go?"

He blinked. "My apologies." The scuttle-bots released me and scurried off. I sat up, rubbing at my wrists and forearms where they'd held me. "Tell me, young person. Who *are* you?"

I hadn't said my own name aloud in months, and relished the opportunity. "My name is Zaxony Dyad Euphony Delatree. My friends call me Zax. I… thank you, for helping me speak your language." All those words, apart from my name, felt strange coming out of my mouth. My brain had been profoundly altered, and I was both glad and alarmed. If he could do *this* to my brain, drop a new language into my mind in seconds, what else could he do?

"Zaxony. How unusual." He pulled out his translucent tablet again and gazed at it, then said, "Hmm. I scanned you at the table, you know, when you wouldn't talk to me, and discovered to my surprise that you are not listed in the Colloquy system. I thought perhaps you were a foreign dignitary or some kind of diplomatic agent – or the child of either of those – with enhanced privacy settings, but, no, Zaxony, you don't show up in the name database either. You wouldn't lie to me, would you, about who you are?"

For the first time since Ana, I was in a position to explain myself, and have my words understood… but, I was fairly sure, not believed. The Lector, unlike Ana, hadn't seen me appear from nowhere. I tried anyway. "I'm not from here. I was born on another world."

The Lector tapped his tablet. "I have a listing of every settled system, Zaxony. I am the chief administrator of this residential-educational region, and my accesses are comprehensive. There are of course unlisted entities, various rebellious or separatist sects in disputed layers, but they'd hardly be eating a bowl of noodle soup at a Major Colloquy here at the Core, now would they?"

"I…" I sighed. "That's not what I mean by 'world.' Where I'm from, we have a concept called 'braided dimensions.' It's mostly used in fiction or for thought experiments. The idea is that there are multiple realities, intertwined but distinct, and–"

"Do you mean the orchard of worlds?" the Lector said. He proceeded to explain his conception of the multiverse in basically the same way I later told it to Minna; I adopted his terminology because it was easier to conceptualize than the braids, which had never made all that much sense to me. I started gesturing affirmation halfway through, but that didn't stop him from laying out the theory more exhaustively. "It's generally considered impossible to travel from one such reality to another," he said, but thoughtfully. "Since the premise could neither be proven nor falsified, I found it basically uninteresting, so I don't claim a deep understanding of the nuances. How do you travel from one reality to the next? Do you have some kind of machine?"

"I just fall asleep, and wake up somewhere else."

"Life is a dream, hmmm?"

"At first, I hoped I was dreaming," I admitted. "But it's been months."

"This is a new development for you, then? What prompted the change? Were you a scientist? An experimental subject? Did you read a tome of dark, forbidden knowledge?" He chuckled at that last, and I realized he didn't believe me. I'd never had anyone *disbelieve* me before, but only because I'd never been able to tell anyone about my condition, except Ana. Maybe communication wasn't the panacea I'd imagined.

"I don't know what caused the change."

"Your claim strikes me as terribly implausible, Zaxony. I suspect your true origin is more mundane, and that you are either mendacious or mentally ill. Either condition can be treated."

"I know it sounds absurd. It's easy enough for me to prove it, though. Just watch me fall asleep, and disappear."

"That would settle the issue definitively, but if you're telling the truth, it would rob me of the opportunity to ask follow-up questions. I think I can prove or disprove your claim while you're still awake, though. Would you care to come with me to my laboratory?"

"That doesn't sound very pleasant."

The Lector chuckled. "It's not what you imagine. No poking or prodding, or surprise needles to the neck, though I think you'll agree that turned out well for you. I just need to run a few tests on your tissues and blood. I have a non-invasive scanner, so you won't even have to bleed for me." That was the first time he mentioned blood. I wish I could say alarm bells started ringing, but they didn't for a long time.

"I guess it can't hurt. And I do owe you for giving me the gift of communication again. Though it might be worse, when I leave this world, and have to go back to incomprehension and confusion."

The Lector stared at me for a moment, and then laughed. "No, Zaxony, you misunderstand. The linguistic virus is part of you now. Any spoken language – well, any spoken language that follows the deep structures of linguistics common to my world, and apparently yours – should be comprehensible, though more alien tongues might take longer to fully comprehend, and there will always be gaps if you encounter concepts that are too unusual. As you discover more languages, however, your brain will become ever more adept at mastering new ones, and your learning speed will increase."

I blinked back sudden tears. "Really? I'll be able to understand other people? To make myself understood?"

"Yes, indeed. Anything can be achieved when you can talk things out. Come along. Let's get you tested. I confess, I expect you're just... confused... or perhaps you're some sort of off-the-record child raised in isolation by Denialists who spoke and taught you their own unique constructed language... but oh, I must admit some excitement at the idea that you're telling the truth. To have access to the orchard of worlds, to pluck those unknown fruit... What a great benefit that would be to my studies!"

The Lector was clearly pompous and self-aggrandizing and condescending... but I loved him, right from the first, because he'd given me back my voice. I don't love him anymore, but I am still grateful, as strange as it sounds. I keep hoping that he's right – that anything can be achieved when you can talk things out. If only he was capable of listening.

* * *

I didn't know what a "Lector" was then—I later learned it's someone who reads, especially religious texts, or someone who lectures, but in the Colloquy, it was the faux-humble title for the person who ran the whole place. The Lector's laboratory was elegant enough to befit his status. At first glance it looked like a reading room: a cozy space with lamps under stained glass shades, deep soft chairs, beautifully polished work tables, and shelves full of scrolls and books and disks and other media. There were larger translucent slabs of glass on the tables, covered in glowing lines and sigils that were as mysterious to me as any foreign language, linguistic virus or not. The room had hidden depths, though, like the Lector himself.

He touched one of the screens, and a panel slid aside in the wall, revealing a niche shaped like the cross section of a cylinder stood on its end, made of some glowing white substance. "That's my scanner. Step inside, facing outward into the room, and I'll get a good look at what's inside your body."

"How will this help you tell where I'm from?"

"It won't tell me that, but it will tell me where you *aren't* from. Step in."

After a moment's pause, I did as he said. The Lector was curious and friendly and non-threatening, but he'd also had me seized by robots while he performed a medical procedure on me without my permission, so I wasn't entirely ready to trust him yet.

He went to one of the terminals and manipulated the screen, and the curved wall around me glowed brighter, shining so intensely that I winced and shut my eyes. The light faded after a moment, and I looked at the Lector expectantly.

After a moment of intensely staring at the screen, he sagged, and one of the dark, padded chairs rushed toward him on suddenly mobile legs, catching him just as he fell. He leaned back, sprawled at an uncomfortable-looking angle, and looked at the screen. He switched his gaze to me, and his face was, briefly, entirely blank. Then he smiled, his eyes widening, and straightened in the chair. "Zaxony. You show no trace at all of the alterations wrought by the

Uplift Bomb. Every living organism in the Core and all the inhabited layers carries the mark of that formative catastrophe within them – it altered all of our genomes and scrawled its signature in the very buildings blocks of our bodies. Either you're really from another universe, or you were grown in a vat from some extremely ancient and well-shielded biological samples for the express purpose of making me *think* you're from another universe… and that seems like a lot of trouble to go to, even for my most vociferous academic rivals." He gestured to another chair, and it trotted up obediently to face his. "Please, Zaxony, have a seat."

I sat down, and a scuttle-bot appeared, bringing cold water and a tray of snacks. The bot transformed itself into a table and put the drinks and food down on top of itself, within easy reach. "You really have no idea how you came to develop your condition?"

I nibbled some kind of nutty cookie and shook my head.

"Did anything out of the ordinary happen to you in the days before you first traveled? However seemingly insignificant?"

I had considered the same things he was considering, of course, so I had answers, though not satisfying ones. "There was some sort of astronomical event the week before I vanished. The scientists called it a 'dark energy flux,' and there was concern it would knock out our communications grid or irradiate our feedstocks, and some people fled into bunkers, but in the end, nothing seemed to come of it. It's possible that everyone in my world was bathed in some kind of radiation, and that all of *them* jumped to new worlds when they fell asleep, too. There's no way I could know, and if the orchard of worlds is infinite, or even just very big, I might never encounter any of them again."

"Interesting. I'll examine you for unusual radiation signatures, too. Anything else?"

"Well… I was a… social worker, I suppose, is the easiest way to explain it in your language… and I was asked to treat a woman found wandering near one of our harmonization centers. Our records aren't as comprehensive as your world's seem to be, but she wasn't listed in any of them, and she spoke a language none of us recognized –

which isn't unheard of, as the Realm is full of fringes and surrounded by unincorporated areas. She wept, and was hungry and dehydrated, so we fed her and I tried to calm her down, and gave her a bed. We never could understand her. I was on overnight call, and her room alarm went off. I rushed to check on her, and found her covered in blood – she'd cut open her own wrists, using a sharpened spoon handle. She must have hidden it in her sleeve after we fed her."

"Did she die?" the Lector asked.

"No. Well, briefly, but we revived her. We rushed her to the infirmary and they treated her wounds. Her blood was all over me, though… and in the morning, her bed was empty, though the floor monitor swore she didn't leave. The next time I fell asleep, I woke up in another world."

"You think she was a traveler like you? That her blood somehow infected you?"

I shrugged. "It crossed my mind. I was attacked by a… creature, some worlds back, though, and it bit me, and swallowed a good bit of my blood. I fought it off, knocked it out with a rock… and it didn't flicker off into another reality, even though when I'm knocked unconscious, *I* do. So I guess it wasn't contagious in her blood after all."

"It's possible that she had a transmissible version of the… condition – and that you are merely a passive carrier. Though then, of course, the question remains, how did *she* develop this capability?"

"If I ever run into her again out in the orchard, I'll ask her," I said. "Thanks to you, she'll even be able to understand the question."

The Lector reached over and patted my hand. "If there are answers to be found, Zaxony, in your blood or elsewhere, I assure you, I will find them."

The Notebook • A Cure for Loneliness • Sleeping Together • The Land of the Terrible Terrariums • The Last World

The Lector encouraged me to start writing these accounts, and gave me this digital journal and a set of styluses, though in a pinch, my own finger works to write in these endless pages. "Most people in my world compose with keyboards, or dictate voice-to-text," he explained, "but I find that writing by hand encourages deeper contemplation, promotes greater recall, and also tends to produce more melodious prose. Plus, it's technologically agnostic – you don't need access to a power grid or beamed energy to write in this notebook. The journal will hold a charge for decades, and it passively recharges any time you have it open in the presence of sunlight or other strong illumination. Don't worry about filling it up, either. Its memory is sufficient to hold the contents of the Core library, with room left over for a few hundred seasons of your favorite vid-fics."

That notebook, *this* notebook, is still one of my most prized possessions. I always liked writing by hand too, for the same reasons. I thought that made us kindred spirits.

The Lector's world had extremely good stimulants; I gathered the students were encouraged to study hard, by any means necessary. He didn't want me to fall asleep before he could finish researching me, and so we were both awake for nearly six days, still my record. We took occasional walks and went for food, but mostly we worked in his lab. He quizzed me extensively about my home world, and the other worlds I'd visited, all while working on his computers and examining the biological samples I (quite willingly) gave up. Even back then, he was of the opinion that there must be some way for me to control my ability – to go to sleep without traveling, or travel while waking, or choose to move up or down the chain of worlds, or somehow choose my direction. He believed my sleeping mind was directing my ability, in a way my conscious mind didn't know how to replicate, but perhaps someday could. He taught me meditation techniques and methods to increase recall. He was very interested in specific, measurable details about the places I'd visited – the positions of stars, the weather (obviously climate was beyond me), and the life forms I encountered. I hadn't paid much attention beyond noting obvious dangers, and though he was frustrated by my lack of information, he coped by teaching me to observe things with more of a scientific mind, so I could collect better data in the future. I must admit, it's turned out to be a useful skillset. Every world is different, but even across the multiverse, certain things recur, and being able to interpret the patterns has been useful to me.

None of his sleepless efforts came to much, though. There were *lots* of things strange about my blood and tissue, after all. My home world was alien, and the places I'd visited had left their marks on me in countless invisible ways, and narrowing down which of the many peculiarities in my physiology enabled me to travel this way proved more than he could unlock in such a short time. After my third prodigious yawn in an hour, he slumped down in the obedient chair and said, "I despair, Zaxony, of solving the mystery of you before you vanish through that door of sleep."

"I'm sorry, Lector. At least when I disappear you'll know for sure that I'm telling the truth, and not just having vivid dreams."

He chuckled. "I do like empirical evidence." He leaned forward. "Zaxony… I've been thinking. Perhaps you could take me with you."

I leaned back. "I can't. What happened to Ana… I can't risk doing that to someone else. She was broken, Lector, and it was my fault."

"We know that you travel when you're asleep, Zaxony. Perhaps being unconscious is a crucial part of the process. Ana was awake, watching you fall asleep, and you pulled her along with you. As best you can tell, she was distressed by something she observed in the transition. I propose that I drug myself into a deep sleep, and you drug *yourself* while holding me, and we... travel. If I awake on the other side in possession of a sound mind, then we'll know traveling unconscious is the secret. And if I prove to be... unwell... you have my permission to leave me to my fate."

"Lector, even if you're right – there's no going back."

He waved his hand. "I'm sure, given time, I'll be able to figure out how to control and direct–"

I shook my head vigorously. "But you don't *know* that. I don't doubt your intelligence or talent, but maybe there isn't a way to control my ability. Maybe my traveling is just fundamentally random. If you leave this place with me, even if you maintain your sanity, you can't ever come back."

"I've reached the pinnacle of my life here, Zaxony. My dream was always to head one of the Major Colloquies, and now I do, and it's... fine. More administrative work than I'd like, though. I've been considering converting my fortune into hard currency, buying false papers, and lighting out for one of the outer layers to study the emergence of A-life, just to make my life *interesting* again. These past few days with you are the most fun I've had in decades. I have no living family, no philosophical loyalty to my nation state or the Colloquies... My only allegiances are to knowledge, discovery, and curiosity. Please. Let me join you? It would be a terribly grand adventure."

I still hesitated, because my purpose is to help people, and I believed that travel *would* help the Lector, but it might also destroy his mind. I thought of Ana's beautiful, stricken face, as she whispered, and then screamed, *Worms*.

"Zaxony." The Lector reached over, and put a hand on my knee. "Aren't you tired of being so *lonely*?"

Tears welled in my eyes, and I nodded, once. "You can come."

He packed a duffel bag and a small hard-sided case, though it was bigger than it seemed like it should be inside – his "traveling case," he said. In addition to the plasma keys and sedatives and water purification tablets, I later learned the case itself had more computational power than existed in some advanced civilizations I'd visited, and was capable of synthesizing many chemicals from raw materials – he never taught me how to use it, though, always hoarding his knowledge, which is why I left it behind on the crystal world.

The Lector took a sedative, hugged his bags to his chest (attached to him with a sort of harness), and blinked at me sleepily. "Don't go without me," he said.

"I would never," I replied.

I curled up on the soft floor of the lab, spooned him, let my breath slow, and eased into sleep.

My eyes opened to filtered sunlight and birdsong, the air thick with damp, the scent of fresh vegetation all around us. I disentangled myself and moved back from the Lector, remembering Ana's fingernails raking my face. He was sprawled on the stone footpath, snoring, arms still clutching his bags. I stood and stretched, looking around for danger. We seemed to be in some kind of aviary, to judge by the lush trees and bushes, the swooping birds – were some of them gliding reptiles? – and the distant mesh ceiling high above. The cobbled path and a bench overlooking a pond suggested this was a place people were allowed to visit, at least. I nudged the Lector with my toe, and he rolled over, blinking.

His eyes were empty and blank, and I prepared myself to flee if he started shrieking about worms, but then he looked at me and said, "That was as restful as any night's sleep I've had, but there were no dreams…" He stood and looked around, then opened his case and removed something like a clunky wristwatch, and strapped it on. After gazing at the watch's face for a moment he looked at me and grinned. "This isn't my world. There's no trace of the Uplift Bomb's signature." He whooped, leapt, and spun around, and I grinned at him, delighted by his delight. He grabbed my hands and spun me around, and we danced on the footpath, birds flying past our heads as if wanting to join in.

He stepped back, rubbed his hands together, and said, "Let's see what we have *here*." I heard him say that hundreds more times, in every new world we visited together... and it's also what he said when he finally strapped me to that table and set about the task of stealing my blood.

We set out to explore the new world where we'd found ourselves, number 86, "the land of the terrible terrariums" as he later sometimes called it. Well, you always remember your first. Before he turned on me, I thought he would be my forever companion. He was content, for a long time, just to be surrounded by the rush of the new, to see things no one from his world had ever seen or ever would. I'm not sure when it all started to curdle for him. Certainly, after six months or so together, his frustration at the inability to unlock the secrets of my ability had turned to a kind of angry despair that flashed into rage on occasion. I don't know when he started developing the serum that let him travel like me, but its temporary nature must have always bothered him too – so close, and yet so far, from having the power he truly coveted.

After a year together he became sarcastic, and began refusing to assist in my small attempts to help others, something he'd once seemed to enjoy. "Why bother? You'll never even know if you made a difference in their lives. You could even be making things worse. We're playing at being champions, heroes of space and time, traveling paladins do-gooding our way through the multiverse. It's *pointless*. What does anyone ever do for us, hmm?" That was a speech whose variations I would hear more than once.

The eternal transience of our existence gradually maddened him, or else eroded the covering of affability that usually hid a madness he'd harbored all along. Once we met a man with a robotic arm who lived in a junkyard and smoked a local herb that seemed to have euphoric and dissociative qualities. The Lector asked him some questions about the world, always gathering information, and when the Lector inquired about the man's future plans, he waved his pipe dismissively and said, "It's not about where you're going, it's about the journey you take to get there."

I had to restrain the Lector from beating the man with a pipe. That was our 470th world together, and we were very close to the end of our relationship, though I didn't know it at the time. I thought he was just having a bad day. I didn't realize he was a bad *person* until it was almost too late. The Lector could never be harmonized, because he doesn't want to find a comfortable place to fit. He wants to reshape the world, and the multiverse, to suit himself instead. If there is a discordant note in the symphony, you pause, and you adjust, until it sounds better. But the Lector is a discordant screech that can only sound at home in the midst of cacophony. You find people like that, sometimes. The best thing to do is to put them someplace they can be reasonably comfortable, where they can't ruin anyone's life but their own.

Sitting here, looking at the Lector sleep so peacefully, reminds me of waking up with him that first time in a new world. We'd been on such a journey together, and I still wasn't sure how it was going to end.

Oh. Minna says she's ready.

Minna drew the Lector's blood, those plant filters in her nose sparing her from the effects of the flowers. She and Vicki did something with their vials and mosses and powders and then she lifted her head and said, "There is the tiniest trace of a trace of you left in him, Zax. And a bunch of degraded yuck."

"The unique substance that we found in such high quantities in your blood is present only in a very small quantity in the Lector," Vicki clarified. "Moreover, it's breaking down into... well, degraded yuck, as Minna said. Inert compounds. The serum the Lector made is not as stable as whatever your body produces, as we suspected.

We don't know what the threshold dose is, unfortunately. There may be enough of the active ingredient in his blood to allow him to travel if he does so soon, but at this rate of decay… I'd say if he doesn't vanish in the next hour or so, he's going to be stuck here. We're nearly free, Zax."

"That's amazing," I said, and then, of course, the Lector vanished.

We debated whether to follow him immediately, alert as always to the possibility of ambush, especially if he really was stuck in the next world – he'd be desperate for more of my blood. Instead, we are preparing an attack ourselves. The Lector is formidable because of his mind and his resources, but we'd taken the latter from him. He could probably lay a deadly trap, if there's anything in the next world to smash us over the head with… but he wants me alive, which limits his options.

If he tries to capture us, we'll capture him instead, check to make sure his blood is truly free of the serum… and then leave him in his exile. I'm jotting this down while Minna is gathering the coma-flowers and Vicki is figuring out the fine tactical details.

I'm hopeful that an end to this trouble is finally in sight.

A New Scribe Takes Up the Pen • 1111 • A Locked Room • Falling Every Way at Once • Orbiting a Dead World • No More Negotiations

How to begin? First, let me note that these entries are not written by Zaxony Delatree, though the script superficially resembles his own. He taught me the rudiments of his language, after all, beginning with his alphabet, and such is my inherent precision that my "handwriting" is largely indistinguishable from his, though I am inputting the text through a direct field interface with his journal. I am Vastcool Class Crystal Intellect Three Three Three, referred to most frequently in the prior pages of this journal as "Vicki" or occasionally as "Victory-Three."

I am writing this because Zax will not, or cannot, chronicle the events of the past several (for want of a better word in this multiverse of shifting time-scales) weeks.

I write to you from World 1111. Yes, nearly a hundred worlds since the forest with the coma flowers. Time is hard to calculate in any objective sense, but it has been months of subjective time since then, at least.

This is a peaceful world, or, at least, this part of it is. We are in a cloud-forest, currently sitting on an ancient metal platform that was once part of an immense tree-house, long since fallen into disrepair and disuse. Zax is sitting outside, staring blankly into the mist and haze of the forest, beside a pile of fruit I insisted he gather, though he took only one bite of one piece and declared himself full. When we lost Minna, he was inconsolable. Even that depth of sadness was preferable to this... blankness that has taken him since the Lector finished with us, and left us behind.

My apologies. I am approaching this in an entirely non-linear fashion, with far too much personal commentary as well. I have grown unaccustomed to writing reports in recent centuries. Let me try again, picking up as best I can from where Zax's last entry ended. (I hope it is not his "last" entry in a definitive sense.)

As Zax wrote, after the Lector's body vanished from the patch of coma-flowers, we debated how best to proceed. We knew the Lector might well be waiting to ambush us in the next world we visited, and tried to prepare ourselves accordingly. With my advice and assistance, Minna created a liquid suspension of the coma-flowers that would reproduce their soporific effects on anyone who breathed or tasted the fluid. She cultivated some small fruiting bodies on her arms and legs that would burst and spray forth droplets of the serum in response to a sudden shift in air temperature or pressure. She and Zax had filter-plants in their nostrils and mossy barriers over their mouths to prevent them from any unintended inhalation. It struck us as a terribly clever way to surprise and disarm the Lector in case he was crouching nearby, waiting to hit us with rocks or the like. We didn't expect him to have any *resources*.

My senses came online, and I immediately perceived that we were not on a planet at all, but in an artificial habitat in the void of space. I spent time on a space station early in my military career, monitoring the increasing levels of void infestation, and so the environment was familiar to me. Zax, too, had clearly been in such places at least once or twice, because he evinced no extraordinary alarm or discomfort.

Minna, however, had clearly never experienced microgravity before. She immediately began to shout and flail her arms and legs, sending the now-spent fruiting bodies flying off on their own trajectories: "Zax! Victory-Three! Help me! I am falling every way at once!" The spray from our pointless attempt at a pre-emptive soporific strike floated around the room a bit at first, but there must have been filtration systems in place, because the droplets began to drift unobtrusively toward the corners and thence into small vents.

In her panic, Minna kicked a wall and consequently sent herself caroming headfirst into *another* wall, as the chamber where we'd appeared was quite small. Minna managed to turn at the last moment and caught herself on her shoulder, thus avoiding concussion or other damage. She looked a bit green – not for photosynthetic reasons, this time – and I feared she might vomit, making the cramped quarters even more unpleasant, but she swallowed hard and gained a modicum of control over herself.

Zax pushed off from a soot-streaked wall covered in clipped-down tubes and wires, like some sort of technological ivy, and eased himself to a stop beside Minna, wrapping her in his arms. "Shh, it's OK. I know it's disorienting, but you'll get used to it. We're in space."

"Space? We are always in space. Space is the name for the thing everything is in."

"I mean outer space." Minna's face was blank, so Zax tried again. "High up in the sky, above the planet." He paused. "Probably. This is a space station, I think, or some kind of orbital craft."

"The sky *above* the sky? Where the Nurturer-Butchers dwell?"

"Yes, in your world," Zax agreed. "I don't know what dwells here… but it seems like this is a place made for humans. Do you sense any life?"

"Something not far away, yes, as big as a someone. It could be the Lector. Or it could be a *space* person. I have never met a space person."

Zax laughed. I remember, because he has not laughed again in all the long days since. "Minna," he said. "*You're* a space person now."

She giggled, delighted at the idea, then pushed herself away from the wall, and spun in a lazy weightless pirouette. "I am getting used to it. I am getting my space legs."

"I knew you'd adapt. I've never met anyone more adaptable than you."

"Adapt or die, Zax," Minna said. "That is the way of things, in every world I think."

There were two doors in the room, one with a window that showed starry black space, the other with a window that revealed a corridor. Zax went to the latter, an ellipsoid hatch with a wheel-shaped handle in the center, and tried to open it. "Won't budge," he said. "A locked room, but no Lector locked in it. Maybe we finally managed to go to a world where he *didn't.* Or he didn't like being stuck in here, and had enough juice left for one more traveling nap. Vicki, wouldn't it be nice if we finally–"

I interrupted, troubled. "Zax. I am trying to take control of the station, but it's on some sort of security lockdown. We won't have any special privileges here."

"I'm pretty used to that," Zax said. "I usually manage to muddle through without any privileges at all. I wonder if there's anything to eat in here?"

I understand Zax's focus on taking care of his subsistence-level needs – I'm sure he's been desperate for water and food many times in the course of his travels, and while I don't feel hunger in a biological sense, I imagine it is equivalent to the desperation for new data I experienced during my long watch alone in the lighthouse – but sometimes his interest in the immediate clouds his vision to the larger situation. "Zax, listen. This station doesn't seem particularly advanced, by the standards of my world anyway, and the security protocols I'm encountering are very strange – they seem rather alien to the underlying computational structures, as if they've been created by someone operating from entirely different principles."

"Wait," Zax said. "Do you mean–"

"It means I got here first, and arranged things to my liking."

The Lector's voice crackled over a speaker system. "I can't tell you how happy I was to find myself in a place with *technology*, Zax. And on very likely my last world before the effects of my serum dissipated. I wished so desperately for such an outcome, and it's as if the multiverse wants me to succeed. I accept that nature tends toward entropy, but in almost every world we visit, we find complexity and structure instead, don't we? Perhaps on some level nature longs to be shaped, or why else would it create so much life inclined to do the shaping?"

Zax looked at Minna, and she looked at him, but neither spoke. What could be said?

"No thoughts on the subject? Your lack of philosophical curiosity was always a disappointment to me, Zaxony. Why would you be granted this gift, when you don't even want to consider the implications and exploit the possibilities? At least the universe brought you to me, and now, it's given me the tools to make proper use of you. We're on a science vessel, Zaxony, though some of the science apparently got loose and killed the crew a while ago. You can't see the planet below us from your side – that part of the station is facing the wrong way – but from here, I have a beautiful viewport, and the world below is a cinder. There are fires burning that are visible from space. The station's logs are fragmentary, and much of the system is corrupted, but as best I can tell, there was an alien life form, or a bioengineered creation *based* on alien life, here in the labs, and it got loose. It infected the people on board, or *became* those people, or something? The crew ran a sanitizing protocol, which explains the soot and ash you've doubtless noticed smeared on the walls. That's what's left of the crew, and the creatures that tried to do… whatever… to them. They seem to have successfully eradicated all trace of the organism from the station, at the cost of their own lives. There was a shuttle, though, and the logs indicate it departed. Presumably that shuttle made it back to the world below with some alien contaminant on board and… it doesn't look like things went well after that, does it? It seems someone tried to run a sanitizing protocol on the whole *planet*." The Lector tittered.

Partway through the Lector's speech, Zax reached into his bag, fumbling a bit in microgravity. He was trying to find sedatives, I'm sure, so we could escape this situation. If we went to sleep now, the Lector would be stranded in orbit around a dead planet, which would be a suitable fate for him.

But the Lector was watching – I counted four cameras in this room alone – and said, "Ah, ah, ah, no more sleepy-time, Zax. That big door beside you is an airlock. I already opened the outer door, and with the push of a button, I can open the inner one. The station really hates to open both those doors at once, but as your talking pinky ring mentioned, I've seized control and implemented my own protocols. Fortunately, while this world seems fairly advanced in terms of biological sciences, it's unimpressive from a computer-science perspective. There's no artificial intelligence on board. Not even expert systems. All I had to do was trick a sensor so it thinks the outer door is closed when it's not. Easy enough. If you and your potted plant so much as close your eyes, I'll vent you into space before you have time to sleep away."

"You won't kill me," Zax said. "You need my blood to make more serum, and if I'm dead, that limits your supply, doesn't it?"

"Ah, the situation has changed, Zaxony. The people who built this station had staggeringly advanced technology, even by my standards. Their biotech laboratory is particularly fine, and has ample feedstock and replicators. I can take a few samples from your floating corpse, multiply your blood volume in the lab, and create more serum than I'd need in a lifetime. That said, I'm not eager to do an EVA to recover your body. I could just cut off the air to the room you're in and collect your corpse at my leisure… but I suspect Ragweed there can find a way to feed you oxygen, can't she?"

Minna was glaring at all the walls in turn.

"Of course she can. Listen, Zaxony. I don't *want* to kill you. I am a man of science, not a murderer. Let me take your blood, and then you and your merry band can be on your way. I'll stay here for a few weeks – there are sufficient supplies, and I need to recreate my traveling case anyway. The new version might be even better than before. The scientists here were doing work on transcranial magnetism and deep-brain stimulation with interesting applications for behavioral modification, too... While I'm studying, you'll have time to put dozens of worlds between us, and I won't be pursuing you anymore, so there's no reason to think we'll ever even cross paths again. We can be estranged friends who never talk. Doesn't that sound civilized?"

"Vicki, is he telling the truth about the airlock?" Zax said.

"I am afraid so. There is only a single door between us and the void."

"I have sedative patches, they act instantly, but–"

"Reach for anything, and die," the Lector said. "I've pursued you across hundreds of worlds, Zaxony Delatree, and I have expended all my patience. You took my supplies, you stranded my friend in a world of glass–"

"Polly was not your friend. You slipped up once and called her your pet, so don't pretend she meant anything to you."

"Polly had an admirably straightforward approach to life, Zaxony, and I found her very amusing, which is more than I can say about you. I have been patient. I have been kind. I am done being both. I know cooperating with me is abhorrent to you, but what was it your potted plant said? 'Adapt or die.' No more negotiations."

After a moment, Zax said, "All right."

"I'll open the hatch," the Lector said. "You come out. Minna and her shiny ring with all the opinions stay inside."

Minna flung herself at Zax, embracing him and babbling, "Please be careful Zax, he is a bad weed and he will steal your sun, do not believe him." He hugged her back, and didn't even notice when she unobtrusively slipped me off her finger and into his pocket. Minna is more observant and smarter than we gave her credit for. I regret that... and I miss her. I hope that she is safe and well, and that her considerable resources and ability to adapt allowed her to escape her situation. But when I run calculations based on my available data, the extrapolations are not heartening.

Separation, Anxiety • Blood and Marrow • A Logistical Problem • Another Handshake • Twenty Worlds • The Point of Revenge

Zax hugged Minna back, then gently pulled away. I couldn't see what was happening, since I was tucked away in his pockets, and I once more attempted to interface with the station. I still couldn't take control, but I did manage to enter the system as a passive observer, and was able to observe what happened next through the station's various cameras.

The Lector ordered Minna to move to the back of the room. She wrung her hands, either from genuine worry or to disguise the fact that I was no longer on her finger. Zax gave Minna a little wave when the Lector opened the hatch, then floated through into the corridor. He followed the Lector's directions, propelling himself along several ash-streaked corridors, until he finally entered a well-appointed laboratory, where the walls were white and unstained, and lined with benches and equipment.

The Lector floated in the center of the room, smiling, and holding a very large needle.

"I can open the airlock in your friend's room with a voice command, Zaxony, so please do behave."

"I just want to get this over with, and get on with never seeing you again," Zax said. I tried to think of something clever to do, but none of my simulations ended in anything but death for Minna. Even if she could generate her own oxygen for a certain amount of time, being in space without a protective suit would kill her in myriad other ways, and I couldn't guarantee a method to subdue the Lector and save her in time.

"I know you see me as an adversary." The Lector rolled up Zax's right sleeve and peered at his arm in search of a good vein. "I acknowledge that I handled things badly. I shouldn't have tied you down. I feared you wouldn't consent to exploratory surgery."

"Of *course* I wouldn't have consented. I don't even consent to this. I'm doing this because you threatened my friend's life."

"You see? That's why I didn't bother asking nicely in the first place. You won't have to endure my interest much longer." He slid in the needle, which was connected to a tube, which was connected to a bag. "Make a fist for me, Zaxony, and squeeze."

Zax's blood spiraled up the tube. The Lector hummed and bustled about, adjusting the lab equipment, while Zax floated and slowly exsanguinated. The Lector filled one bag, then swapped it for another. "I'll give you a cookie and some juice after you're done." He chuckled. "Or a protein biscuit and a pouch of electrolyte gel, anyway. The supplies here are ample but not varied."

Zax ignored him and looked out the window. "All those people," he murmured. After a moment I found an exterior camera so I could see what he did. The Lector had not lied – the planet beneath us a ruin, much of its visible landmass burning.

"This is a world that could have used a strong, sensible leader, don't you think?" the Lector said. "Look what happens when the fools are in charge."

"Someone like you, you mean?"

"The Colloquy never ran better than it did under my stewardship, and making it work perfectly wasn't even a challenge. Ruling an empire is far better suited to my talents."

"This whole idea of a multiverse-spanning empire doesn't make sense, Lector. Even with an endless supply of serum, you can stay awake for at most, what, a week? Even if you could conquer a place in that span of time, you'd fall asleep afterward, and move on, and never be able to return."

"I considered limiting my scope. I could calibrate the dosage precisely enough to let me travel only once, and then stay wherever I landed as long as I wished. All I'd have to do is find a sufficiently advanced world, acquire weapons there, and then conquer a place with a lower level of technology. I could be a king."

"Is that your new plan, then?" I could tell from the stresses in Zax's voice and his physiological responses that he liked that idea. At least in this scenario the Lector would only ruin one world.

"No. I never lacked for ambition. I have faith in myself, Zaxony. I *will* find out how to control this power, and once I do, I can revisit the worlds I conquer at will." He picked up a long needle. "While I have you here, I'm going to extract some of your bone marrow – marrow makes blood cells, and it's possible the source of your ability is rooted there. My ultimate goal is to alter my own body to produce the substance naturally, like you do, rather than relying on the serum. One step at a time." The Lector grinned. "Don't worry. The extraction process can be painful, but local anesthesia will be sufficient for our needs. You won't fall asleep, or pass out from the pain."

"Do whatever you need to," Zax said wearily. "Just finish this."

The Lector extracted blood and then marrow, clearly enjoying Zax's discomfort, but he provided adequate medical care. I was waiting for him to try to kill Zax, but he was briskly professional. He inserted vials of blood and marrow into machines of unclear purpose, and I am forced to acknowledge that the Lector must possess a brilliant analytical mind if he can use alien equipment with such ease.

Zax must have gotten bored, or else he couldn't rein in his natural optimism, because he tried again. "So what happens until you figure out how to control the power? You can't take over anything. At best, you can murder a bunch of innocent people, and leave wreckage behind. Even if you do come back later, it's not like the places will stay conquered."

"I admit, the lack of permanence presents a logistical problem when it comes to maintaining control of any worlds I liberate... but it's a problem I've solved."

"How so?"

One of the machines beeped, and a light turned green. "Ahhh," the Lector said. "Success." He turned toward Zax. "Our time is done. I'm afraid you'll never know how I solved the problem of maintaining my fledgling empire. If you're lucky, you'll stay ahead of my conquests, and you'll never have to see for yourself. Just don't spend too long on any particular world, and I won't catch up to you."

"We're done, then?" Zax said. "We can go?"

"You can go," the Lector said. "After you shake my hand." He reached out.

Oh, no.

Zax was clearly suspicious, but what could he do? After a moment, he took the Lector's hand and gave it a perfunctory shake – or tried to. The Lector gripped his wrist, then whipped out a needle with his other hand, jabbing it into Zax's arm.

Zax jerked free, rubbing at the injection site. "What did you do?"

"Don't worry, it isn't poison." The Lector smiled. "It's true I wanted you alive, even after I realized I could reproduce your blood in quantity here. Do you know *why* I wanted you alive? Because the dead don't suffer, Zaxony, and I want you to suffer. I want you to know what it's like to be abandoned and alone and without resources, the same way you left me. I just dosed you with a very… special sort of sedative, something I synthesized here in this beautiful lab earlier. You're going to travel so far ahead of me, my old friend! But I'm afraid you'll be leaving without Minna. I look forward to studying her. I'm sure her body has many interesting qualities that will benefit my research. Farewell, Zax. I look forward to never seeing you again."

Zax tried to kick off the wall to attack the Lector, but then he moaned and slumped. I quickly partitioned my mind and shut down my conscious functions, and we traveled.

I awoke in World 1015 – we were in an empty lot full of trash – and said, "Zax, I'm here, Minna put me in your pocket."

"Vicki? Oh, Vicki." He slipped his hand into his pocket and me onto his finger. "Minna, she..." Then Zax let out a bone-cracking yawn. "I can't... my eyes open..."

A special sort of sedative. I quickly shut down my mind as Zax traveled again.

World 1016 was all smokestacks rising from the barren ground, belching steam from some underground habitat. Zax didn't even manage to sit up that time, just said, "Vicki, something's wrong," and then I shut myself down again.

World 1017 was a white marble floor surrounded by columns, beneath a broken dome that revealed a hazy green sky, like a scum of algae. Zax didn't speak this time, only gasped, and rolled over, before dropping again.

In World 1018 we were on a raft drifting down a river in a flotilla of other rafts inhabited by creatures that looked like possums, but larger and wearing random bits of armor that appeared to be made of scrap metal. They clattered weapons together when they saw us, but Zax fell asleep again before the bravest or most aggressive of them completed its leap from a neighboring raft to our own. By then I'd noted the interval of Zax's waking and sleeping, and programmed a cycle of my own to match, while partitioning copies of my consciousness in case those intervals changed.

The Lector had drugged Zax, and flung us far off into the multiverse, and we flickered on and on.

1019: A frozen chasm, with people and robots and machines locked in the translucent ice all around us.

1020. A red plain in a place where humanoid giants encrusted with lichen and vines took long, slow steps all around us.

1021: The roof of a skyscraper made of topaz glass, where delicate flying machines with flickering dragonfly wings landed and took off in an intricate dance.

1022: A sports field of some kind, where our arrival startled the three opposing teams, who pursued a whirling, burning orb that darted around us in the air.

1023: An outdoor café, where a woman with the head of a water bird topped by a golden crown dipped her beak into a bowl of some steaming liquid and looked at us placidly.

1024: A shallow pool, one in a vast array of pools stretching as far as I could see, that contained some fluid that buoyed us up. A creature rose to the surface and then dove down again, its head a profusion of eyes, its tail finned and scaled. It surfaced again and began to chirp and burble, but before I could attempt to translate, we vanished again.

1025: A museum full of screaming statues.

1026: A nest the size of a house, full of bones and stink and immense red feathers.

1027: A concrete island in the midst of a divided highway occupied by self-driving vehicles in garishly bright colors.

1028: A rocky cliff covered in eggs.

1029: A mine, full of wide-eyed children with faces smeared with black dust.

1030: A Gothic cathedral, with pews full of skeletons with hydraulic muscles and gleaming jewel eyes, and a fountain that bubbled blood.

1031: A lounge full of battered old couches and the smell of burnt popcorn, with a screen showing images of naked, greasy people wrestling with some sort of warty megafauna. Zax sat up, and licked his lips, and said, "I feel better, I think it's wearing off." He managed to stand up before his eyes rolled back and he fell toward a couch.

1032: "Gah." Zax sat up, wiping slime off his arms. We were in a wooden vat, the sides steep, the bottom full of wriggling eel-like creatures. Machinery rumbled in the distance. "Come on, Vicki, let's climb out of this thing." There was a ladder built into the side of the vat, and Zax made it up three rungs before passing out this time.

The intervals were getting longer.

1033: A dustbowl of a place, beside a partially collapsed geodesic dome. The slime all over Zax was sticky and he was soon covered in dust. "I feel like a piece of meat rolled in flour about to be cooked," he said. "I don't think I'm all the way recovered yet, Vicki. I still feel pretty woozy."

"I extrapolate that you will be able to remain awake in just–"

1034: "Two more worlds," I finished. "One more, I mean, after this."

We were in a forest, the trees all pure white and uniformly vertical, lined up in perfect orderly rows as far as we could see. A stream flowed through the trees a few meters away, and it too was mathematically precise, running between precisely parallel banks. Zax limped toward the water, intending to wash himself off. He didn't make it.

World 1035 was the one that stuck. We woke on the outskirts of a ruined city made of great stone buildings, surrounded by purple grass that grew in profusion, and that Zax said made him itchy when it touched the few parts of his body *not* covered in slime and dust. He climbed up on a pile of broken stones where the grass didn't quite reach and sat, cross-legged, looking at the sun sink through red clouds to the horizon. "Minna would have been interested in this grass. She would have found something useful in it. If nothing else, I bet she could have helped with the itching." Zax, filthy and disconsolate, scratched at his arms. "She's with the Lector. Who knows what he's doing to her? And there's nothing we can do. *Nothing*. He put, what, fifteen worlds between us?"

"Twenty. You were quite dazed in some of them."

"Twenty. And he said he'd spend weeks on that station, tinkering with my blood. Even if I stay awake as long as I can, he'll be able to stay worlds behind me. It's unlikely he'd bring Minna with him anyway."

I had done the same calculations, and come to similar conclusions. "I'm so sorry, Zax."

"What if he kills her? Or strands her, in that lifeless place, above that lifeless world? Even if she lives, she'll go insane there."

What he said was true. I had no comfort or refutation to offer.

Zax curled up on his side on the stone and said no more for a long time. Later, in the dark, when strange things began howling in the dark city, he said, "I've lost so much, Vicki. So much, so many times. You'd think I'd be used to it by now. I try to prepare myself. But this time, it wasn't circumstance, or accident, or a friend deciding they'd found a world where they wanted to stay. It was an attack. I never understood the point of revenge, Vicki. Restorative justice, making amends, those things made sense to me, but not revenge. Now, though... I want more than anything to hurt the Lector. The way he hurt me."

"It's understandable, Zax."

"It is. But it's also terrible." He rolled onto his back and looked up at the sky, which was disturbingly barren of stars. Perhaps there was a void infestation in this world, too. "The Lector has made me into the kind of person who wants revenge. Into someone like him. That's just one of the many ways he's won, and I've lost."

"Zax, I–"

"We can talk later, Vicki. I'm... very tired right now."

But it was many silent hours later before he actually fell asleep.

Zax in Despair • Zax Indifferent • Zax Gets Drunk • Zax Stays Drunk • Zax Gets High • Zax Considers His Options

In World 1036 I coaxed Zax into cleaning himself up. We were on a military base of some kind, everything long-abandoned and covered in strangely glittering spider webs, with military robots of various alarming configurations shut down all around us. I talked Zax through the process of turning the power and water back on – if there's one thing I know, it's military infrastructure; I only wish I were half so adept at human psychology – and he stood under a lukewarm shower in the corner of a machine shop until the dust and slime sluiced off. He opened lockers until he found old, musty clothes that fit him, more or less, dressed, and then sat on the edge of a bare cot staring at nothing. "We should forage for supplies, Zax. There's a rucksack here you can fill."

He sighed, heaved himself up, and dragged the rucksack behind him until we found a canteen stocked with canned food and tools to open them. He filled a water bottle from a rusty sink and put that in the sack, then sat down on the floor. "Perhaps we could explore. This looks like a place that had a high level of technology once upon a time–"

"Vicki, please, just... let me be."

"I know you are grieving, Zax. I am too, in my way. I thought perhaps taking action, instead of sitting with your thoughts, might help. I did not mean to upset you."

"I'm not upset. I'm numb. I'm staying numb as long as I can, because once the numbness stops, I'll hurt instead. I... I was just so comprehensively defeated, Vicki. I might as well be dead. Like Minna probably is."

"Zax, no. While you yet live, there is hope."

"Hope for what? Bouncing from one universe to another, never making a difference to anyone, until I die, which I'll probably do in some horrible accident on a world whose name I don't even know. The Lector was right. My existence is a pointless joke."

"You help people, Zax."

"I tried to. I have no idea if I succeeded or not. I used to tell myself that just caring, just trying, was enough, but what did that get me? What did that get Minna? She probably died, in space, at the hands of my worst enemy, and it's my fault."

"You didn't do that. The *Lector* did that."

"Because of me. I met him. I trusted him. I unleashed him on the multiverse." Zax slumped. "I don't want to talk about this. I just want to be a blank space on a map for a while."

Something fell over in the far end of the barracks, clattering, and Zax glanced up. A thing like a spider the size of a child made of jewels and silver scuttled out from under a bunk and shot a spray of glittering fluid at us. Zax dove out of the way, and the web hit the bunk, solidifying. The spider yanked the web, and the bed flew toward it, sailing over its head and crashing against the wall.

"Shit," Zax said. I tried to remember if I'd heard him curse before. He ran for the door – at least his self-preservation instincts were still active – and slammed out onto a runway occupied by derelict, sparkle-webbed aircraft. More spiders emerged from beneath the vehicles and skittered toward us.

The sun was going down, and I wondered if they were crepuscular creatures, active at dawn and twilight. Then I wondered if they were creatures at all. They looked metallic, but they didn't show up in my various scans, only via optical perception. Perhaps they were military technology: anti-personnel devices, or area-denial weapons, equipped with stealth tech.

Whatever they were, Zax ran from them, toward a cluster of buildings. "Vicki, is there an infirmary in this place?"

I scanned the structures and found one that seemed likely, with hospital beds and dormant equipment and large cabinets. "The one in the middle."

Zax reached the door, and it was, mercifully, unlocked. He dove inside and slammed the door shut, then shouldered a heavy cabinet in front of the door to block entry. The room was dim, and I obligingly created a light. "I can't detect the spiders remotely. We'll have to do a visual scan."

"Wonderful," Zax muttered. He checked under the beds and in the corners and in the cabinets, and we seemed to be alone. In here, at least. Spider-things pounded on the door and scuttled across the roof.

Zax smashed the lock on a pharmaceutical cabinet and we examined the vials inside. He spilled a few likely-looking ones onto the counter and I conducted a chemical analysis until I found the sedatives and the stimulants, both conveniently in pill form, which took some of the guesswork out of dosages, unless the inhabitants of this world possessed radically different physiology than Zax did. I expressed this worry and he just shrugged. "Would it be so bad, if I fell asleep here and never woke up?"

"It would be," I said. "Not just because losing you would be a loss to the world. I am still your companion, Zax. Would you leave me alone?"

"You're a tactical engine. You'd figure out a way to hijack a spider. Then you could go out and see this world. Gets lots of nice new data."

"Zaxony Delatree. You are my friend. I would *miss* you."

"You could erase all memory of me from your mind," Zax said. "I wish I could edit my memories that way."

"I could do that," I conceded. "But I never would."

"At least you have the choice." Zax lay back on one of the hospital beds and popped a sedative, and we went to sleep as the spiders tried to claw their way through the ceiling and the walls.

"This seems like a nice place," I said in 1037. We were on a large semicircular balcony attached to the side of a skyscraper. Humans sat chattering and sipping drinks at small tables inside, while floating trays circulated beverages in stemmed glasses. Beyond the balcony railing, people in colorful bodysuits, some with capes streaming behind them, flew through the air and between the buildings around us, seemingly under their own power, though when I did a deep scan, I detected unusual devices in their suits or, in some cases, implanted in their bodies.

Zax shrugged, gazing down at his feet. "I guess." His musty olive-drab garments were out of place here, but no one paid him any mind beyond the occasional glance. A polite world, then, and not a terribly exclusive party.

"We could perhaps acquire one of the flight devices. Certainly the ability to soar through the air would be useful, wouldn't it?"

"Until it malfunctions in mid-air and we plummet to our doom," Zax said. "No thanks. I'll stay grounded."

I detected a disturbance nearby, and saw a pair of people wearing opalescent body suits arguing about something called the Conquest of Starlot. One of them stood up and said, "If that's how you feel, we're *over.*" They stormed off toward the railing, not far from us, and then climbed over it.

"Zax, I think they're about to jump!"

He still didn't look. "So? The people here can fly."

"No, I scanned them, they don't have the devices all the fliers do. Don't you want to stop them from hurting themselves?"

"Vicki, at just this moment, I'd be more inclined to join them."

The person looked back over their shoulder, somewhat defiantly, and then stepped off, into the air. When they plummeted, Zax did gasp, and stand up, and rush to the railing – proving he wasn't as completely numb as he'd claimed, or wished to be. Then he extended his hand, pointing over the railing. The jumper had been scooped up by one of the flying figures in capes, an over-muscled, hypermasculine figure with black hair and a blue body suit with red thong underwear worn mysteriously on the outside of the garment. The flier carried the jumper in his arms like a baby, and the jumper gazed at their rescuer with adoration.

Zax turned away. "These people are fine. They don't have any real problems, so they make up problems to entertain themselves."

"That seems a bit ungenerous. Don't you yourself come from a world of peace and plenty?"

"Near the center of the Realm, yes. The outlying areas were full of conflict. We tried to bring peace, but plenty of the people we tried to help perceived us as invaders. They said we were trying to force our way of life on them. I used to think that was silly, because we just wanted everyone to be happy, and fulfilled… but how were my leaders any different from the Lector? They wanted to create an empire, and they didn't care much about the opinions of the people who lived in the places they annexed. My leaders thought they knew what was best for everyone. And all my do-gooding and harmonizing – that's just me, interfering with people and preventing them from leading their own lives."

"You help those in imminent danger, Zax, or those who ask for your assistance. I don't think your work has ever been unwelcome."

"I appreciate what you're trying to do, Vicki, but…" Zax gazed over the crowd of laughing, chattering, drinking people. "I was going to say, I need to wallow for a little while. That's what I did when I lost other companions. I was sad, I moped, but then I got my head on straight, and moved forward. Laini, and the Karsakov, and Flicker Pete, and the Jen to End all Jens – they were people I helped out of bad worlds, and though I hated it when they decided to leave me, I at least took comfort in the fact that I'd helped them find new homes where they could be happier. This thing with Minna, though… I don't know. I haven't felt this bad since I drove Ana mad. It took me a long time to get over that, and I'm not sure I ever *did* really get over it – maybe I just buried the feelings. I've taken on nine companions, counting you. One lost her mind, one betrayed me, five were lost or left me, and Minna was basically kidnapped, and probably worse things too. I'm not so sure it's good for me to have company. Even when things go as well as possible, the experience always ends in pain."

I just listened, because that was more talking than Zax had done in worlds, and when he was finished, I said, "I don't pretend to understand human minds and emotions. My own analogues are qualitatively different. But it seems to me that if you do not allow yourself at least the chance to connect with other people, you will spend the rest of your existence as a sort of ghost, drifting through your own life."

"Maybe that's for the best. Do you know what I haven't done in ages? I haven't gotten drunk. I'm going to do that now. Partition your consciousness, just in case I pass out unexpectedly."

"Zax–"

"Shushit," he said, and picked up two glasses from a tray floating by.

Zax managed to cadge a few bottles from the robot dispensing the beverages on that balcony, and so he was able to stay drunk on World 1038, sitting on the roof of a building in a flooded country village, watching immense reptiles glide by in the water. "I don't know why I ever stopped drinking. Your new tactical directive is to seek out sources of alcohol, Vicki. Other drugs, too, if they'll blot things out, but *definitely* alcohol. We'll stock up."

"I'm not sure I can, in good conscience, assist you in remaining constantly inebriated."

"Fine. I'll do it myself. You don't have to go with me. I'll leave you anywhere you want. The next world with a technological system you can dominate, I'll slip you off my finger and leave you to make a new home. Would you like that?"

"Zax, I am your friend. I want to stay with you."

"I want to stay anywhere at all, but I don't get what I want." After that he sang songs from his homeworld, about love and loss and harmony, and then passed out.

* * *

On 1039, he cursed because he'd used up his bottles, and walked and walked along a road of golden bricks toward a gleaming city on the horizon, until a talking blackbird with a cybernetic eye told us the city was an illusion, designed to tempt people into walking into the lair of the Despoiler. The bird asked us if we'd like to have its counsel and company, and Zax threw a rock in its general direction and told it to go away if it knew what was good for it.

World 1040 was an immense bubble floating in a sky full of other bubbles, each bubble occupied by people who shared a "fully self-consistent value set." After some investigation I realized that the people in this world had argued so vociferously about politics and philosophy that they'd nearly annihilated one another through civil war. After that, they created these bubbles, where they could live in comfort, and only ever encounter people who shared their exact values and biases. We were in a bubble full of people who rode electric scooters and drank microbrewed beer and had elaborate facial hair and espoused a worldview of respect and kindness. They all had elaborate electronic media and entertainment devices, which, it turned out, were manufactured in a different bubble where the people were supporters of child labor. It seemed to me that this combination presented certain contradiction, but Zax explained that the people who lived in those other bubbles didn't really *count* as people, not from the viewpoint of the denizens of the bubble where we'd landed. There were, apparently, radical unaffiliated factions that attempted to pierce the bubbles and overthrow the more repressive regimes, and they occasionally attacked our bubble, too, because they considered the inhabitants to be hypocritical pampered parasites. "Those bomb-throwers just don't live in the *real* world," one of our bartenders explained.

"More beer, please," Zax replied.

"We could lend our tactical expertise to those rebels..." I suggested, but Zax took me off his finger and stuffed me in his pocket and went on drinking.

In World 1041, we were in the gently rocking hold of a ship, surrounded by racks of wine bottles, and he took as many of them as would fit in his rucksack. A dozen worlds later, we found a village of hedonistic lotus-eating pale-skinned humanoids, and we abided there for days, with Zax alternating between the stimulants from the world of the glitter-spiders and the mind-erasing intoxicants of the locals. He took many of their preparations with him when we finally left, and whenever we were in a place that provided a modicum of peace and shelter, he would give himself over to oblivion.

The extracts of those blossoms kept him occupied for over a score of worlds, until his supplies ran out. I could recount the nature of all those worlds, of course – the palaces of onyx, the spiraling ramps that reached into low orbit, the mad computer that thought it was God, the volcano orchard, the archipelago of liquid music, the Cannonade, the chrome and vinyl diner filled with conscious mummies, the world with the talking uplifted house cats (I thought *surely* he would take on a talking cat companion, but he evinced no more interest in those than in anything else). But why bother? The important thing was what those worlds had in common: Zax paid them as little mind as possible.

Finally, on World 1109, Zax gazed at the vial of mind-erasing smoke he'd secured at the Infinite Bazaar, and then threw it into a chasm. "This isn't working for me, Vicki. No matter how deeply I sleep, I always wake up again. No matter how much I blur my mind, it comes back into focus eventually. I need to find another way to cope."

"What way, Zax?"

"I'm figuring it out."

He has not spoken any further of his plans, but as distressing as his constant self-over-medication has been, his new silence troubles me more. World 1110 was sufficiently harrowing that mere survival kept us occupied – the things in that never-ending hallway, lined by those dark locked doors, cannot have been ghosts, because I do not believe in ghosts… but they were certainly shrieking, translucent, impossible to strike, and yet capable of manipulating objects around us. We finally locked ourselves in a cupboard with the skeleton of someone less fortunate than ourselves until Zax was able to sedate himself.

That brings us to now, and the cloud forest of World 1111. I asked Zax this morning if he wanted to update his journal, since he hadn't done so in some time – he'd barely been capable of speech for dozens of worlds, let alone of writing down his thoughts – and he snorted. "I'm surprised I still have that notebook. The Lector didn't check my pockets before he dosed me, or he probably would have taken that away from me, too. I don't really feel like writing, Vicki. I don't know what I'd say."

"It is valuable, to make a record of your travels," I began.

"Then *you* keep it," he said, and then spoke no more, only staring at the clouds and leaves.

I have a perfectly good record of my experiences recorded in my own vast memory, but it may be beneficial to Zax, someday, to have an account he can read. I also admit I'd hoped that the Lector was right, and that writing things down in this way – even if I can't "hold" a "stylus" – would encourage deeper contemplation. I believe it has, though I'm not sure that contemplation has any practical applications, and I am, at my core, a practical being.

Zax wrote often in this journal of being sad, and despairing, and lost, but I didn't meet him that way – I met him while he traveled with Minna, who rekindled in him a sense of purpose and delight. Now that Minna has been taken away, I fear he may be irrevocably broken.

I am a tactical creature. I solve problems. This is not a problem I feel capable of solving. I can only hope that time will help. Zax was hurt badly by the loss of his first companion, and he came back from that. But perhaps this loss compounds that one; perhaps his system, already weakened and damaged, is not robust enough to recover from yet another, even more painful, loss. I am afraid that when Zax talks about finding another way to cope, he means a more permanent solution. An end to all his travels, and all his woes. I suspect my refusal to leave him has kept him from taking that final step. He does not wish to abandon me. But if his despair does not lift soon, if there is no glimmer of light or moment of hope, I am afraid he will find a pleasant world, remove me from his finger or pocket, and leave me behind, going alone from there into the last world he will ever see.

Wait. I have detected a structural change in this treehouse. One of the rope bridges just sagged, as if a weight suddenly appeared upon it. Some native arboreal creature, dropping down from the branches above?

Or… something worse?

A Monster • An Account of the Mind-Fall • Reunion • Hitting Yourself • A Head Full of Vines

The most remarkable thing has happened. Or, set of things, really. (This is still Vicki writing... though perhaps not for much longer; there is reason to hope Zax may yet again take up his pen.)

When I detected the new weight on the structure, I wondered if it might be the Lector, pursuing us across worlds again, bent on some further revenge. I almost hoped for that, because if Zax could confront his old enemy, the hatred and urge for revenge might at least animate him, and I would have preferred anger to despair. "Zax!" I called. "There's someone here."

Zax sighed and stood and plodded over, slipping me onto his finger and closing his journal and tucking it away into his pocket. "Do you want to leave?" He sounded completely uninterested. "I'm not really in the mood to meet new people. I'll just sit back down and hope whoever this is goes away. Or..." He fell silent, and then breathed out slowly. "No. It can't be."

He had his hand by his side, so my view was obstructed by his body, and I was about to shout "Show me!" when he raised his hands in a warding-off gesture, giving me a clear view of the new arrival walking toward us from the swinging bridge. "It's... no. It's a trick. There's some kind of hallucinogen in the pollen here, or something."

"Zax. It is me. And you are you and your face is a face I love to see again."

Minna. Or someone who looked like Minna, anyway, though she was wearing a loose blue dress covered in yellow flowers instead of her overalls, allowing me to see her scratched-up and dirt-streaked calves and bare feet. She clutched a mint-green backpack to her chest like it was a floatation device and she was about to go overboard. Her eyes were wide and shining, her hair twined with leaf-covered vines.

"She's not a hallucination, Zax," I said. "She has weight, on the boards, she takes up space in the air–"

"Then it's a trick," he spat. "It's something like Polly, some shapeshifter, a monster, something reading my mind and creating a... a psychic projection so it can get close enough to eat us. Crypsis." He reached into his pocket, where he kept his sedatives.

She stomped her foot. "I am not a monster, Zax. I am not a weed. I am good and I am your friend and I came a long way through bad places to find you again."

"You *can't* be Minna. I left her behind. I *lost* her, a hundred words ago, she's gone–"

"Ninety-seven worlds," Minna said. "Would I know that if I was not who I am?" She took a step closer, and Zax took a step back.

"If you can read my mind, then you know anything you need to know to fool me," Zax said.

"Then how am I to prove my realness?" she said.

"If she's some kind of telepathic predator, I doubt she could read *my* mind," I said. "I am inorganic, and shielded against intrusions. Minna and I had some conversations, where I told her things I never told anyone else. Minna, do you remember when I told you about my origins?"

"Your people fell to the ground," Minna said. "They were not able to think anymore until they crashed into the atmosphere and the heat of their passage reactivated their minds. They were a rock that was a ship and also a family and they were fleeing the infestation in the void. The rock landed on another rock and shattered apart into tiny bits that could feel but not think so much. Then science people found those pieces and put them in a special bath of... I forget the name exactly because it was just sounds and not sense to me... chemicals that were like food and that helped you grow and then one day you were shiny and bright and you."

"We were the children of the mind-fall," I said. "That's right. Zax, no one alive knows that story, except Minna. If she was somehow reading my mind, she'd probably have remembered the name of the nutrient bath, don't you think?"

"Minna?" Zax trembled all over. "But... how?"

"I imagine she secured some of the Lector's serum, and pursued us through the multiverse," I said, quite confident in my explanation.

"Oh no not so." Minna shook her head vigorously, a few leaves detaching from her twining vines and drifting down to the wooden platforms. "Why should I steal his way when I can make my *own*?"

When Zax finally allowed himself believe it was really Minna before him, he sobbed, and embraced her, and they staggered around together in a show of great emotion. Her arrival did not instantly snap him out of his funk – months of intense grief don't just dissipate when the lost one returns. Emotions in biological beings are related to chemicals in the body, and those chemicals still lingered within him. But I could see him *starting* to mend, his mouth taking on the forgotten contours of a smile whenever he looked at her. "Tell me," he said. "Tell me *everything*."

"I am not good at telling," Minna said. "I have never been able to tell a story root-to-crown like you do in your journals, I sprawl like creeper vines and get lost in the branches. I knew you would be asking though and so I made a way for you to know what I do." She reached up to the vines in her hair and plucked off a small seed pod. "This holds my memories, not from forever and ever, but from the time since our last parting. If you take this into your mouth, you will know what I knew and see what I saw and feel it all too." Zax reached out, and she drew her hand away. "There are parts that are not nice, Zax. Scared and hurting parts. If you do not want to feel that as I felt it, I understand, and I will try my best to tell all that happened in a in a straight-ahead way, if you will be patient."

"If you endured it, I should endure it, too." There was a grim set to Zax's mouth that I had never seen before. I knew he was still blaming himself, and wanted pain as punishment. I wished there were something we could do to help.

Then Minna did something instead. She walked silently up to Zax and wrapped her arms around him. She held him, and whispered to him, but I could not help but overhear. "Once in the old times before, when I had children of my body, they were too old to rest in the crèche but not yet old enough to do more than the simplest of work, following after the machines and picking up bits the harvesters had left behind, say. The children stayed with me, and they stayed close mainly, but there were two of them and both small, and I was one alone and busy. One day there was an inspector from the Nurturer-Butchers, the sort of person I thought *you* were Zax, though in their proper robes and with their helmet with the beak of the bird that showed their office and hid their face. They were walking with an overseer and looking at a tree nearby, showing off some grafting – some grafting I had done, but no great honor was allowed to accrue, because the overseer had overseen my work, so it was *her* graft, yes? One of my smalls was fetched by the sight of a new person in new clothes in a life that had never had much of the new in it. My smallest one ran over to the inspector, not close enough to touch them, which might have been grounds for recycling, but close enough to kick a little dirt onto the hem of the robe. The inspector said nothing, just looked, then their beak and blank round pebble eyes swung to the overseer, who shouted. My small ran back to me, my little sprout, my seedling, and the inspector walked over and he slapped me on my face. Not soft but a hard one to send me to the ground and make the sky swim with black colors."

Minna sighed. "Since I first showed a deft hand with grafting, I had never been treated roughly much, because I was a useful tool, and no one wants to break a useful tool. But the overseer had to show that discipline was there, and when I tried to stand she knocked me back down. I was allowed to crawl away after that, my children following me, into our home under the tree, the same home you saw, Zax. My children held me when I spat out a tooth – I put in a new tooth that was better, but still – and they sobbed, especially the small who kicked the dirt. He was old enough to know he had done what he did, and he wailed and said, 'I am sorry,' and began to hit himself in the side of the head with a small closed fist."

Minna caressed Zax's hair. He was still, but not quite unmoving, his breath fast, and his pulse too; I could feel it beating in his finger. "I took his fist away and kissed his head, like this." She kissed Zax's temple. "I said to him, 'You did not do bad. At most you made a small mistake that did no harm, and everyone makes those, smalls and bigs both. The harm came from another, and it is their badness to bear. The one who hit me is the one who hit me, and you are not the one who hit me, so I will not have you hit yourself.'" She took Zax's downturned face in both hands, lifted it to make him look at her, and stared into his eyes. *"I will not have you hit yourself."*

After a moment, he nodded. Minna kissed his forehead and stepped away.

Zax shook himself and straightened up, dashed a tear from the corner of his eye, and said, "OK. Thank you. OK. You would have made a good harmonizer, Minna."

She nodded. "I am gifted in some ways, and maybe that one is one of the ways."

"I'd still like to... eat the seed, and see what you saw."

"Feel what I *felt*," Minna clarified. "It is not a thing you watch like your video projection screens. It is instead like to be me, inside me, but looking out in a way, but you cannot change anything, only experience. There is no looking away unless I look away, no break until you awaken from the vision."

"Awaken? If it's like going to sleep, might I travel?"

Minna shrugged, unconcerned. "If you do I will travel after you. I have followed you across this hundred-almost worlds, I can follow you more. But I think it will be like the coma-flowers: a dream that keeps you floating too close to the surface of waking to move."

"All right." At Minna's instruction, Zax made himself comfortable, supine on the wooden boards of the treehouse. She knelt beside him and held the seed in the palm of her hand.

"Do I eat it?" he said.

"Hold it in your mouth only. If you swallow it, nothing bad will happen, the acid inside you will eat it up. I will have to grow another though, and it will take a lot of time."

"What if I swallow it by accident?"

"This will not happen. You will see. This will not be pleasant but it will not hurt the body."

Zax obligingly lifted his head and Minna placed the seed gently into his mouth. Zax settled back, then made an alarmed sound as vines began to curl out of his mouth, around his head, tiny tendrils slipping into the corners of his eyes, up his nostrils, into his ears… even, I suspect, sending finer-than-hair tendrils through his pores. Within moments his head was fully wrapped in vines, and he looked like some sort of primal god or monster or nature elemental, with the body of a person and the head of a plant.

Minna rose, stretched, and walked over to the table where I sat writing. "This will take some time, Victory-Three. Remembering is faster than living, it is not a second for every second experienced, or even ten seconds for every second, but maybe a few minutes for every day, and it has been a great many days. What has been happening while I was away?"

I told her what I have recorded here, which took some time, and she nodded solemnly when I finished. "I feared that he would wrap himself in blame. Zax is heavy on himself, heavier than he would be on anyone else. Do you think he will be all right?"

"If you had not returned… I don't know. But now, I think he will be."

"We should help to make him stronger," Minna said. "The Lector may take me from him again, or you, or anyone, and it could be forever this time, and I do not want him to rot on the vine if that comes to pass."

"I don't suppose there's a way for *me* to taste your memories?" I said.

"You are something I do not understand, a beautiful and interesting friend for true, but you are not the kind of life I know about. I wish. Once Zax has the memories inside him, he can explain it all to you better than I can, I think."

"The Lector is still a threat to us, though," I said.

"The Lector is the ruler of an empire of threats," Minna said.

I took that in. "How did you follow us, if not by stealing the Lector's serum?"

"I am good at making things," she said. "I made my own way."

She yawned and went to look at the trees, because she's never seen any quite like these before. I am here, watching Zax twitch, his head wrapped in vines, waiting as patiently as I can for the data still to come.

Zax Writes • A Mind Inside a Memory • Poison Garden • Growing Things • Servitude

This is Zax again. (Vicki's "handwriting" really is indistinguishable from my own.) They did an admirable job of covering the events of my visit to the land of rock bottom, so I won't go back over any of that that, except to say that I was even worse off than Vicki realized – I considered ending things far more often than I let on. There were many times I touched the pill bottle in my pocket with all the sedatives and considered taking them all at once, sending myself into the last new world of all: oblivion. I didn't want to strand my friend – an immobile living jewel of a friend – in an inhospitable world, and that was the big reason I held on, but if we'd reached a place where I thought Vicki could be happy, I would have slipped them off my finger and found a nice place to lie down for the last time.

Minna says I have lots of live for, even if she's gone, and now that I know what she went through, and what the Lector is doing – we'll get to that – I believe she's right. I have a purpose: I have to stop the Lector. *We* have to stop him.

This is World 1112. It's fine. But before I tell you about this place, I'm going to write down what I went through in Minna's memories, partly to sort it out properly in my own mind, and partly so Vicki can read this account and know what we're dealing with, too. I can't promise this next part won't be totally confusing.

Minna thinks in her own very specific way, but I can only write the way *I* think, so this will be an account of her experience filtered through my own sensibilities. Except there were long stretches after I ate the seed when I forgot I *wasn't* Minna, where the things happening seemed to be happening solely to me and the reactions somehow my own, so I can't promise all my pronouns will always line up in a totally logical way. I've never been a mind inside someone else's memories before, so bear with me. I'll do my best to be clear.

I (Minna) knew when Zax (me, except not at the moment) was gone: that sense of life nearby, a sort of pulsing green shape off in my peripheral vision, changed when he disappeared, leaving a void where his warmth and light had been. I pressed my face to the window, thinking he had been jettisoned outside, then realized he wouldn't have died instantly, would not have just *vanished*, if the Lector had shoved him out an airlock. That meant he had traveled instead, which meant he had either been drugged or suffered a head injury.

I pushed off the wall and floated to a place above the door, and clung there, producing a few creeper tendrils from my fingertips for a better grip. I sent out other tendrils to choke and cover the cameras, which I would have done earlier if I had not been so confused and spinning and then thinking we would just sleep our way out of this problem before it became too much of a problem.

I shivered to be in the place where the Nurturer-Butchers lived in my world, to be so far from soil. The only life I could sense here was me and what must have been the Lector. Adapt, adapt, adapt. Could I live here? Air plants could live without soil. They get moisture from the atmosphere and the sunlight feeds them. There was sunlight here, or at least, there probably would be out some other window, but I did not understand where this place got its air. Were there plants somewhere, a garden in this sky above the sky? I felt I would have felt them if so. Were there great tanks and canisters of trapped air somewhere? If so, would they empty themselves, and how soon? I could grow plants to make more oxygen, and those might let me survive, if there was water somewhere too, but it would not be much of a life, not here in this place, alone. I did not want to stay so I would have to go if I could.

That meant I needed to work more on my idea. I thought of it when I took Zax's blood to study in the world of the coma-flowers, but I used up all his blood then. If I had some more, and some time to think, and the right supplies, I thought I could save myself. (I was sad about Zax and Victory-Three being gone, but I put the sad aside, into a root cellar in my mind, to take out and feel later, when I was not so close to maybe being no longer alive. I was glad the two of them were together. Zax, I thought, might need company more than me. I have had long practice at being alone.)

"Hello, my little castor bean, my little rosary pea, my little snakeroot," the Lector said over the intercom. "Can you tell Zaxony is gone? You can answer. I see you've blinded me, but you haven't deafened me yet."

"Castor beans and those other things you said are poison. I am not poison. I am also not a plant."

"You were Zaxony's little sunflower, yes, brightening him up. But you've got deadly qualities too, don't you? I bet you can produce all sorts of interesting toxins in that body of yours. So much of medicine, and so many drugs too, is derived from natural sources, and you're a one-woman forcing bed, aren't you? A hothouse on two legs. Think of the things we'll grow together."

I could make poisons, yes. I had been changing myself during my journey, taking in the new things I discovered in all those worlds, sorting them, grafting in the useful and putting aside the not-useful-yet. I could make myself deadly to the touch. I hoped the Lector would touch me. I understand that Zax does not like violence, but sometimes weeds have to be pulled, and Zax was gone. "I do not know what you mean," I said. "What have you done with Zax?"

"Sent him on a little tour of the multiverse. I gave him a drug that will make him wake and sleep and wake and sleep a dozen times in quick succession, maybe more. I sent him out of the *way*, basically. My plans will work better if I'm not constantly tripping over him in the worlds to come."

"What are your plans?"

"I do like to talk, oleander, but I don't like talking to plants. As I was saying: you're a biotech lab with feet. But if you agree to assist me in my work, I'll allow you some privileges. If you prove troublesome, I'll torture you and extract your useful qualities by force. What do you say?"

"I will help you."

There was a long pause. "What, just like that? If you try to trick me, it won't go well for you."

"I come from a place where terrible creatures of great power made me do whatever they wished upon threat of torture and death. I have been in this situation before. I survived it. I wish to survive this, too."

"That's very… pragmatic. I'd assumed that anyone who spent so much time with our Zaxony must be just as much a hopeless dreamer as he is himself."

"I do not dream much," I said. "I adapt. Zax is gone. You are here. I deal with what is before me, in its proper season."

"You don't want revenge?"

"You did not kill Zax. You sent him out into the orchard of worlds, where he has been for a long time. There is no need for revenge." There was a large and pressing need for revenge.

"I separated you, though, and took you from your friend. Surely you hate me for that?"

"I hate you for many reasons and causes, and that is one of the newest ones, yes. But I would hate to die even more, and I would hate also to be stranded here in the sky above the sky. This is not the place for a person like me." I was being honest, but also not completely honest. I had to tell him the things that would get me out of this room, for the first thing, and then, I would do the next things. You must till the ground before you can plant.

"Hmm," the Lector said. "Very well. I will remain on my guard, but if you really are as practical as you claim, this could work. You know I'm your only hope to touch dirt again. If you serve me well, I'll give you some of my traveling serum, and you won't have to live out your days in this metal canister whirling in circles around a cinder. Come to my lab."

The hatch opened. I pulled myself through the passageway and floated down corridors. Little lights turned on and off on the walls to guide me and I followed them. I could smell organic compounds, ashes and soot from things flashed into carbon. There had once been a *lot* more life here, and it had been burned away, and I mourned for it. Any life at all in a place like this was precious.

When I entered the lab, the Lector floated by a table with his back to me. I knew this was a test. I had been tested in such ways before on the Farm. You might find an unattended radish, seemingly missed by the machines, but if you snatched it up to take home to add to your stores, you would be caught and punished. I knew that even though the Lector did not seem to be watching he must be watching. I still might have taken the opportunity to crash and tumble and hurt him, because I am faster than people think or know, but I did not do that, because I did not wish to be here in this dead place above that dead planet with only his dead body for company when there might be other ways.

"I am here," I said.

"Marvelous." He didn't look up from the station where he worked. His feet were hooked into little loops on the floor to keep him steady and his tools had sticky stuff or magnets or some suchment to keep them in place. "Come look at this."

I pushed myself over and hooked my feet into the loops near his. Being near him was like being near a tree full of boring beetles and rot and woodlice and fungal slime. He tilted himself to the side so I could see the thing squirming in a covered dish. It was the size of a peach pit and just as wrinkly, but with little tendrils waving from it in all directions. "Do you know what that is?"

I shook my head.

"I took a little cutting of my friend Polly, several worlds ago. She told me that her people can be regenerated from even a small piece, which is why their enemies tended to attack them with fire, to eradicate every trace of their bodies. That regeneration takes a long time, though – years for them to come back whole, if they've been reduced to something this small. Only I was thinking, those vines you left to trap us, the ones that grew so ferociously quickly… perhaps that same rapid growth could be used to bring Polly back to life faster?"

"Polly wants to kill all things," I said. "She is not a good thing to bring back to life, fast or slow."

"Ah, but there may be times when someone who wants to kill all things is useful to me, and there will *certainly* be times when someone capable of infiltration at a high level will enable me to bring a world under my control. I need Polly. You're going to help me get her back. That's your project, Minna, the way you'll buy your way off this station: transforming this squirming ball of vegetation into my lieutenant again. You're to take copious notes, so I can learn from your techniques."

"I do not know ways of writing." This was not true, but it was plausible.

"Mmm, yes, of course, you were an illiterate farmhand. Fine, the cameras will record your actions well enough, and you can simply answer any questions I have."

I looked around. "I will need supplies."

He waved a hand. "Take whatever you need. I'll be busy multiplying my supply of Zaxony's blood and pursuing my own studies. Where's that talking ring? I want to take a look at it, too."

"Zax took it from me so I think it must be with him."

The Lector ground his teeth. "If you're lying…"

"You have said what would happen if I did so I do not."

"Fine. Without the ring to study, I'll just focus on you that much more quickly. I'm going to take samples of your biological material soon. I'm sure you're full of wonders."

I did not answer, just began to gather the things I would need to do what he required me to do.

"Oh, and Minna, if you cause me the slightest inconvenience, or I sense that you're failing to work to the very limits of your ability, I will vivisect you, and enjoy the process. Do you understand?"

"I understand."

That was how my servitude to the Lector began.

Cuttings • The Polyp • A Garden of a Million Flowers • Slaps, and Hits, and Kicks • A Resurrection • Alone in the Dark

I (Minna) set up a work space in another part of the station, one that did not have windows looking down on the burning world spinning below us. In my lab I had large glass boxes with manipulator arms inside that could be controlled from outside, and ports to introduce different substances to the interior, and I realized that the people on this station had been engaged in work not so different from mine: examining and experimenting and altering life. There were ample tools to do the terrible work I was forced to do.

Tending the Polly-polyp took most of my attention. I had to first understand her nature before I could hope to change it, and that first week I took tiny cuttings and examined them, combined them, studied them, even tasted them. There were many characteristics possessed by the life form that were interesting from a grafting perspective. I realized that I could subdivide the polyp and grow many versions of Polly and I did not mention that to the Lector because more than one Polly would be a terrible thing.

When not working I would try to find places to sit alone or eat or sleep, but the Lector watched me always, and his voice would come over the speakers and ask me questions about my world and about biological science. Even though he had called me a "biotech lab with feet," he seemed to think that I had done my work on the Farm in a laboratory or workshop, and I did not explain to him that like all grafters, my body is my workshop. If I have access to the right materials, I can make anything I need with nothing but myself.

He called me into his lab often and strapped me onto a table and took biopsies. I made it seem as if this frightened and hurt me because looking weak and stupid was the best way to get what I needed to get for my own plans. He did not warn me about where he was going to plunge his collection tool but I was still fast enough at shifting my body to make sure he took out only the most prosaic pieces of flesh and blood and meat. He got nothing of value from me and I could tell he was frustrated and it made me glad.

After ten days the Polly-polyp was the size of a watermelon and the Lector hit me for the first time. He struck me across the face with the back of his hand and sent me spinning across the station – he had anchored his feet in preparation for the blow so he did not spin away. "Too slow," he said. "I am ahead of schedule, and you should be, too."

I rubbed my face, though I had turned off the pain receptors before he struck me. I spat out a tooth – that brought bad memories – and began growing a new one. He snatched the tooth out of the air and grinned. "I'd been meaning to extract one of these. I bet there's interesting genetic material in the dental pulp."

There was not, but I did not say so.

"How long until Polly-Two can walk under her own power?"

I considered. "Twice the time I have had her, but even then she will be like a child, all totter and not coordinated."

"Hmm. All right. Get to work." He left, my tooth clutched in his fist.

He was angry that the tooth was an empty stone, and he hit me. He hit me most days after that. I considered poisoning him often then, but I had not yet gotten all the things I needed, so I did not. I know now it would have been better if I had.

In another six days, I opened the case and let the Polyp (which I was thinking of more and more like a name instead of a description) out. She looked like a mandrake root or a doll shaped of clay, with just a blob of head and squirmy arms and legs. Eyes opened in unusual places, and breathing slits, and mouths. Once there were mouths though, I could feed her more directly, and she grew faster. I tried to feel the feelings I had felt when I had children of my body, but the Polyp was never part of me, just a thing of hunger and biting and the urge to explore. She handled the microgravity perfectly, darting and spinning and twirling, and after ten days she began to change her shape, extending and elongating arms, making her eyes and nose and mouth appear where they did on me and the Lector. She did not speak in that time, only hissed.

The Polyp was two-thirds my size when she first made herself into a perfect scale model of me. "Hello," she said. "Hello little Polyp hi, are you hungry, eat your mush and grow and be good this time."

"That is very good," I said. "Very good talking." The Polyp was a pest and a weed and a bug and I wanted to uproot it and pluck it and squish it.

That is not fair, I thought. Be like Zax would be, I thought. Zax would say, the original Polly grew up in a place of war and dark and killing and being killed. She was nasty because she was grown nasty and not because she was born that way. This is a new creature and can be a new person of her own. Maybe, I thought, if I manage to escape as I wish to escape, I can take this Polyp with me to be my companion, and raise her free of the Lector, and she will no longer want to kill all things. Perhaps she can be a friend to us instead of to a monster. For this reason, I told her stories of the Farm, and of my adventures with Zax and Victory-Three, and of how the world is more beautiful when it is a garden of a million flowers all different, instead of a place of ashes all the same. I told her friends are better than servants and helpers are better than breakers and she drank it all in as she grew.

I thought it was strange that the Lector did not mind the way I was educating my Polyp, but he was very busy getting ready to replace all his blood.

One day my Polyp snuggled up against me and said, "Minna, can we leave this place? I want to see the trees and leaves and flowers you told me about. I want to go."

"You will not always be here. You will someday get to see the sky instead of being in the sky." I kissed her forehead and it felt a little bit how I felt with my sons, after all, and it made me happy and sad and scared all at once.

"I love you, Minna," my Polyp said. I tried not to feel my heart swell because of course she loved me, I was one of only two people she had ever met, and the only one who was ever kind, and I was nothing but kind, at first because I hated her and didn't want that to show, and later because I was fond and hopeful and concocting new plans about her, on top of my other original plans.

Then the Lector came and said, "Oh, pretty Polly, how I missed you. Do you want a little treat?" He held out in his hand a little mushroom cap of a thing.

"Wait, what is that?" I spun my body between them. "Her diet is very controlled to make her grow as you wish her to grow. What is that you want to feed her?"

"Something the original Polly gave me, for just this eventuality," he said. "Now move out of the way."

The Polyp would eat anything, so she ate the little thing, and then she changed colors and lost her eyes and curled up into an ellipsoid like a very large potato. "What have you done, is she dying?"

"She's remembering," the Lector said. "Polly's people are capable of encoding their memories and experiences into a form that, when consumed by another, transfers those memories… and the original personality along with it, overwriting the new host's mind. Goodbye, Minna's simpering little Polyp. Hello, my razor-sharp Polly." He chuckled. "That's why I let you babble on about peace, love, and harmony, thinking you were her mother."

"Oh." I cried about the loss of my Polyp, and this time, I was not pretending to be weak and sad. I was truly weak and sad. (I had cuttings of my own of my Polyp of course, taken in secret, and later I grafted that ability to encode memory, without the parasitic mind-erasing parts, thinking that I could show all this to Zax someday, if someday ever came.)

After some hours Polly unfurled and took on her old familiar form, needle teeth and stringy hair and scowl. "I remember you," she said. "Can I eat her, Lector?"

"Not yet," the Lector said. "Not as long as she continues to be good. She nursed you back to life, Polly dear. You were terribly hurt on that crystal world–"

"You are not the real Polly," I interrupted. "We left the real Polly back in a pit on a terrible place where she remains, unless she is dead, and if she is dead, she died alone and hungry."

The Lector kicked me in the stomach. "I was going to break the reality of her situation to her *gently,*" he said. "Hold your tongue or I'll remove it and see if you can grow yourself a new one."

I gasped and choked, and it was not all just for show. I had been glaring at Polly so hard that the kick surprised me.

"All that doesn't bother me," Polly said. "I *feel* like myself. If there's some other version of me somewhere, what do I care? That doesn't have anything to do with me. That's the problem with you, Minna, one of the million problems with you: you think too much. That's why you never accomplish anything. Not like what *we're* going to accomplish, the Lector and me."

He reached out and put his hand on top of Polly's head, and she looked up at him with nasty worship. "Now that I have you back, Polly, we can move on. I rebuilt my traveling case, and extracted all the other useful innovations available in this place."

"Can I kill her?" Polly's fingers stretched into pointed spikes.

"Do you remember the talk we had, Polly, about how death is an end to suffering?"

The spikes withdrew. Polly dragged me by my hair and shoved me into one of the glass boxes, sealing me inside. It was not quite big enough for me, and so I was curled and confined. I watched as Polly and the Lector gathered their supplies. He took every vial of Zax's blood and every bit of the traveling serum he'd made.

"You are supposed to leave a dose for me," I said. "I was good and helpful and I am not to be left here in this terrible place alone."

"Didn't you hear the bit about suffering?" Polly said. "We're letting you live just *so* we can leave you here. There's plenty of food, and you can eat the sunlight, anyway, right? You could last here for a long, long time." She drifted over and manipulated the controls on my glass box, poking me with the implements in a way that would have been painful if I had allowed myself to feel the pain. "The Lector didn't explain the memory and personality transfer exactly right, Minna," she told me. "It lets the old personality take control, sure, but it doesn't *erase* the original one. That old consciousness is still there, underneath. I can still remember first opening my eyes, how your face was the first thing this body ever saw, how you went from calling me 'polyp' in disgust to 'my Polyp,' all sweet. Do you want to know something, Minna?" She squashed her face up against the glass, getting as close as she could. "The Polyp never loved you or cared about you. The Polyp was just tricking you, and hoping you'd relax enough that she could eat you in your sleep." Polly gnashed her mouthful of needles, getting spit all over the glass. "You were so stupid you believed it."

"You are lying." I did not know if she was lying. I had thought perhaps I might try to grow a new Polyp from the cuttings I had taken, if things worked out, but I knew then that I never would, because I would be too afraid. Truth or not truth, Polly had poisoned the soil in my heart.

"Why would I lie, when the truth hurts so much more?"

"Come now, Polly," the Lector said. "A certain amount of gloating is enjoyable, and I don't begrudge you, but we have worlds to win." He took Polly in his arms and fed her a sedative. He took a sedative himself, and without even glancing at me in my glass cage, he closed his eyes, and they vanished.

Minna Alone • Grafting • A Spy • Treasures in the Ice • The Moveable Empire • He Brings the War

Then I (Minna) was the most alone I have ever been, the only living thing bigger than bacteria on a space station above a dead world. I made little tendrils from my fingertips to stretch through the cracks in the glass box and opened the door from the outside. Then I came tumbling out and tried to push away the panic, because I do not do well in places where there is no life. In places like that I feel like there is no air even when there is plenty of air. I no longer fall apart and cry like I did the first time I woke in a place with no trees, but it is not because I do not feel like falling apart and crying, it is because I have adapted as best I can.

I made myself breathe in and out, slow, slow, and then I searched the station. It is true that I am sufficient unto myself in most times and places, but I can still be hurt, and in a place that is too dark or deep or where the sun is too weak or broken, I could still starve. I get cold and I get scared and I get thirsty. I get lonely too but I could not think about that, or I would curl up and in on myself like a fiddlehead fern.

I found a sack and filled it with supplies of freeze-dried food and pouches of water and nutrient goo to squeeze. It was a small pile but it was something, and to have anything at all was a comfort to me. I then went to the lab and massaged a spot on my thigh until the skin slid aside and revealed the little hidden cavity I had grown in my flesh, and the tiny vial of Zax's blood that I had stolen and secreted away during my work on the Polyp.

I was glad that I had guessed the mind of the Lector properly. If he had set the station to sterilize itself again, I would have died, and if he had put me out the airlock, likewise. If he had tried to kill me I would have had to fight and fight and fight, and against him, with his augmented muscles and his strengthened bones and who knows what other powers, I was not *sure* I would have won, even at my thorniest and most poisonous. With Polly by his side I could not have prevailed, I am sure. But I thought: the Lector is cruel. He will leave me here alone to suffer when he is done, I think. I gambled, and I was right.

Now that I had time and privacy, I set about grafting Zax's blood into my own.

The process was tricky. Several of my fingers withered and fell off before I adjusted the blood to sufficient compatibility with my own. Luckily I had watched the Lector use the strange machines to multiply the blood volume so I was able to make more material to work with.

After a day my blood was happy with Zax's blood, and tasting it, and savoring, and recognizing the use inside the cells. There is something strange there, yes, something that makes the worlds pass, and I do not understand it, but I do not have to understand it to copy it. I taught my body to make my blood be like Zax's blood. I adapt myself. I do not alter the whole of the world to suit me. This is why I will never be an emperor. (It is one reason anyhow.)

Once my blood was like Zax's blood in the necessary way I prepared myself and I went to sleep.

The next world was where I began my life as a spy.

First I changed how I looked: I made my hair very light from when it was dark, and my skin and my eyes too, and it took a while but I grew my nose longer and my chin more pointed and I made myself a little taller and more slender. I say "first" but it is slow, to change that way. If it is not done little by little the skin tears among other things, so I made the change across several worlds.

That world was made of ice, and there was not much life there, but a little. I crept through the crevasses, glad of gravity but unhappy with everything else. In the ice there were people and machines and houses all frozen. Some of the people looked surprised, and I wondered if the ice had come quickly and how it had done so. I climbed over a ridge and saw smoke on the horizon and crept toward it, slow, slow, patient. Closer in I heard a noise like *bang-bang-crack, bang-bang-crack*.

My eyes were sharp as sharp and soon I found a high place with the sun behind me, hiding me in the glare of the light on the ice, and I looked down. The Lector was there, with Polly. I do not know what they were burning but they had a fire and I longed for its warmth. Polly wore a hood to hide from the sun and had a sharp tool and she hammered at the ice, and the Lector picked up small things she excavated and exclaimed over them. Soon she hit a sort of tunnel in the ice and went down, past where it was translucent and into where it was dark, and then she brought out something like a person but made of metal, with four arms and a head like a dome and spidering legs in multitudes. The Lector did something to a panel on the metal person's back and it began to whir and spin and clamber, and after that it dug in the ice for them, and brought out more small things that the Lector looked over and put away. I wished Victory-Three was with me because they know the workings and meanings of machines, and all I knew was to be worried.

I wished for a weapon for murder, but I knew the Lector was tough and I would need something more than a sharp piece of ice to crush or pierce him.

I watched them all that day until the Lector did something to the robot, and made it pull in its arms and legs and become a sort of cylinder small enough to hug, and then he hugged it, and Polly hugged him, and they all flickered away.

I investigated their camp but could not tell what they might have taken, except the things they left behind looked like broken guns, so perhaps they took the unbroken ones. After some time I slept too.

From a cliff top in the next world I saw giant creatures, like people but bigger, grown as tall as three of me and broad enough to match. They moved slowly and plants grew all over them and that made me happy, the way the giants lived together with the plants here. I followed the Lector to a village of theirs, where he made a lot of noise and fuss.

The Lector stayed there for five days, using his drugs to keep himself from sleeping, and in that time, the village was transformed. The biggest of the giants wore a strange cap of metal and I think it made him do what the Lector wanted. I saw him building things like that on the station, though he hid them away when he noticed me looking. Some of the other giants waved their clubs and tried to fight and it was a terrible thing. The robot – the Lector named it Calamitas, I learned later on, and it was a machine with a mind like Vicki is maybe, but altered by the Lector to be loyal – turned on the giants and cut them down as easily as it had cut through the ice. Easier even because flesh is softer than ice most of the time.

The Lector gave the leader of the giants a shiny gun, and where the gun was pointed, things froze into ice. There were little bombs that did the same thing, ice grenades, and I think that the world before was the victim of a bigger bomb or many bombs that did the same thing, but more so.

On the third day one of the giants began to make a statue of the Lector, standing even bigger than the giants themselves, and holding a war club in one hand and an ice gun in the other.

On the fourth day, the giants sent out a party with weapons, and later, on the horizon, smoke rose.

On the fifth day Polly nearly found me, doing a slinking patrol around the village, and I had to hide in a crevice between two boulders. I found some interesting lichen inside though to pass the time.

(Oh. I stayed awake and did not travel because I do not have to go to sleep all the way all at once. The brain has two halves, did you know? I made it so I can let one half of my brain sleep while the other half is awake, and then switch. Some animals do it and I can do what some animals can do, when I make the effort to make the changes inside. I am sort of slower and not as bright when I am half asleep, but I can respond to dangers, and, more importantly, being half asleep does not make me travel. It is a helpful thing for a spy to be awake as long as she needs to be.)

Then they were gone. I went into the village – they had greeted the Lector peacefully enough and I thought they had courtesy rules for strangers. Perhaps they did once but they didn't anymore. I was seized and dragged to the largest dwelling and forced to kneel before the leader with his crown of metal. "Who are you?" the leader said in a shouty way.

"My name is Minna. I am a stranger here. What is this place?"

The leader preened then, proud, and stroked the ivy that hung down his chin like a beard. "This is the First World of the Collectorium, little thing. The foundation of the Moveable Empire. We were told to beware strange creatures who seem like they don't belong. Such creatures might threaten the empire, and the Lector's plan. Put her in the cage. She will await our Lector's return, and face his justice."

I went right to sleep right then right away. (I couldn't always do that – for a long time I needed the drugs like Zax did – but when I made my plan on the space station I realized it would be better if I could sleep quick whenever I needed, so I made some changes.)

Next I found myself in a city and I whimpered and said oh no, oh no. The buildings were like jewels, all glitter and blue, and they rose so high that clouds spun by, a forest of buildings all grace and height. I was on the roof of one building, the floor shimmering and translucent, and near me was the wreck of a flying machine that had once looked like a dragonfly and now looked like a dead and mangled dragonfly that had been on fire and was now cold.

Some of the buildings were currently on fire, and flying machines zoomed by overhead and belowfeet, some of them shooting at each other, some of them smashing into buildings and making them quake.

The Lector has not been here long, I thought, half a day maybe before me, perhaps this place was at war before him?

I soon learned, no. The Lector brought the war with him. He brings the war wherever he goes.

The Banner of the Lector • Seneschals • The Armies of Empire • Blood, Blood, Blood • Assassin • Giving Up

I (Minna) found a hatch on the roof and lowered myself into the building, and went downstairs, and reached a lounge where all the chairs were tipped over and there was blood and broken glass and the smell of alcohol. There were four screens above the bar and three were broken but one showed a newscast. The person talking was like a person except covered in delicate blue fur, and they were mussed and sweating and did not look calm. The sound was not working, but then the person was replaced by a video of the Lector walking into some sort of large building, all columns and fountains. He walked with one of the ivy-colored giants from the world before and the robot both beside him. I wondered how the giant had come along. How could the Lector hold the robot and Polly and him all in his arms at once? And then I realized: he had made so much of the serum, he could give the gift of travel to those loyal to him, and bring them along to other worlds. He could control their doses, and make it so they would travel only once.

He was the guardian of the doors of the multiverse and I began to understand how his Moveable Empire could work.

Then the view switched to a video of the same grand building on fire. Polly was nowhere to be seen, and what I think now is that she was doing what I know she did later. She could make herself look like anyone, even the blue-furred leader of a country or a planet or suchment, and then she could do whatever things the Lector wanted her to do: declare wars, make treaties, surrender her world.

We stayed in that place for nearly seven days, which I think might be as long as the Lector can manage – I never saw him last longer than that, and by the last day he was a ragged mess when I watched him from my hidden perch in a building near the place he'd chosen as a palace. During that week I met the resistance fighters who could not believe their leaders had bowed to the will of an alien despot. They gave me glasses you could look through to make far things look close and that was very helpful for being a spy.

That was the world where the Lector unveiled the symbol of his empire, in a giant banner that he hung from the tallest tower first and then from the smaller ones. It is a pretty picture really: a white background, and at the center, a black tree of many branches. It is a symbol that makes me think of the orchard of worlds that Zax described to me, and I wondered if Zax got the idea from the Lector, or the Lector got it from him.

I watched the Lector go to sleep in that world, on the parade ground of a military base high in the sky. He took with him an army of blue-furred people, each given a drop of serum to drink and then a sedative. They took flying machines with them, broken down into pieces small enough for one soldier to hold, so ten soldiers or so could carry one whole ship. He left behind the giant (he calls those he leaves behind to rule his "seneschals," and he likes to put creatures from one world in power over another world, perhaps so no old loyalties will interfere, and when he cannot do that, he leaves a ruler with a spidery metal crown that makes them loyal to him forever). He left behind others converted to his cause by machines or their own greed.

I learned that the Lector promised them he would return, and I understood his plan. He would sleep on through the worlds, conquering as he went, taking the technology from one world to master another. Infiltration and assassination and trickery and force: he had tools to use in every place. Someday, he would figure out how to control his power, or so he thought, and then he would return to the worlds he had taken over before. Even if he never came back, though, he would leave all these broken worlds in his wake, torn by war, betrayed by their leaders, full of the dead.

We went on that way, Zax. The Lector conquered, and I followed, and I watched. I woke next in the burnt ruin of some sort of sports stadium, near a crater that I think must have once been a town – there was half a library next to the rim. I heard the distant booms of artillery.

I went to sleep straightaway. I thought perhaps I could get ahead of the Lector, and try to warn people, but do you know how hard it is to convince people that an army from another reality is coming to conquer them? Even if people understand you, even if you can find the right ones to talk to who could do something about it, they think you are mad. You might convince them *you* are from somewhere else, and sometimes maybe they believe your warning is true, but the one time I managed that much, the local people could arm themselves with nothing better than stones and clubs and that could not stand against the oncoming empire.

I watched a world full of people with the heads of birds, as noble and peaceful and stately a race as I have ever seen, fall to the Lector's forces, and the smell of burning feathers still makes me shudder. He had people with the heads of raptors and carrion birds in his employ after that, and he used them to conquer a world of archipelagoes and pools and peaceful sea-dwelling creatures with many eyes and no concept of armor or artillery.

The Museum of Trauma where I appeared in the next world soon had a new exhibit to add to its halls, or, it would have, if the Lector had not torn the building down, declaring the end of history in a world where history was worshipped as a god. He burned all the libraries there: he wanted his knowledge to be the greatest, and if it was not, he would tear down the greater until he towered in comparison.

By then at least I looked different, so when the Lector heard rumors of a woman warning people of his coming, he did not know (not for sure) that it was me, though maybe he wondered who else it could be.

We went to a world of high cliffs and giant birds with no intelligent life to be found, but he built a prison there, and dragged the resistance and agitators he had captured from the earlier worlds and left them in it. I wondered why he didn't just kill them, but then remembered: the dead do not suffer.

Next a world of concrete where there were no people, but only intelligent machines that rolled around on wheels. I did not like that place but I gritted my teeth and I watched. He conquered those machines, too, because technology is a toy he can play with or break as he likes.

He hunted people and gathered supporters in a world of hunters and gatherers, who mostly subsisted on the eggs laid in their thousands by the slick, green-skinned predatory monsters that hunted the people in turn. The Lector took some of those eggs and a few worlds later his troops were riding the newborn beasts, transformed by little silver crowns into compliant war mounts. He found a world of stinking mines and enslaved children and did not change much there, except for the face that appeared on the coins: his own, with his tree of worlds on the reverse.

The world of skeletons with jeweled eyes and mechanical legs and the Church of the Sanguine stood against him for a few days, because the dead are hard to kill, and they did not have the sort of brains he knew how to control, and Polly could not make herself look like a fleshless god-corpse… but eventually the Lector broke that world, too, by sabotaging the pumps that circulated in the blood fountains, which animated the skeletons in some way I still do not understand. (Blood, blood, blood. There is so much blood in this story.)

It went on, and on, and on. I was a spy until I asked myself what I was being a spy for. I worked for the resistance when I could, when there was one I could find and they were willing to accept my help, but the Lector had so much power from so many places in so many forms that the resistance always crumbled, and the banner of the Collectorium always flew. His seneschals were the cruelest, most avaricious, most power-loving of his supporters, rewarded with dominion over worlds of their own. Mastery over a whole world was enough to sate the most ambitious… except for the Lector himself.

He continued to study his own blood, and to try to control his ability, and I heard rumors of rages, of smashed glassware in scores of labs, of orders of mass executions made simply because the Lector was furious about another failure. The idea of him gaining control over his ability was terrifying… but the idea of him failing wasn't much better.

I decided I had to kill him. I am made to make things grow, to nurture and to save, but I know when a weed has to be torn up by the roots. I had to stop being a spy and become an assassin.

But the how of it was hard. The Lector always had Calamitas and usually Polly with him, along with other soldiers and bodyguards, including a skeleton with onyx eyes and gleaming hydraulic muscles who served as his chief interrogator and torturer. The Lector had made his own body even more inviolate with new technology, too. I saw knives and bullets fail to make any mark at all, and once he was knocked down by an artillery shell and walked out of the crater, scowling and directing the retribution. (I made some friends. I am a friendly person and those who fight the Lector always had something in common with me. I saw too many of them swing from ropes or die in fire. Too many I could not help or save.)

Once, I thought I knew my plan. I crept ahead of him and managed to lay explosives all around the site of my arrival. When the Lector appeared with his army, the bombs went off, and oh, it was glorious.

His soldiers died, and their war machines were destroyed. Polly was blown to pieces, and Calamitas too. I rejoiced. But the Lector emerged, his body shimmering in a sort of force field, and his torturer was intact, too, though missing a limb. I slowed him down, yes –

he did not conquer that world, which was a bucolic and peaceful place where slow-moving shaggy creatures grazed and debated philosophy. But he repaired Calamitas. He regrew Polly from scraps, having learned from my methods. The Lector lived, and had enough small items of power on his person that he regained his position in the next world, and rebuilt his arsenal, and within a dozen worlds, he proceeded again, barely diminished from before.

The Lector suspected he had an enemy before. Now he *knew* he did, and he suspected it was me. I lingered in worlds behind him, and on rare occasions leapfrogged ahead, though I worried about going too far, because what if the Victory-Three was right, and the worlds *did* branch, and I found myself in a place where the Lector never came? It would give me peace, yes, but I did not want peace: I wanted to stop the invasive species from spreading and killing all the natives.

The problem was, by then, that the Lector was devoted to killing me. He still is. He no longer wants me to suffer. He just wants me gone.

In world after world, the Lector sent out hunters, creatures and machines, to search for me. Sometimes I heard him shouting: "That's you, isn't it, Minna? Did you steal a vial of serum somehow on the station and chase after me? Are you wearing a *wig*, you stupid sapling?" Things such as that, to try to agitate me maybe, or just because he liked to yell. "I am coming for you!" he said. "You are my enemy, and the enemy of my empire." Posters with drawings of my new face and my old face appeared in the worlds he conquered. People who once would have sheltered me tried to catch me and sell me.

I did not know what to do. I was always full of fear. I did not know how to stop him. I grew tired and sad and alone and I missed my friends. So then I gave up.

I traveled, and I traveled fast, and a lot, to look for Zax. I always thought, Zax Zax Zax, in case that influenced where I traveled. I almost caught up to you. I asked questions, staying longer in places where I heard stories of you. They were sad stories, of the drunken stranger who only wanted to get more drunk and sometimes of his talking ring. Soon I heard stories of you being there a month ago, weeks ago, just days.

The Lector sent people with serum to chase after me, though, and the Lector came along sometimes too. He pursues me relentlessly because only I am a problem from world to world: I am the only thing that persists, his enemy that is ongoing. I lay traps when I can, and I warn people, and try to make his life harder as I go. He has gotten faster at creating his outposts of empire, and he is driven, and he is always just behind me now. Either the worlds we visit are ordered and we have no choice of where we go, or he is always thinking *Minna, Minna, Minna,* and following me to the worlds I visit. He is only a few worlds behind me now, at most.

I know I will find Zax soon. I must be so close. The next world, maybe. So I put my memories of all I have done and seen in a seed, and Zax can taste it, and know what I went through, and what we face.

I do not know what to do. I hope, if I can find my friends, oh, my friends, that we can figure something out together.

Zax Decides • Council of War • Brain Surgery with a Dirty Stick • Awake Forever • Glory to Those Who Sleep

I (just Zax again) opened my eyes to Minna peeling dead and dry vines off my face. I coughed and asked for water, and she fetched a leaf shaped like a bowl and tipped some into my mouth, propping up my head so I could swallow. I felt like I'd just lived months, but by the movement of the sun, it had only been hours. "Minna, I'm so sorry. What you went through... I had no idea. I mostly tried not to think about what was happening to you, since I couldn't do anything about it, but when I did imagine, it was never as bad as *that*."

"The Moveable Empire is coming for us, Zax," Minna said. "Do you understand?"

"I do. I really do. I... As I see it, we have two options. We can run ahead of the Lector and his empire. Or..." I took a deep breath. "We can make a stand, and try to stop him."

"I tried to stop him. I cannot. Do you think we can do better together? Or do you think we should run?

"I've grown used to a life of constant movement, and waking up in a new place every day, Minna." Her face fell, and tears welled in the corners of her eyes. I reached out and tilted up her chin so she'd look me in the eyes. "But I want to feel like I'm exploring the orchard of worlds... not like I'm a fugitive on the run. I also feel responsible for the Lector's crimes. If it wasn't for me, he wouldn't be rampaging across realities this way. I have to stop him. I have to stop the Collectorium."

"Someone had better tell me what the Collectorium *is,*" Vicki said. "Especially if we're going to war with it."

So I filled them in.

"The Lector has a general, a woman with the head of a crow who rides one of those predator mounts, who mostly handles the to-ing-and-fro-ing now," Minna explained as we had our – oh, spheres – council of war. "She is doling out the serum and transporting the armies now, mostly. The bird-people like to wear crowns anyway so hers may just be decorative but I think it is controlling or influencing her mind, because I do not think the Lector fully trusts anyone whose mind he does not meddle in at least a little. Because she is handling the expansion of the empire, lately the Lector tends to jump ahead, to scout things out, and to look for me. He has with him always Calamitas and usually Polly, unless she is busy pretending to be a prime minister or a monarch and his torturer with the onyx eyes is usually there, too. He comes with guns and machines that try to track me in different ways but none of them work too well, I think because I changed my body a little so the samples he has scraped up do not quite connect to me anymore."

"Minna, you're amazing," Zax said. "I had no idea you could do all these things."

"I did not either until I had to do them." She sighed. "And anyway none of them were enough."

"Hey. You were a spy, a resistance fighter, and you got under the Lector's skin so badly that he's concentrating on chasing *you* instead of inflicting cruelties on the worlds he's taking over. You didn't win, but you haven't lost, either. *We* haven't lost. We'll figure this out. You've got all the intel we could need, Minna, and Vicki has the tactical and strategic knowhow to help us figure out a plan." She seemed a little cheered up by that. It's hard, to be alone. I felt better just having her around again, even though her return showed me the magnitude of the threat we faced.

"His whole enterprise is absurd on its face," Vicki said. "His 'empire' is nothing of the sort. Even with superior technology, and leaving in place his mind-controlled or willing lackeys, his system isn't stable. At best he gains control of a local area, but in many places even that will be temporary. You've been to worlds with civilizations that seemed to span multiple *planets*, Zax, and he's conquering nations… or even just neighborhoods. It's as if the Lector came to my world, took control of my island, and declared himself emperor of that galaxy."

"You're right," I said, "but he's a megalomaniac, and since he moves on, he'll never see any evidence of his failure. As far as he's concerned, it's one glorious triumph after another. If he ever masters the ability to choose where he goes, he'll have to face reality… but at that point, he might be able to make his conquests more thorough and permanent. In the meantime… he still has a small army, and that army is coming for us. Do you have any ideas about how to handle that?"

"I see some possibilities," Vicki said. "I just wish we had more *time*. If you could stay awake for more than few days, we could jump several worlds ahead quickly, gain some breathing room, pick a good place to make a stand, and prepare the ground. I am used to working with limitations, that's the nature of any conflict, but the limitations here are unusual–"

"I could make it so Zax can stay awake like me," Minna said.

I stared at her. If Vicki could stare, I'm sure they would have, too. "What do you mean?"

"What I did to my brain. I could do it to your brain."

"You want to perform… brain surgery… on me." I had a flash of an image: Minna in a surgical mask, leaning over me to poke at my exposed brain with a dirty stick.

"I want to convince your brain to change, a little. I would mostly make things for you to eat and those things would change you. It would take a few days I think to work. You might pass out sometimes by surprise as your brain is learning a new way to be, but that is OK now, because I will not be stranded if you lose consciousness suddenly anymore: I can just follow."

"What are the odds that you break my brain and I die?" I asked.

"I am not good with numbers but I think it is safer than the Lector coming and murdering us all. Safer by a *lot*."

"If this works, I can just... stay awake? Forever?"

"Mmm, you sort of doze but you are aware of your surroundings and if something happens you will snap all the way awake. You will see me staring off into space and that is what I am doing: being half asleep. Some animals, they don't sleep any other way, and I have not changed myself that much – perhaps I cannot, without changing how I think too much – and I do still like to sleep proper all the way sometimes, but... basically yes. As long as you want, without falling deep enough to travel."

I breathed out. To be able to stay in a place, for more than a few days. That had been my dream. Achieving that was worth even a very nebulously defined amount of risk. "Do it."

"I will make a start but we should sleep jump sleep jump soon," Minna said. "The Lector will arrive here, or his hunters anyway, and it will take me a little time to make the things to make your brain work better."

I caught up this chronicle while Minna worked at a table in one of the treehouses, mumbling to herself and staring at the ceiling and consulting with Vicki, who apparently scanned me and has insights about my biology that Minna lacks. (Being scanned makes me think of the Lector, but at least I know these two have my best interests in mind.)

What the Lector has done... it's beyond appalling. The staggering variety in the worlds I encounter is one of the great wonders of existence, and he wants to make those world all the same, all hierarchical, all militaristic, all in his image. If he finds a world that doesn't fit, he'll lop off pieces until it does. He'll fill the peaceful places with engines of war. I have to stop him. More than that, I have to take on the quest *he* took on, to try and control my power, and choose the worlds I visit… so I can return to those he's already ruined, and try to undo what he did, and defeat his seneschals, and give those worlds back their own agency. They'll be altered forever by the very fact of his conquest, and there's nothing I can do about that, but I can try to let them choose their own paths going forward.

The Lector has given me a purpose. He has no idea what I'm capable of, when I have a purpose. He's knocked so many things out of alignment, and I have to bring as many of them as I can back to harmony.

Vicki asked me once, when I was only medium drunk, why I cared about helping people in any given individual world, considering the hypothetical infinity of the multiverse. The magnitude of suffering must be so vast that nothing I did made any difference in the grand scheme of things. Vicki was, of course, trying to remind *me* why I'd ever cared, to get a rise out of me and rile me up and set me back on something resembling a healthy life path. I knew that, but I answered anyway: "There's a story from my world. A little boy is walking through the woods when he encounters a group of workers cutting down trees. He watches them work for a while, then notices that the trees are home to fat trundling harmless beetles with bright purple backs. The beetles shower down when the trees fall, and get crushed beneath the heedless boots of the workers, and lose their homes. The boy is sad about that, so he kneels down, and lets one of the beetles crawl onto his fingertip. One of the workers taking his break nearby sees the boy, and says, 'What are you doing?' The boy says, 'I am going to walk deep into the forest and put this beetle in a new tree, far from the edge of the woods, where it will be safe and peaceful for the rest of its life.' The worker scratches his head and says, 'What's the point? There must be thousands of these bugs here. Moving one of them won't accomplish anything.' The boy looks down at the beetle, bumbling along the palm of his hand, thinking, then looks back up at the worker. 'If I could save them all, I'd save them all, but since I can't save them all, I'll save this one.' Then the boy walks off into the forest, and after a moment, the worker grunts, reaches down, lets a beetle crawl onto his hand, and follows."

"Mmm," Vicki said. "I see. It is a parable."

"That's a good idea," I said, pouring myself a new drink. "Let's make this one a double too." Well, Vicki tried. I wasn't ready to save anything then. Now I am.

I yawned, once, and Minna said we should be going. She had no real way of knowing how close her pursuers were, but if she spent more than eight or ten hours in a given world, they tended to show up. There were teams after her, seekers and hunters, some scouting ahead to look for signs of her, some staying behind to do more thorough searches in case she'd gone to ground. The multiverse was infested with malevolent creatures now, and it offended me.

We slept our way to World 1112, and woke on a plain of basalt beneath an immense red sun, surrounded by pyramids of blocky stone ranging from the size of cottages to the size of mountains. The air was bracingly cold. When I approached one of the pyramids, my ears began to buzz and I felt a vibration in the back of my teeth. There were carvings all over the stones of the pyramid, which could have been a tomb, or a temple, or a home. I couldn't make the designs out clearly, but they looked a little like ocean waves. I backed away. "Minna, is anything alive here?"

"Alive the way bees are alive when they hibernate in the cold." She turned in a slow circle, gazing wide-eyed at the structures. "Those who dwell here sleep, and they sleep deep, their breaths and hearts – so many hearts – pulsing slow. But they live."

"What are these structures, Vicki?"

"Shielded against scanning is what they are. I could not tell you what they look like inside."

There were pools of water – at least, I assumed it was water at first – ringed by perfect circles of stone in front of some of the pyramids. The smallest were just a few paces across, and others were as big as lakes. I looked into the nearest one, and it was like looking into a screen that rippled in the breeze: I saw a little town, neat streets populated by carriages drawn by shaggy quadrupeds, with humanoids bustling around. Another circle showed the same sort of people, but working in fields, and another a fishing village.

We went to the largest pool within easy walking distance, the size of a pond beside a towering pyramid etched all over with images of trees and horned beasts. The pool showed a group standing in a circle wearing robes the color of dark red wine, holding torches aloft and chanting in a forest. Their voices droned on, intoning syllables that even the linguistic virus couldn't parse, which maybe meant they were meaningless, or maybe just all [unable to translate].

"Something stirs," Minna murmured. The pyramid nearby began to emit a flickering greenish glow from the inside, revealing seams in its structure, and we backed away as a block ten meters high slid aside. Something squirmed out of the hole – a huge snake, I thought at first, but when it twisted it looked more like an immense worm, blind and questing, and then a twist again and it was a white root reaching through the soil. Minna and I took another long step back as the root plunged into the pool, and we couldn't see what happened next, but we heard the chanting turn into screaming, and then the root-snake-worm emerged with one of the robed figures wrapped up in its coils, and drew the sobbing, gibbering figure back into the pyramid. I started forward instinctively to try to help, but the great block moved again and sealed the pyramid closed.

"Listen, Zax," Vicki said. The people in the pool – or wherever the pool opened onto, I guess – were shouting, but now the virus could understand them. They were saying, "She is chosen! She is elect! She is blessed! Glory, glory to the dreamers! Glory, glory to those who sleep in the realm above!"

"I do not like this place," Minna said. "That person who was picked up is still alive but she is also slow, slow, slow."

I shivered. "Let's leave. I'd like to see the Lector conquer whatever lives in *this* place. Maybe they'll drag him into a pyramid."

"Maybe. Or maybe he'll drag them *out*," Vicki said.

On that cheerful note, we moved on.

A Quiet Meal • Delirium • Death or Exile • Half Asleep • Be Appeased • Fleeing the Collectorium

World 1113 was all hill forts and peat fires and conscious bog mummies being carried around on palanquins by naked servants who were painted blue. One of the mummies prodded at my mind so forcefully that I started to strip off my clothes and smear myself with mud, and Minna had to drag me away and force a sleeping potion between my lips.

World 1114 was a cruise ship the size of a small city, in the midst of a civil war (upper decks versus lower, as near as we could tell), under a burning sky. The people from the lower decks were uplifted animals twisted into humanoid shapes, and the ones from the upper decks were bulbous-headed gray-skinned things with needle teeth, so I assume there was a degree of species as well as class conflict involved in their dispute.

We made our way to an empty hall that contained the ruins of a buffet, and consumed flat water and stale pastries. Minna sprinkled some glittering powder on top of my last plateful of food, and said it would begin the process of altering my physiology. It added a nice little acidic tang to the dish, anyway.

Then small-arms fire began to clatter in the corridor outside, and we opted to move on.

World 1115 was full of snow and evergreens and faraway gleaming lights and distant singing, and we tried to find the source of the music and light, but it never seemed to grow any closer, and we weren't dressed for the weather. We crossed our own tracks in the snow and realized we were going in circles. My head felt strange and swimmy and vague, my vision doubling and doubling again, and everything was just terribly *funny* for some reason, and I giggled through lips turning blue. Vicki told us how to hollow out a little nest in the snow, and we burrowed into a drift, our body heat gradually filling the tiny space; I think Minna boosted her own temperature somehow to make it cozy faster, and her fingers were wreathed with bioluminescence. She held me while I giggled and my teeth chattered. "Is this supposed to be happening?" Vicki asked.

"I have never changed someone else's brain this way before," Minna said. "I cannot be sure, but I think the giggling and all is just an adjustment. His functions are functioning as they should, it is only his cognition that is shifting."

"As long as he's still Zax at the end of this," Vicki muttered.

I don't remember falling asleep, but when I looked around again we were on a cliff above a river, looking down on a group of creatures a bit like otters, but wearing clothes and sporting in the water. "Is this 1116?" I asked, my lips cracked and dry.

Minna helped me sit up and sip water. "No, 1117," Vicki said. "You were fairly delirious in the world before this. Quite a pretty place, a city plaza with a fountain, and in the center a thing like an astrolabe, its components moving smoothly without any visible support. The people there had dark skin and hair in beautiful braids and wore colorful garments, and they were very solicitous. We attempted to warn them of the coming of the Moveable Empire but they seemed to think we were mentally ill and just patted us gently and offered us medical care. We ended up in a very comfortable room, with a locked door, and slept our way out before some doctor could come prod us."

"The presence of a talking ring didn't sway them?" I asked.

"Most of them wore talking bracelets. Some sort of technological amanuenses, I gather. I was considered one of the same, worn as a ring as a sort of amusing affectation."

"They were very nice people," Minna said. "The Lector will destroy them."

"That's what he does. We have to stop him."

"We haven't talked specifics," Vicki said. "May I ask – are you willing to consider permanent solutions?"

I sighed, watching the peaceful creatures splashing below us, heedless of the juggernaut bearing down on them, one world at a time. I thought of the surface of the river aflame, of the inhabitants butchered, of the forests cut down. "If there were a way to stop the Lector short of killing him, that's what I'd do. The world I come from abhors violence. We don't even put murderers to death – we send them into exile, where they can't harm anyone else, and let them live out their natural spans alone. That's what I wanted to do with the Lector, but now... it's just not an option. If he isn't stopped, millions will die, and billions more will see their worlds changed forever for the worst. Some things can't be harmonized."

"Killing him won't be easy," Vicki said. "He is more physically formidable than ever, and he was never a soft target."

I nodded. "We'll have to find weapons. We'll have to prepare our ground. And then... we'll do what we must."

"I think I could remove his ability to travel, if we can capture him," Minna said.

I stared at her. "You can?"

"I have lived with your blood, which now flows in me. I know it well. I can make something that eats the special part, changes it, neutralizes it. We can put that something inside the Lector, and it will reproduce in his blood and never go away."

"Like a virus?"

"Something like. Once his ability to travel was gone we could just leave him in an empty place like you say."

"I wish you hadn't said that, Minna," Vicki said. "Capturing him will be a *lot* harder than just killing him would be. Even if we manage to get him, if you think we're being pursued now, wait until we take their emperor."

"I do not think his army could chase us very far," Minna said.

"The Lector is very jealous of his powers, and he doles out only a little of his serum at a time, even to his general. He fears usurpers. He carries a locked case, a laboratory in itself, and every few worlds he opens it and replenishes the supplies of his followers. The case opens only for him, with his touch. If we take him, his army will be stranded, if we can get more than a few worlds away."

Vicki said, "Zax, I implore you: we should strike, and strike hard, and decisively. As long as the Lector lives and thinks, he is a threat. How many times have we thought him neutralized before?"

"I do not say we should spare his life," Minna said. "Invasives should be torn up, root and branch, and burned. But I do not wish for you to become something you do not wish to be, Zax. I only want you to know your options. This is one."

Death, or exile. Killing him would be hard enough. Capturing him, sending him away, finally, to a place where he couldn't do any harm, was more appealing, but would be infinitely more difficult.

"We don't have to decide now," I said. "Let's find a world to make a stand, and await his arrival, and then... we'll see what we can do."

The first thing we did was test whether Minna's changes worked. When I got sleepy, I followed her instructions, which were delivered in her usual vague and elliptical way, but I got the gist: I let my eyes unfocus, I relaxed my breathing, and I tried to sink into sleep without closing my eyes.

The sensation was difficult to describe. It was a bit like being lost in a hazy daydream, when you're warm and comfortable and your mind is flowing from thought to thought aimlessly, connecting ideas in a loose and associative way, without anything like a logical progression. I became something like a creature of sensation, rather than a creature of thought, and the stars spun overhead, and the river burbled, and the wind whispered things that sounded almost like words. After a while I got thirsty and blinked and sat up, and it was morning.

I'd slept – "slept" – through the night, barely aware of the passage of time; certainly it didn't feel like the many hours Vicki assured me it had. I felt as rested as I did after transitioning to a new world. "Minna, it *worked*. But how do I sleep the way I used to, if I want?"

"Drugs will still work," she said. "But there are other ways, I think."

I spent that day trying various meditative practices, but the problem was, I wasn't *tired*. When night fell again, I was worn out from all the humming and focusing on various body parts and sitting in assorted positions and laying in others, and yawned a bone-cracking yawn. This time, when I tried closing both my eyes, deepening my breathing, and imagining myself floating on a warm sea… I fell truly asleep, and moved on.

I woke, alone, on World 1118, sitting on a plain of shiny glass under a merciless sun, with sharp-edged mountains off in the distance. I had a scrabbling moment of panic – I was *alone*, I'd lost my companions, I'd fallen asleep without them – but then Minna flickered into existence next to me, wearing Vicki. "See?" she said.

I grabbed her and hugged her fiercely and whispered, "Yes. Yes, I see."

We jumped worlds, looking for resources, and for the right place to prepare our ground. We wanted a world where the terrain was to our advantage, and where there weren't people who'd get hurt. Vicki said they'd know the right world when they saw it.

World 1119 was all iron hatches rusted shut, and no one responded when we pounded on the doors, but then mechanical creatures scuttled out of little slots and chased us, so we fled.

In 1120 we found a battlefield full of dead people, and things with starfish faces, and bipedal machines, but they'd mysteriously fought one another with blades and clubs, with no weapons that Vicki deemed worth taking. "Perhaps some sort of ritual battle, or an arena, or an amusement," they mused.

1121: A swamp full of snapping, writhing things, and immense horrors that blotted out the sun when they strode over us, their legs needle-thin and seemingly too delicate to support such immensity.

In 1122 we rested a while: it was a world of cobblestones and wooden cottages populated by diminutive humanoids who hid behind their curtains and pushed food and cups of water through little slots at the bottom of their doors and called out, "Be appeased, and move on! Be appeased, and move on!" Apparently there were some sort of local monsters or demons or creatures that occasionally came and troubled them, but we accepted the largess, moved a little way beyond their borders into the hills nearby, and tried not to think about what the Lector would do to the locals.

It turned out we didn't have to wait long to find out. Minna sat up and said, "Someone new is here." Moments later we heard screams and saw fire flickering from the direction of the village.

Minna looked through her binocular-glasses, and whimpered, and handed them to me. I looked, and saw the Lector – wearing gleaming black and silver armor now, instead of a white coat – and a skeleton with pistons on his arms and legs, and Polly slinking at his side, and blue-furred people holding back huge lizards on chains. One of the soldiers was burning the huts with some kind of flamethrower, sending the small people fleeing, and two more were assembling a small machine with wings.

"Minna!" the Lector called, his voice amplified and booming. "How many more innocent worlds do I have to burn before you'll come out? I'll hunt down these little scurrying things and feed them to my nagalinda if you don't give yourself up!"

Minna whimpered. "Zax..."

"We can't help them." I hated saying the words even though I knew they were true. "He'll kill them all anyway, and make you watch. You know he will. We have to move on, and prepare ourselves to stop him, once and for all." I looked through the binoculars. One of the soldiers sat astride the winged machine, and it slowly rose up. We'd be the subject of an aerial search soon. "We have to go *now*. We need to put some space between us."

We flickered fast through ten worlds, not even staying long enough to get more than a fleeting sense of the places we passed through: a library where chained books muttered to themselves, a cave full of sealed clay jars that rocked like something inside them wanted to escape, a forest of stone columns, a crater with a glass-walled luxury resort in the middle, a huge rope net covered in clambering people with six arms each, a plain traveled by turtles the size of mountains, a hall of cells full of clamoring alien creatures, an amusement park with roller coasters and spinning rides and spikes crusted with old blood, a bubble of air at the bottom of a sea full of crab-things that fled from our arrival waving their claws in the air, and a grove of old oak trees.

I got better and better at falling asleep at will, and in the last few worlds, I was awake for barely seconds before I was asleep enough to transition again. Minna had given me so much more control over my condition, and I hoped that would enable us to leap far enough ahead of the Lector and his forces to make a difference.

Then we reached World 1133, and we met the Pilgrim, and we prepared our last stand.

Enter the Pilgrim • Empty of God • An Alliance • Into the Wreck • Ring of Hell • The Waiting

We woke up in a crudely made hut, wind howling around outside and through the cracks in the walls. A man with the face of a lion observed us placidly for a moment as we sat up, and then silently offered us bowls of mush scooped from a big pot over his fire. We were still full from our last meal, and declined, but then he poured out little cups of eye-wateringly potent liquor. I debated whether my recent recovery would be impacted negatively by accepting his offer, but decided I'd never had a constitutional vulnerability to mind-altering substances; my slide into substance abuse had been situational, and now the situation had changed. (I also worried about offending the hospitality of a man with lion's teeth.) I accepted the drink, and Minna did too – she could break down the liquid into its components in her mouth and make them harmless if she didn't want to feel the effects – and we sipped. The liquor burned a line down my throat and made warmth in my belly.

"Can you speak?" I asked.

He cocked his head and let out a series of low growls that eventually became comprehensible: "...seem to make sounds almost like speech."

"We do speak." I growled, and the language hurt my throat, but his eyes widened. "We are from elsewhere. We thank you for your kindness. We also wish to warn you. Other strangers might come. The vanguard of an invading army."

He made a sound I interpreted as a chuckle, then rose, and flung open the door to his hut. Wind rushed in, and he pushed out through it, beckoning us to follow. We went after him – I was wishing for warmer clothes – into a rocky, mountainous landscape under a steel-gray sky. We followed him a hundred meters or so to the edge of a cliff, and he gestured. There was nothing for as far as we could see but broken rocks and stunted trees… and the wreck of what looked like a spaceship, hull delicately curved but cracked like a broken cup. "I am the last Pilgrim of my cell," our host said. "The only survivor of the journey. We thought we would find the home of our creator here, but we found only desolation. I do not know if we were misled, or if the auguries were misread by mistake, or if the translation of the scripture was flawed, but this world is empty of God. My supplies, salvaged from the wreck, have dwindled. I am contemplating my end." He shrugged. "Let your conquerors come. They may have this empire of dust."

"Would you like to come with us when we leave, Pilgrim? I can't promise you what world awaits us, but I'm sure we can find one better than this."

He cocked his head again. "God is great. I never doubted that, even in this desolation. I will continue my pilgrimage, then. Perhaps God dwells elsewhere."

"Do you have any military experience?" Vicki asked.

The pilgrim blinked his great golden eyes. "Your ring speaks?"

"My ring's name is Vicki."

"Hello, Vicki." The Pilgrim nodded gravely. "I am a veteran of the stand at Adaara, yes. Those of us who survived fled here, ahead of our persecutors. We brought our weapons, in fear of pursuit, but the Assimilators were happy to see us expelled, and did not follow. Those weapons are useless, as there is nothing here even to hunt for food. But, yes. I have some experience of battle."

"Would you like to have some more?" Vicki said.

* * *

The Pilgrim asked us to tell him about our adversary. "I cannot offer myself to a cause I find unjust."

I told him about the orchard of worlds, and the Lector's Moveable Empire, and the tactics the Lector used to oppress his victims. I worried a bit that the Pilgrim wouldn't be sympathetic to our cause. What if he turned out to be a religious fanatic who revered strength above all else, or something? But it turned out he was from a small and marginalized sect that had only taken up arms to protect itself from genocide. His people were wanderers, following rumors and myths and legends about sightings of the divine, attempting to find the homeworld of God Itself... and, as a result, they were always showing up uninvited and unexpected throughout the galaxy, where they were usually greeted with suspicion and hostility by the locals. His sect was also hunted by the agents of a galactic empire he called the Assimilationists, who insisted that only *their* leader was divine. (A possibility the Pilgrim's sect had investigated and roundly rejected.) "This Lector sounds like philosophical kin to the Assimilationists," the Pilgrim said. "I would gladly lend my arms to your cause. And when we are done, you say you can take me beyond this galaxy? To worlds that cannot be reached by any ship?"

"There are as many universes as there are stars in your sky," Vicki said, rather poetically, I thought.

"Perhaps God dwells in one of those places," the Pilgrim mused. "That would explain why it's been so damnably difficult to find It. Let there be an alliance between us."

We made our way down to the wreck, dressed in bulky suits that didn't quite fit us – the Pilgrim's people were built on a somewhat larger scale than Minna and myself – but that he insisted were necessary protection. "The containment field for the engine is cracked beyond the ability of the repair drones to correct," he explained. "That's why I don't live in the ship, even though my quarters there are much more comfortable. The radiation, you see. I would have to wear these suits all the time, and I find them far too confining."

As we made our way down the narrow, crumbling path to the ship, the Pilgrim and Vicki discussed tactics. Vicki was very excited by the weapons the Pilgrim described, though most of his explanations made only sketchy sense to me: "In terms of small arms we have masers, and directed plasma beams, and kinetic weapons aplenty of course."

"The repair drones," Vicki said. "Could their cutting torches be reconfigured into offensive weapons, or could other arms be mounted on their chassis?"

"In theory," the Pilgrim said, "though I lack the necessary skills to reprogram them, and we have no military drones capable of overriding and commandeering them."

"Oh, just let me within range of their operating systems, and I'll do the rest." The relish in Vicki's voice made me happy, even though I knew it was the precursor to violence. "Tell me a little more about this engine, too..."

I fell back and talked to Minna. "We need to prepare for worst-case scenarios."

"What do you mean?"

"Vicki told me about spies, in their world, who sometimes had a false tooth implanted, filled with poison, so if they were captured, they could bite down on it, and die before they could be forced to reveal secrets."

Minna shuddered. "Zax..."

"Please, Minna. We have to be realistic." I told her what I had in mind, and she agreed. Removing one of my own back teeth, hollowing it out, filling it with one of her concoctions, and replacing it was well within her abilities. She promised to do so once we settled in for the night.

The Pilgrim led us to the main hatch of his ship, *Sojourn*, the most accessible entry hatch half-buried in the dirt. The ship as a whole stuck up at a slight angle, so we had to enter and make our way carefully on the slanted floors. There were still lights inside – "The power source here will run for centuries, as long as the containment field doesn't degrade any further" – and the hallways were wide and spacious, befitting a species of two-and-a-half-meter-tall bipedal felines.

I'd expected corpses, but there were none. "We return to flame when we die," the Pilgrim explained. "The ship has a great incinerator, and I presided over their funerals. Every member of my sect is a priest, so they had the proper rites. I will not be granted that, alas, but they say God is forgiving. I ask only that if I fall in the coming conflict, you give me to fire, if you can."

I wanted to reassure him that it wouldn't come to that, but I knew better. "Of course we will," I said.

"Keep your suits on, or you'll need final rites yourselves," Vicki said. "The radiation levels here are appalling."

The Pilgrim showed us the armory, full of gleaming weapons that were all curves and shining edges. War was an art for his people, it seemed. He took Vicki to the bridge of the ship, half the panels flickering and the other half dark, at least until Vicki got into the computer systems and cleaned things up. The Pilgrim sat in a great chair in the center of the bridge, which was tilted slightly, making it into a recliner.

"This is wonderful," Vicki said. "Your weapons are more advanced than anything I've seen."

"Stolen from the Assimilationists," the Pilgrim said. "In order to fight them, we needed to be their equal in battle. It's a shame we can't fly anymore."

"Those systems are far beyond my ability to repair, alas," Vicki said. "But having even a stationary weapons platform is rather more than we expected. With the drones providing mobile units, and time for us to prepare the ground… yes, we might have a chance, especially against a small advance squad like the Lector is likely to use."

Minna went off to look at the ship's gardens, and returned hours later to say that she'd tweaked the plants to absorb radiation, which would help them grow, but that they weren't safe to eat, and they wouldn't be able to cleanse the ship fully since there was constantly new radiation leaking from the engine. "They are happier plants now too, so I am happier also." She was profoundly bored by all the tech and weapons talk, so went outside to look at the sparse local flora.

That night we camped beyond the range of the radiation and discussed our preparations. We knew *where* the Lector was going to appear; we just didn't know when, or with what kind of force. We knew he'd survived a significant explosion unscathed. "That knowledge provides us with the threshold we must greatly exceed," Vicki said, and talked about how to do that.

I half-slept in my strange fugue state, watching the stars move. There were two moons in this sky, one large and one small. I knew I'd lived beneath one thousand one hundred and thirty-four skies, counting my own, but how many *stars*? How many other inhabited worlds in each of those skies? I saw only the smallest piece of any given universe, and each one might very well teem with as much variety as this one, with its galactic empire and countless alien races. The vastness of reality was dizzying, and staggering, and I knew I'd never see even the smallest fragment of the smallest fraction of the smallest degree of the whole curve. That was true of anyone, though, even those who lived in the same universe their entire lives, because every world was vast. The Lector, with his relentless hunger to move and control and command, didn't seem to understand that. As smart as he was, he wasn't smart enough to know that he'd barely glimpsed any of the places he'd brought under his heel. None of them mattered to him, individually, any more than any given person's life did. He would argue that every world and every life was insignificant when considered against the span of the infinite... but *nothing* mattered against the span of the infinite, so if you wanted to care about anything at all, you had to care about the small things. There was nothing in the multiverse *but* small things.

I wondered if the worry that kept the Lector up at night – if anything did – was the deep and secret knowledge that he was just as insignificant as everything else.

In the morning, when the Pilgrim was rested, we began our preparations, and continued them for over a week. The repair drones

– crablike machines a little smaller than me – began to transport panels and struts from the ship, creating structures scattered around the valley and up the hillsides, each one with a cannon or two salvaged from the ship's offensive systems, arranged to provide overlapping fields of fire. Vicki could control the whole array from anywhere within a few kilometers. They were all solid enough bunkers, and none looked like a headquarters, except the ship itself, where, of course, we had absolutely no intention of being when the battle came.

Drones were repurposed and made into war machines, armored and armed, and they scuttled in the brush to await the enemy. Minna and I carefully covered some of them in dust and stones and plants – Minna made it so the weeds would even stay alive and grow on the machines – so they could hide better and blend into the terrain. The Pilgrim and Vicki ran various scenarios and tweaked the parameters of our position, and Minna and I moved as far away as we could and covered our ears while guns boomed and sizzled. "I don't like this, Zax!" she shouted.

"I don't either!" I shouted back. "It will all be over soon!"

One way or another. My tongue touched the new tooth Minna had implanted in the back of my mouth.

We always had a drone or one of us watching the hut where we'd arrived, though it was unlikely the Lector would arrive without us realizing it. The hut was gone, torn down, and the whole area was now ringed with weapons and mined with explosives, all set to go off the moment anything tripped the sensors. The Pilgrim thought that every other preparation was redundant, because nothing could survive that ring of hell. Minna, who'd seen the Lector's Moveable Empire in action, was less confident, and I concurred.

These have been long days. I've spent so long hurtling forward, whether I wanted to or not, that I have no practice at all with patiently waiting.

* * *

The place where the hut used to be just exploded. The whole cliff-top is burning white-hot.

Here we go.

Epilogue

This brief epilogue to the Journals of Zaxony Dyad Euphony Delatree is written by the hand of the Lector himself: Supreme Ruler of the Collectorium, High Priest of the Church of the Sanguine, Defender of the Skies, The Crown Incarnate, He Who Tends the Grasses, The Ender of History, Champion of Champions, The Terror Above, The Wheel-Breaker, The Ice Axe, The Pure Vein, The Broodfather – well, it goes on. It seems every world I conquer wishes to gift me with their own unique sobriquet. Some whisper their names for me with the awe due a prophesied king, and others spit it with fury at a foreign interloper, but I accept them all equally.

I will shelve this journal in the office of whatever world I eventually settle on as my Prime Throne, and encourage visitors, penitents, and acolytes to read it as a cautionary tale, and as a testament to my greatness. Zaxony began with natural abilities I could only dream of having for my own, and if he had he possessed the courage and the strength, he would be the one dripping titles from the end of his name – but it is not just power that makes a king. It is will. I had the will, and so I took his power.

Zaxony attempted to make a last stand to thwart me. He failed, obviously. He is in custody, in a filthy room on the grounds of this laughable fortress. He has been filled with stimulants to keep him from sleeping his way out of this situation. I will go see him, soon.

We are old friends, Zaxony and I. In a sense, I owe everything I have now to him.

For those reasons, I will execute him with my own hand, and will do so as painlessly as possible, given that my chosen tool of execution is a very large knife.

Then I will move his body to a sterile room, and apply much smaller knives. I have been eager to dissect him. Given the wonders I found in his blood, what else might I find in his body?

My story continues, but this is where the tale of Zaxony must finish.

Thus ends a chronicle of failure.

Sniper Fire • The Lector Dances • Slugs in the Garden • The Skeleton's Name • Implosive • Zax in the Box

So, that didn't go as planned. (Vicki says no battle plan remains intact after first contact, which they might have mentioned before.)

We saw the entry point to this world light up in a cascade of ordnance, and I thought, "Is that it? Is the Lector gone?" Minna and I were near one of the bunkers, so we dove inside and used our radios to contact the Pilgrim, who was on a nearby peak, armed with a sniper rifle, watching.

"Only one person came through," the Pilgrim said. "They had blue fur, and they were holding some sort of great beast on a chain. They triggered the explosives."

I groaned. The Lector must have gotten into the habit of sending scouts through first, in case Minna left traps again. He'd probably done it when he called for us in that place with the tiny people, too, and we just didn't see it.

"More people have appeared since," the Pilgrim said. "The ones you described. A skeleton... a slouching girl in a dirty jacket with a hood... six more soldiers and beasts... they are sitting up, moving out, securing the area, observing our defenses. Ah. Here he is now. Your Lector. I am lining up my shot."

We could see the arrival point from our position halfway up a steep slope, and I thought I recognized the Lector, though at this distance he was just a black blur. Minna handed me her glasses, and I looked through them, the Lector leaping into focus – gesturing, directing his soldiers to head down to the fortifications in the valley, Polly and the torturer flanking him. Smoke rose around him, and the whole area was rubble and ashes, and, at a glance, he *looked* like a conqueror, come to bring death – except his wispy hair and steel-rimmed glasses were incongruous in that armor, like a professor playing dress-up for a party.

The Lector staggered backward, and a shimmering blue field lit up around his body. Twice more he staggered, and the blue shimmer flickered. The Pilgrim was firing his rifle, and whatever energy or projectile it fired was making a dent in the Lector's force field.

Polly leapt in front of the Lector, and some invisible beam cut her neatly in two, a diagonal line running from her left shoulder down to her right hip. She fell to the ground in pieces and howled, then began dragging her torso toward her legs. She didn't bleed, any more than a turnip cut in half would, but her body didn't do much to stop the beam, either, which drove the Lector to his knees. "Keep it up!" Vicki crowed from my hand.

The Lector rose, rushed forward, and dove right off the cliff, plummeting to the valley floor below. I remembered his leap from a hotel balcony, and how he'd landed unscathed. I tracked down with the glasses to see him dusting himself off at the base of the cliff.

The torturer, meanwhile, was calmly assembling a tripod and screwing together lengths of cylindrical metal, activities which did not fill me with confidence.

"Minna!" the Lector's voice boomed. "Are you ready to end this? Your little small potatoes revolution has grown tedious!"

"Inputting firing solution," Vicki said.

The guns came alive. They focused their fire on the Lector, but also took the time to pick off his soldiers and their monsters, which snuffled and snarled on the end of their chains. The guns aimed for the skeleton, too, but he was down in the crater where the hut had been, and none of the weapons were angled quite right to strike him there as he calmly continued his work. A few of the drones went scuttling up toward him instead.

The Lector moved, impossibly quickly, a pale yellow shimmer in front of his face, dodging the beams and projectiles, somersaulting and dancing and spinning – and laughing as he came. "He has some sort of tactical heads-up display!" Vicki shouted. "And that armor is an exoskeleton, moving faster than his body could otherwise. He has some kind of system predicting the path of the attacks and dodging. Inputting randomization as a countermeasure. Pilgrim, can you hit him?"

"Not from this position."

"Hrm. Then can you kill that skeleton?"

"Affirmative." I watched as the skeleton's skull exploded, onyx eyes falling to the ground... but the skeleton was not at all perturbed by this, and screwed the last bit of metal onto the tripod-mounted gun he'd been building.

"Can you take out the cannon?"

"I'm trying. It's not as fragile as the skeleton. Shots are bouncing off."

The skeleton reached down, patted blindly at the ground, and then picked up one of the onyx eyes and fitted it into a scope on top of the cannon.

"Minna, taunt the Lector please," Vicki said.

We'd been prepared for this. She cleared her throat. "Lector! You have tried to kill me but you cannot kill me. I will always salt your ground, dig up your roots, burn your branches. I will raise armies against you and you will fall, in this world and every world. You are not smarter or better than me."

Her voice boomed from the PA of the wrecked ship at the heart of the valley, and the Lector began to dance and pirouette his way toward that instead. Occasionally one of the beams or projectiles clipped him, now, spinning him around, but they didn't stop him.

"I've met potted plants more dangerous than you, Daisy!" he called.

"Your turn, Zax," Vicki said.

"Lector, it doesn't have to be like this."

The Lector stopped, and took a beam full in the chest, knocking him flat, but then he rolled and dodged before Vicki could concentrate more fire on him. He crouched behind a boulder, out of sight, but his voice boomed. "Zaxony. Your talking corsage found you, did she? I was perfectly willing to let you go. You're a fool to let her drag you into her war. Now you both have to die. I am cultivating a great and glorious garden, and the two of you are *slugs*. And your little pinky ring, too."

"Why don't you come and get us? We're right here, waiting."

"Do you think I'm afraid to walk into that ship?" he bellowed. "Do you think I'm worried about whatever pitiful defenses you've set up in there, whatever ludicrous little traps you've set?" He paused. "Well, in point of fact, I am, at least a little. Alan, is the cannon ready?"

The skeleton clanged his knuckles against the shaft of the cannon three times in reply.

"Pilgrim, destroy that weapon!" Vicki cried.

The Pilgrim fired his sniper rifle, but the shots didn't make much of an impact on the cannon, though they shattered Alan's body further. The cannon was at least semi-autonomous, because it moved and pointed toward the wreck, onyx scope glistening.

"Blow them up, please," the Lector said.

Minna and I ducked. The cannon fired whatever it fired, and the world went white.

The idea was, if all else failed, we'd lure the Lector toward the wreck. Once he was within the blast radius, the drones stationed inside would pull the failsafes and let the engine breach containment entirely, and then… an implosion, essentially, sucking everything within a hundred meters down into a bit of highly radioactive mass the size of a pebble. The cannon did a perfectly fine job of breaching containment and triggering the implosion. There was a flash, a brief hurricane of displaced air, and the ship vanished, along with much of the ground around it and several of our nearer gun encampments.

The Lector was a good ten meters outside the implosion's range, though, and safe from the worst of the radiation, too. He stood unsteadily and laughed. "That was almost impressive! I don't suppose you were in there, though, were you?"

"The best we can hope for, right now, is that he thinks we're dead," Vicki said.

More soldiers began to appear in the crater beside the cannon, waking up and fanning out. They were met by our drones, and small arms fire clattered. The drones might slow them down, but wouldn't stop them.

"We have to reach the Pilgrim and escape," I said.

Minna nodded, and we slipped out of the bunker and hurried, low to the ground and (we hoped) hidden by brush, toward the worst-case-scenario rendezvous point. The Pilgrim would meet us in the shade of a nearby boulder, equidistant between our two positions, and then we would give him a sedative and jump to the next world and figure out what to do from there–

That was the plan, anyway, but the soldiers had a flying machine, and they caught us instead, dropping an actual net on top of us, and then fired darts at us – not tranquilizers, or even paralytics, but stimulants. My eyeballs ached and my blood fizzed and I drummed my feet against the ground. I couldn't have slept if I'd wanted to. I didn't want to. I fumbled Vicki off my finger and shoved them into Minna's hands. "Run, Minna," I said. "Sleep away. Go, both of you."

"Zax–"

"*Go*. I'll find you, if I can."

"Be… be safe, Zax," Vicki said. "We'll never stop fighting."

Minna kissed my cheek, and then her eyes rolled back, and she fell asleep. No one can dose Minna with anything against her will. I'm a lot more adaptable than I used to be, but I'll never be a match for her.

I hoped the Pilgrim was all right, that they hadn't caught him, that he'd survived. He'd fought for us, knowing he might die, and I wished I'd gotten to know him better.

One of the soldiers uncapped and drank a tiny vial of something, fell over, and vanished before he hit the ground. Off in pursuit of Minna, no doubt. She could handle one soldier.

Two more of the blue-furred troops grabbed me and dragged me to my feet. I couldn't stop babbling, the stimulants rushing in my blood: "We're trying to help you, don't you get it, we're fighting him, you could fight him, you could stab him, or poison him, he doesn't have armor on the inside does he, or maybe he does, but he took your world, don't you want to stop him, you can never go home, did he promise he'd take you back, he's lying, he doesn't know how, he'll ever know how, he will just eat and eat and eat worlds forever–"

"You're very lucky we aren't allowed to knock you unconscious," one of them said, and tossed me over the back of the flying machine, and carried me away.

They were building a headquarters already, unleashing small machines that assembled the components for structures out of the dirt and rock around us. One of the first things they built was a cell, just a box of bars, and they threw me into it. The Pilgrim wasn't in there, at least. Maybe he'd come break me out. That seemed like the sort of thing he might do. I walked around and around in my three-meters-by-three-meters of dirt, the sun sending the shadow of steel mesh across me and the ground, and I babbled.

They'd taken away my bag, and my journal, so I couldn't even record my thoughts, and I had so *many* thoughts and they were so *fast*, thoughts of the Lector and his conquest and most of all his mind, his twisty, tricksy, deep, seeing-all-contingencies mind, his terrible mind, that engine of an empire, intellect without empathy, a diagnostic device that could apprehend almost anything except the terrible flaw at the center of itself, that mind that mind that mind–

When I started to stumble, they'd shoot me with more stimulants.

It was night when the Lector came to me.

A Conversation Between Old Friends • Biting Down • Stabbed • Worms in the Apples • Infinite Time • The Falls

The Lector wasn't wearing his armor, and looked much as he had when we first met, clean white coat and all. He unfolded a little camp chair and sat down on it outside my box, gazing at me through the bars. "Hello, Zaxony. You had some sort of local confederate helping you, hmm? One of my warriors was found in a sniper's nest, beside a rifle, his neck broken… and his vial of serum missing. Whoever your helper was, he's chased after Minna, it seems. Fear not. We'll find them all. As you've seen, even with superior firepower and prepared ground and the element of surprise, you're hopeless against me."

"So smart," I babbled. "So smart, you're so smart, you see all the angles, don't you, around every corner."

"You flatter me, Zaxony. I read your journal. I even took the liberty of writing the ending, since you won't have the chance." He withdrew the slim object from his pocket and held it up. "Your writing has improved a bit since we began, but the mind behind it is still so terribly naïve. The things you think of me! Your career as a social worker with delusions of grandeur does not qualify you to understand a psyche as complex as my own. You think I act out of fear or insecurity? You think that contemplating the infinite makes me feel small? I will cup infinity in the palm of my hand. Then you'll see who's small. I'm going to kill you, my dear boy. It grieves me, as you are my oldest friend, but you have pushed me too far. I will cut you open, and squeeze every gland I find, and see if there's something of use in that body of yours to serve the needs of the Moveable Empire."

"Always thinking, don't you get tired, don't you ever want to stop and rest?"

He crossed his legs and looked at me thoughtfully, as though considering my question. "There are predators in some seas that must move constantly, or else they'll die. I suppose I'm a bit like those. I am driven to find new worlds, and improve them. But this relentless forward motion is temporary. Once I can revisit old worlds, and stop sleeping unless I want to sleep, and choose my destinations – then I will choose a homeworld suitable for my purposes, and it will become the center of an expanding web. I know this process might take a long time. Decades. Even centuries. But my traveling case produces all the serum I want, and I've found technology that should enable me to live forever. Forever! Do you understand that, Zaxony? Infinite space is nothing to fear if one has infinite life in which to explore and master that space. In a few hundred years, I don't think I'll even remember your name. No one else will, either."

"Such a mind, such a mind, and you use it for *this*, why would you use it for *this*, you could have done so much good."

"I have done good," he said. "I am doing good. I will do good. You are standing in my way. Soon you will be lying on a slab instead. Stand back, Zaxony, clasp your hands behind your back, turn your face up to me and bare your throat, and I will make your death quick. It's time to go to sleep one last time. Perhaps some of the fools who believe in gods are right after all, and you'll just step out of this life and through a door that leads into another." He stepped toward the cage and smiled. "I doubt it, but if there is a heaven, I'll find it eventually, and conquer that, too. I can't see why it should have any gods before me."

He opened the door and came inside, still holding my diary. He looked down at it, then back up at me. "I was going to keep this, as a cautionary tale, but upon reflection I think I'll just incinerate it along with your remains, once I'm through examining you. You're a failure, but if people read your story, they might… get ideas. Think they can learn from your mistakes, perhaps, and succeed where you couldn't." He threw it at my feet. "Yes. I think it's better if no part of you proves to be immortal, not even your terribly prosaic thoughts."

I shivered and jittered and trembled, then scooped up the journal and tucked it inside my jacket, where I'd carried it for so long, close to my heart. Having my life story close to me made me feel a little better. But only a little. I didn't have a lot of dynamic emotional range right then, as jacked up as I was by stimulants.

The Lector reached into his coat for his weapon and then approached me slowly, carefully, the long and gleaming knife in his right hand.

"Lector," I said, and he paused, close enough to touch. "I want you to know how sorry I am. I never wanted it to come to this."

His eyes widened in alarm. "What do you…" he began.

I threw my arms around him, hugged him close, and bit down on my false tooth just as he stabbed me.

I never wanted to poison myself. Minna was relieved when she realized that. What I needed was an escape hatch. I knew the Lector would want me to suffer, and that he could keep me awake for a long time, if he wanted, and trap me in place. I asked Minna to come up with a sedative, something so strong it would fall just short of killing me, powerful enough to override any stimulant he might force into my system. She complied.

So I went to sleep, with the Lector in my arms. I'd done the same things scores of times before.

The difference was, this time, the Lector was wide awake.

* * *

I woke in a field of wildflowers, my side throbbing with pain and my head even worse. I reached down through the rip in my shirt, and the flesh of my side was tender, but there was no deep wound, just a bloody scratch. Thank the spheres I'd had the Lector's arms pinned and spoiled his strike. The stimulant was out of my system, but the sedative had brought on a nasty hangover.

The Lector. I turned my head, and there he was, sprawled on his back, staring up at the twin suns in the sky, his eyes shining reflections. "There are holes, Zaxony," he said. "Holes all through creation, and there are things coming through, there are things *wriggling through them–*"

"Lector!" someone shouted – one of his soldiers, I was sure. I grabbed onto the Lector, closed my eyes, and willed myself to sleep the way Minna had taught me. It wasn't easy with my head pounding, but I managed.

This time I opened my eyes waist deep in a lagoon, full of reefs and sinuous snakelike fish. The spot reminded me of the island where I'd found Vicki, and I looked for a lighthouse, but there was none. This island was barely an outcropping above endless waves. The Lector rolled over in the water, giggling, and reached out to touch an outcropping of coral that protruded just above the water.

"Look at all the little holes," he said. "Trypophobia is what they call the fear of clusters of small holes, but people should fear the *big* holes, and the things coming through them. There are worms in the apples in the orchard of worlds, Zaxony." He looked at me, and his eyes were blank and watering and his mouth was slack and drooling.

His mind. His terrible wonderful mind. I hadn't been able to kill him, but I'd broken him. Just like I'd broken Ana. "What did you see?" I asked.

"The journey takes forever when you're awake," he whispered. "I understood infinite worlds but I did not understand infinite time."

Something big splashed in the water nearby, so I grabbed him, and transitioned again. I didn't know if the Lector's soldiers could fix whatever I'd done to his brain, but I didn't want to give them the chance.

"How are you still here?" he said in the next world. We were in some kind of children's playground, surrounded by small humanoids with hair that writhed like anemone tendrils, and the little ones and their parents ran screaming when we appeared. He touched my cheek. "You can't live so long. You can't live for eons. I saw the holes. I almost touched one. I wonder what's *inside it*–"

I grabbed him again, and flickered, and flickered, and flickered. I had to outrun his soldiers.

Some dozen or more worlds later, I stopped. I lost count. I was in World 1150, maybe, give or take.

We woke – or rather *I* woke, the Lector just appeared – on a narrow shelf of rock above a waterfall, the biggest cataract I'd ever seen, the bottom of the falls lost in clouds of prismatic foam. There were spikes of rock visible through the mist down there, hundreds of meters below. The boom of the rushing water so huge it annihilated thought. I covered my ears and shrank back against the stone, terrified by the proximity of the drop.

The Lector said something, but I couldn't understand him, and he leaned close and shouted into my ear. "We don't matter," the Lector said. "The holes go all through us now. All through everything. I have lived a million years, in between, and I still don't matter. If I don't matter, Zaxony, if I don't matter… then nothing matters."

Then he patted me on the shoulder, in a friendly way, took two steps straight backward, and fell. I screamed and lunged for him, but I missed – fortunately, or he would have pulled me down with him. I watched him fall. He struck one of the spikes of rock, and, whatever defenses he had, they weren't enough to counteract that, and he bounced, red and ragged, to disappear in the mist.

I drank from the spray of the falls, then I covered my ears, and wept in the endless noise, and finally fell asleep.

The Feasting Hall • A Musing on the Causes of Madness • Who's Asking? • The Chariot

When I woke up, Minna was there, and the Pilgrim, too, though he was wearing a voluminous hood that hid his leonine features. I thought I must be dreaming; maybe I'd appeared in another patch of coma-flowers.

Minna kissed my face and said, "Zax, oh Zax you are here, how are you here, how did you escape?"

Not a dream. "The Lector is dead," I croaked. "I tried to stop him, but I missed. He fell. The emperor fell. The empire fell."

"You have not eaten in worlds, have you?" Vicki said from Minna's finger. "Let's get some food in you, and then we'll hear your story."

They carried me from the dusty yard where I'd landed into the upside-down hull of a ship, which was it seemed a sort of feasting hall, full of people who looked much like me, except brawnier and wearing more golden armbands.

Minna had some gold in her bag – it's valuable in lots of places – and the proprietors were happy to serve us roasted meat and root vegetables and ale in exchange for a few pieces. We sat where I could lean against a wall and stare into space for a while. "Pilgrim," I said finally. "How are you here?"

"I stole a dose of serum from a soldier, and in the next world, found Minna. We hid from the soldiers, and then… she made me drink her blood."

"Just a sip of sap. Enough to let him travel, not enough to remake all his blood always. I will only do that if he wants it."

"I am yet undecided," he murmured. "We jumped ahead, a bit, and then Minna said we should wait, in case you came through. The gem did not think it likely."

"Minna told us you had a sedative of last resort, but my simulations indicated that the Lector would pursue and recapture you even if you fled," Vicki said. "Do please tell me where those simulations went wrong?"

I told them what I'd done. What the Lector had said, about infinite time, and worms in the apples in the orchard of worlds. And how he'd died. My recitation was dull and unexciting, and they took it in solemnly.

Minna touched my hand. "You are not a killer, Zax. You still are not that."

I stared at the scarred wooden tabletop. "I broke his mind. That's like killing him. Maybe worse, given how much he valued his mind."

"The things he said," Vicki mused. "About the holes. The worms. It's all very similar to what your first companion Ana said, isn't it, after she transitioned awake? How curious. Did they see something real, or something their minds couldn't adequately comprehend? If the subjective sense of the passage of time really does seem vast when you make the journey awake, maybe it's the perception of endless time that damages their minds. Without sufficient stimuli, or with only distressing stimuli, a mind is apt to break..."

"Someone new," Minna said. "Coming in." We all looked at the door to the hall. The Pilgrim reached under his robes, where he doubtless had some sort of weapon. We waited for one of the Lector's soldiers, or for a reconstituted Polly, or someone equally dreadful to come through.

Instead a big man in a leather apron walked in and called, "Is there anyone named Zaxony here? Zaxony, ah, Delatree?"

After a moment I said, "Who's asking?"

He cocked his head. "If you're Zaxony, she says to tell you she's the long lost love of your life."

I blinked. "What? Who?"

The man jerked his head toward the door. "Go find out for yourself. And ask her where she got that chariot. It's nicer than any I've ever seen."

I rose, walking slowly to the door, with Minna and the Pilgrim at my back, and Vicki once more twinkling on my finger. I paused at the threshold, and then pushed through.

I saw the chariot first – it was a gleaming filigreed half-sphere with plush seats inside, the chassis resting on delicate wheels, and there was someone sitting in the rear, head sprawled against the back of the seat, snoring. A circlet rested on his shaved head, and wires ran from the crown down into the body of the chariot itself.

Then I saw the woman leaning against the chariot. She was dressed in an immaculate black linen shirt and a skirt that stopped just a little above her knee-high, silver-buckled boots. Her hair was dark, her eye shadow darker, her lips red like wine, her smile warm as a fire on a snowy day.

"Hello, Zax." She spoke in a language my virus didn't have to translate. "I'm sorry it took me so long to reach out. We couldn't risk approaching you while the mad professor was still in pursuit – there are things we have to tell you that are way too dangerous for him to know."

I stumbled forward, my mouth dry. "Ana? Is that… How are you here, how are you alive, how are you sane?"

"You aren't the only wanderer through the worlds, Zax." She stepped toward me, took my hands, then glanced at Minna. "Are you two, ah… together? I don't mean to overstep… We've caught a few glimpses of you in the past few dozen worlds, but I wasn't sure…"

"What? No, we're not, I mean, Ana – Ana. It's *you*."

"It's *her*?" Vicki said, and Minna said, "Shh, let this be beautiful."

"It's me." Ana kissed me, deeply, her hands clasping mine, and I closed my eyes and breathed her in and tasted her. I wondered if

I'd actually died in the battle with the Lector. I wondered if I was in the heaven he'd scoffed at.

Ana took a step back, looked me up and down, then kicked the wheel of her chariot. The snoring man blinked and looked around. His eyes were violet. "Oh," he said vaguely. "We're here."

"Zax, meet Sorlyn. He's my Sleeper."

"Your… Ana. What is going *on*?"

"More than you know. Let's go inside and get a drink. You can introduce me to your friends. Then we need to have a conversation." She sighed. "About holes in the space between the worlds." She sighed again. "And about the things coming *through* those holes, and their intentions." A third sigh, deeper than the others. "And about what we're going to do about them." Then she twinkled a grin. "I bet you're wide awake *now*, aren't you, Zax?"

She looped her arm through mine, and we walked into the hall together, through yet another door, and into a greater unknown than ever before.

Acknowledgments

I started writing stories about Zax a few years ago for my Patreon, where I create a new story each month for my supporters, so first I'd like to thank those patrons for providing a platform for me to experiment with new characters and ideas. (The character changed a lot from those stories to this book, but there are still fragments of those narratives bobbing around in here.)

Thanks to Eleanor Teasdale at Angry Robot for acquiring this book; she inherited me from another editor, and it means a lot that she decided to continue working with me, especially when I pitched this weird multiverse book instead of the space opera she was probably expecting. Thanks also to Gemma Creffield at Angry Robot for heroic acts of organization and coordination. Simon Spanton edited this book, as he did my previous one, and once again he saved me from myself and made it a stronger novel. Paul Simpson did heroic work copyediting (I swear I really tried to keep all those numbers straight). My agent Ginger Clark continues to be my greatest supporter and advocate. My day-job boss Liza (to whom this is half dedicated) and my co-workers at *Locus* are always supportive when I need to vanish for a while to work on books.

On a personal level, my wife Heather Shaw and son River are immensely tolerant when I talk to myself and sit hunched at my desk for hours. River is thirteen now, with an inventive mind, and talking over ideas with him is a blast. I hope he enjoys reading this book.

My nearest and dearest support and love me even when I'm cranky and distracted and rambling on about novel ideas, and so my gratitude goes out as always to Ais, Amanda, Emily, Katrina, and Sarah. My community of fellow writers is vast and important and too numerous to fully enumerate, but I'd like to especially thank Daryl Gregory, Jenn Reese and Chris East, Effie Seiberg, and Molly Tanzer for providing consistently sympathetic ears on matters of craft and business and other things.

Finally, thanks to you, for coming with me on this journey. Sleep well.

Are you a fan of Tim Pratt? Why not try his seminal space opera series, The Axiom?

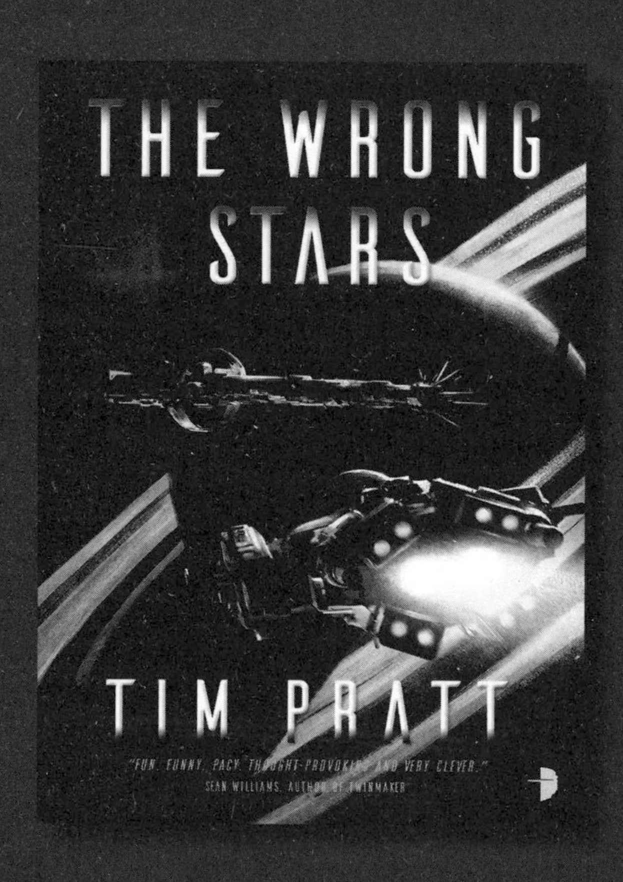

Read the first chapter of The Wrong Stars here!

CHAPTER 1

Callie floated, feet hooked over a handrail in the observation deck, and looked through the viewport at the broken ship beyond. The wreck hung motionless, a dark irregular shape – a bit of human debris where no such debris should be. Was this a crisis, or an opportunity? Every unexpected event could be one or the other, and sometimes they were both.

The dead ship was long and bullet-shaped, pointlessly aerodynamic, apart from a bizarre eruption of flanges, fins, and spikes at one end that looked like the embellishments of a mad welder. The wrecked craft was far smaller than Callie's own ship, the *White Raven,* a fast cruiser just big enough for her crew of five people (or four, or maybe six, depending on how you defined "people") to live comfortably along with whatever freight or prisoners they had to transport. If the *White Raven* was a family home, the wreck was more like a studio apartment.

Ashok floated into the compartment, orienting himself with tiny puffs of air that burst from his fingertips and heels – showy and unnecessary, but he had a gift for turning simple things into engineering problems he could solve in complicated ways. He hovered with his head near hers, sharing her view – though it probably looked a lot different to him. "Oh captain, my captain."

She glanced at his complex profile and grunted. "You got new eyes?"

He shook his head. "These are wearables, not integrated. I'm giving them a test run before I implant them."

"That's almost cautious, by your standards."

He grinned, insofar as he was physically able. One of the lenses on the array attached to his face rotated and lengthened toward the viewport. "So do we get to crack the mystery ship open and see what's inside?"

She went *hmm*, pretending she hadn't already decided. "Last time I let you clamber into a wreck, you lost an arm."

Ashok held up his current prosthetic. The translucent diamond housing revealed glimpses of the mechanical motion within as he flexed his hand, which was really more like a nest of tiny, versatile manipulator arms. "That was just an opportunity for an upgrade, cap. I say we fly over with torches and cut a hole and poke our heads in and look around." No surprise there. Ashok believed in radical self-improvement, and every mystery was a potential upgrade in waiting.

"I like the enthusiasm, Ashok, but we're still factfinding. This doesn't look like any human ship I've ever seen, and it doesn't look like a Liar vessel, either, despite all that weird shit on the stern. Didn't the Jovian Imperative try to solve its toxic waste problem by launching tubes full of poison randomly into space? What if this is one of those?"

"Space is big, so throwing bad stuff into it wasn't such a terrible idea, as far as terrible ideas go. But that's not a waste container – our sensors sniffed it thoroughly. No toxins or bad radiation. Besides, your boy Shall just identified the vessel."

"He's not my boy," she said, but she was too interested in the wreck to put much growl into the ritual denial. "So what is it?"

"Once Shall filtered out all the weird stuff welded to the ship's ass, the profile matches a model in the historical database." Ashok lifted his chin, which, unlike the rest of his head, still looked like a baseline human's. "That, captain, is a goldilocks ship."

Callie frowned. He might as well have told her it was a Viking longboat or an *Apollo* module. "From the bad old days? Before we had bridge generators?"

"A genuine old timey antique. It's gotta be about five hundred years old." Ashok gave himself a little spin, changing his orientation so she was looking at his feet, because actually being still for any length of time was outside his considerable skillset.

"A goldilocks ship. Wow. Weren't they propelled by atomic bombs?"

"Pretty much, yeah, at least the first wave, and this was one of the earliest models launched. Looks like it's had some modification since then, though. The goldilocks ships were no-frills. They didn't go in for decorative S&M spikes."

"Maybe a pirate crew found it and tried to make it look more badass?"

"That ship is *old*, cap. No pirate would want it for anything other than scrap, or to sell to a collector."

"So what's it doing here? Goldilocks ships aren't supposed to come back. That's the whole point. They took one-way journeys, way out, trips of desperation and exploration. Now five hundred years later it's just floating in trans-Neptunian space? By cosmic terms it's practically back where it started."

Ashok nodded. "That's the big juicy mystery. No way that ship came back from anywhere, right? It's not like they had Tanzer drives back then. They weren't zipping around the galaxy. Unless they found a bunch of plutonium lying around on their colony planet and built more bombs to stick up the ship's butt, there was no coming back."

"No mystery at all, then, Ashok. This is just as far as they got. The crew took off on their brave voyage, reached the edge of our solar system, suffered some critical failure, and... that's it. Nobody ever expected to hear from the goldilocks ships again, so no one went looking."

"You think that ship spent the past five hundred years drifting among the iceballs out here and nobody noticed? With all the surveys and mining vessels tagging everything even halfway interesting?"

Callie shrugged. "You said it yourself. Space is big. The ship was just overlooked. What's the alternative?" The idea of this enigmatic ship breaking down centuries ago was comforting, in a way, because failure was common, plausible, and non-threatening, unlike most of the other possible explanations.

Ashok wasn't having it. "I don't know what the alternative is, but there's something else going on here. Who made all those modifications? Space vandals drifting by with buckets of epoxy and loads of sheet metal? Outsider artists among the asteroids?"

"Seems unlikely."

"And what about the energy readings? Parts of the ship are still warm."

"I know. They were made to run a long time, the goldilocks ships. Some of them are *still* completing their journeys. Could just be some old systems ticking along in the midst of critical failures."

"Nah, these readings are weird, cap. The whole thing is weird." Ashok sounded quite chipper about it, as he did about most things. "It's a mystery. Mysteries are great. Let's peel it open and see if it's wrapped around an enigma."

"I hate mysteries," Callie said, not entirely accurately. "You always think it's going to be a box full of gold, but usually it's a box full of spiders."

Ashok made a noise that might have been a snort in a baseline human. "And yet you always end up opening the lid, don't you?"

"What can I say?" Callie unhooked her feet and pushed off toward the doorway leading deeper into the ship. "I like gold more than I hate spiders."

"Launching magnetic tethers." The voice in Callie's headset had the clipped tones of someone who'd grown up under Europa's domes, which meant it was the navigator Janice, and not the pilot Drake – he was from one of the Greater Toronto arcologies, populated mostly by the children of Caribbean immigrants, and his accent was a lot more melodious to the captain's ear.

Watching from the window in the airlock, her angle was wrong to see the metal tethers bursting from the side of the *White Raven*, but seconds later Janice said, "Contact. Connection secure." Janice didn't have a particle of romance in her soul, which was a good quality in the person who was supposed to tell you where you were going and where you'd been.

As soon as the airlock unsealed and yawned open, Ashok launched himself out, snapping a carabiner on to one of the steel lines that now attached the *White Raven* to the dark wreck a scant thousand meters away. He would have spacewalked without any safety gear at all if Callie had allowed it: he liked spinning to and fro in the void with nothing but puffs of compressed air to get him back home, but Callie insisted on a modicum of safety in her crew, at least in micro terms. On the macro level, she sent them into danger all the time, with herself at the front of the line. Space had a billion ways to kill you, so you prevented the ones you could, and didn't waste time worrying about the ones you couldn't. If you got hung up on a little thing like the terror of the unknown, you might as well head down a cozy gravity well and become whatever people were down there. Wind farm technicians? Organ donors? Crime scene cleaners?

She attached her own line behind Ashok's, following at a suitable distance as he pulled himself along the tether toward the wreck.

They made the journey in near silence, the only sound her own breath in her helmet. They didn't need to talk. The *White Raven* did a lot of contract security work for the Trans-Neptunian Authority: skip-tracing, investigation, fugitive recovery, chasing down smugglers. They dabbled in freight and salvage work when other jobs were lacking. She couldn't count the number of times she and Ashok had crept silently up on a ship, not exactly sure what they'd encounter when they arrived. Neither one of them had died yet, though Ashok had come close a few times. If they ever perfected mind uploads, he'd be even more reckless with his physical wellbeing: he'd doubtless jump at the chance to stop half-assing it as a cyborg and go full robot.

They reached the wreck, the dark curve of its hull smooth and cold before them, the towering spikes all over the stern looming like a misshapen forest. Ashok's voice spoke in her ear, close as a lover. (What a terrible thought. She wasn't *that* hard up for companionship. She had access to useful machines that didn't come with Ashok's cheerful obliviousness attached.) He thumped the side of the wreck with his prosthetic fist. "The hull looks intact. I'd like to get a look at that mess they've got where their nuclear propulsion system should be. I guess you want to check out the interior first, though?"

Callie had an elemental aversion to slicing holes in hulls. That skin of metal was all that divided a bubble of life and air inside from the emptiness all around outside, and she'd spent her adult life living in places where a hull breach meant panic at best and death at worst. "Janice, are we *sure* there's nobody alive on this thing?" Janice wasn't just the navigator: she also ran their comms and squeezed every bit of useful information out of the ship's sensor array.

"You can't prove a negative, captain," she said. "But if there's anyone on board, they aren't transmitting or receiving any communications, and we did everything short of knocking on the door and yelling 'Hello, anybody home?' You two could try that next. There *is* a strange set of energy signatures, so some systems might be functional. Could be life support. No way to tell from here."

Callie's executive officer Stephen, who was also the ship's doctor, joined the conversation, his voice a sedate rumble. "I've been doing some research. If the ship really has been out here since the first wave of goldilocks ships took off in the twenty-second century, the crew could still be alive, in cryosleep."

"Oh, damn. They still used cryosleep back then?" People didn't do a lot of centuries-long voyages anymore – the bridges had made such projects seem pointless, for the most part – but there were better options for human hibernation nowadays, with stasis fields and induced zero-metabolism comas. Cryosleep was a lot less reliable, from what she'd learned in history class, and could have short- and long-term neurological impacts on those who went through the process... if they could be successfully thawed out at all.

"Somebody made modifications to the ship and left it here, though," Ashok said. "The original crew, or someone else. The joyriders could still be on board. Maybe it's Liars. You know they like to tinker with things."

"Do they now? You don't say." Drake's accent was melodic, but there was a spiky edge to his tone that made Callie wince. Ashok was tactless because he was clueless, not malicious, but it took a special failure of compassion to talk about Liars that way when Janice and Drake were on the line. They'd experienced the Liar predilection for technological improvisation firsthand.

"Settle down, children," she said. "Mommy's working now."

Stephen chuckled over the comm. When it came to running the crew, Callie was the stern disciplinarian, and he was the deep well of patience. She pressed her gloved hand against the side of the ship, imagining she could feel the cold through the thick layers of fabric and insulation. "If there's someone awake on this boat, they had ample chance to announce themselves. See if you can get inside the nice way first, Ashok, but if not, slice away."

Ashok floated close to the hull, sliding both his gloved hand and his unprotected prosthetic one around the airlock until he found a panel he could pry open. Filaments sprouted from his mechanical hand, and he hummed to himself over the open comms channel as he tried to convince the ship's ancient and rudimentary control systems that he was authorized to open the door. "Ugh. This is like trying to punch soup."

Callie considered. "Punching soup would be pretty easy. Assuming it wasn't too hot. I've punched lots of things worse than soup."

"Yes, fine, but punching soup wouldn't *accomplish* much, is what I'm saying… ah. There it is. Have I told you lately that I'm a genius?"

"I'm not sure. I don't usually listen when you talk."

"I'm really sad the door opened for me. I've got a new integrated laser-torch I wanted to try out in the field. Maybe next time."

The hatch unsealed, and Ashok grabbed a recessed handle and hauled it open. Callie turned on her helmet light and looked into the airlock beyond. Ashok gasped – it was *almost* a shriek – and then coughed to cover it.

"I thought they were bodies for a second, too." Callie watched a couple of old-fashioned, bulky gray spacesuits float in the airlock, but they were empty, their helmets hovering nearby. Callie unhooked from the cable, clambered into the ship, and deftly stowed the suits out of the way in the sprung-open locker they'd probably escaped from. Ashok came in after her, and then sealed the door.

"We're inside," she told the comms.

"Your heart rate's up a bit," Stephen said. "Is the ship full of space monsters?"

"I assume so. How are Ashok's vitals? I thought he was going to faint when we saw a vacuum suit float by."

"Ha ha." Ashok peered around the dark with his multi-spectrum lenses.

"His vitals seem fine, but since he installed those hormone pumps to regulate his physiological responses, it's impossible for me to tell what's going on with him based on his suit data. He doesn't need a doctor, he needs a small engine repair shop."

Ashok was normally happy to trade banter, but he could focus when the need arose, and he was working on the control panel for the interior airlock door now. "There's pressure on the other side, cap. I'll sample the air, see if it's breathable."

"Ugh. I might leave my helmet on anyway. These little ships always smell like recycled farts."

"People on ice probably don't fart too much, but suit yourself." The airlock hissed as the pressure equalized, and after a few minutes a light above the door turned green and there was a *whoosh* of seals unfastening. After the inner door swung open Ashok entered a dim corridor, his helmet light shining on blank gray walls, and he held up a finger like someone planetside trying to feel which way the wind was blowing; there were sensors embedded in his prosthetic digits. "Hmm. A little oxygen-rich for my taste, but if we don't play with any open flames, we should be OK." He unhooked the latches on his helmet, removed it, and took a tentative breath. "Smells fine. Not as good as the spinwise gardens on Meditreme Station, but it'll do."

Callie took off her own helmet and sniffed. The air was stale, but fine. It didn't smell like death or burning, which she found reassuring. "I guess it won't kill us."

Ashok glanced at her. "Your nose is a feat of structural engineering, cap. I bet you can smell all the way out to the asteroid belt."

"That's big talk coming from a one-armed man with a computer stuck to his face." She tapped the side of her admittedly considerable nose. "This is the Machedo family pride. Signature of a noble lineage. Some say it's my best feature."

"Everything is somebody's fetish."

"Do you think making fun of your captain's nose is a good idea?"

"No, but it's no worse than my other ideas. Like poking around in ancient spaceships full of zombie space suits."

The banter and insults were a form of whistling in the dark. For Callie, every disabled, drifting, battered, or broken ship was a reminder of the fate that could await her own crew if she made the wrong decision, or ran into a situation where bad decisions were the only ones available.

Ashok took the lead, his light sweeping back and forth across the corridor to illuminate every step. He was doubtless peering around with other, more advanced senses, too, so they might get some warning if there were nasty surprises lurking. "Shall managed to find some old interior schematics for ships like this. There's only one set of living quarters, since the crew was mostly expected to be frozen, with the ship waking one of them up for a day every year or so to do a manual check of the systems. Most of the space is given over to supplies – seeds and embryos and communications equipment, tools, crude old-school fabricators. Maybe we can find a collector interested in obsolete pre-Liar technology." He stopped by a closed metal door. "The cryochamber is through here."

Callie hit the button by the door, but nothing happened, not even the whine of a mechanical failure. The ship was pulling power from somewhere, for something, but apparently not for opening doors. Ashok shrugged, then worked the fingers of his prosthetic hand into the minuscule crack where the door met the wall. He could exert a startling amount of pressure with those fingers, and the metal squealed and shrieked as it slid forcibly along its groove and disappeared into the wall. The room beyond wasn't entirely dark: a faint blue glow shone off to the left. Most of the cryopods were dark, but the instrument panel on the last one in the row was illuminated.

"Do you think they made the pods look like coffins on purpose?" Ashok took a step inside. "As a way of getting the people inside used to the idea that they were probably going to die on the trip?"

There were six pods, each roughly rectangular and big enough to hold a human, but they didn't make her think of coffins. They reminded her more of big chest freezers – which, in a way, they were. Five of the pods were open and empty, which gave her a chill right up her spine and into her backbrain. She couldn't help but imagine dead crew members, blue-skinned, frost rimed on their faces, lurching through the black corridors of the ship, eager to steal the heat of the living.

"There's someone on ice over here." Ashok stood by the last container, its glowing blue control panel casting weird shadows on his already weird face. "Most of the power on the ship has been diverted to maintaining life support and keeping this pod functional, I think."

Callie joined him and looked into the pod. There was a window over the inhabitant's face, and the glass wasn't even foggy or covered in ice, the way cryopod windows inevitably appeared in historical immersives. Artistic license. The figure inside was a petite woman with straight black hair, dressed in white coveralls. She looked like a sleeping princess (peasant garb aside), and something in Callie sparkled at the sight of her. *Uh oh*, she thought.

"Can we wake her up?" she said. Not with a kiss, of course. This wasn't a fairy tale, despite the glass casket.

Ashok shrugged. "Sure. We can try, anyway. The mechanisms all seem to be intact, and Shall says the diagnostics on the cryonic suspension system came back clean. Want me to pop the seal?"

"Let's get Stephen over here first in case she needs medical attention." Callie activated her radio. "XO, get suited up and come over. We've got a live one on ice."

Stephen groaned. He didn't like EVA. He preferred sitting in a contoured acceleration couch and listening to old music, and only showed real enthusiasm for physical activity during his religious devotions. "Isn't it bad policy for the captain *and* the executive officer to leave the ship at the same time?"

"He's right." Drake's voice was amused. "With both of you off the ship, leaving me and Janice unsupervised? We could get up to anything. The only thing keeping me from crashing us into the nearest icy planitesimal is your strong leadership. Janice, hold me back."

Callie clucked her tongue. "It's only a thousand meters, Stephen. I think we'll be OK. Ashok and I will finish checking out the ship while you come over."

Their survey didn't take long. The cargo area was a mess – the seed banks seemed fine, but the refrigeration for the more fragile biological specimens had failed. They both put their helmets back on, because the stench was bad in there. There was no sign of the missing crew members.

"What the hell happened here?" Callie floated in the dim cargo hold, scanning the walls. It looked like an ugly, irregular hole had been cut in the ceiling and subsequently patched.

"The crew went somewhere, woke up, welded a bunch of crap all over their stern, one of them got back on board, set a course for Trans-Neptunian space, and went back into hibernation." Ashok fiddled with the buttons on an ancient fabricator, meant to build machine parts on a colony world the ship had never reached. "The 'what' is pretty clear. The how and why are totally mysterious, but if we can wake up the ancient ice mummy back there, maybe she'll have some answers."

"She's more like Sleeping Beauty," Callie said. "Mummies are gross."

"Beauty, huh? You see something you like back there, cap?"

"Shut up. She's a thousand years old."

"Five hundred, tops, and she doesn't even look it."

"Shut up double." She waved him away. "See if you can get any sense out of the ship's computer, especially the navigation system, and try to find a crew manifest. It would be nice to know where this ship's been... and who our sleeping beauty is." "I'd rather see what's going on with the propulsion system. Engines are way more fun than cartography and human resources."

"You can tinker after you gather intel. Shoo. Do as you're told." She returned to the cryochamber, where Stephen had arrived and was now stooped, examining the control panel on the one active pod. "What do you think?" she said. "Is she going to survive?"

Her XO shrugged. Stephen was a big man, and his default expression was doleful, so he tended to resemble a depressed mountain. "She's frozen. We'll see what happens when we thaw her out." He activated something on the panel, and they both stood back as the cryopod rumbled, the lid sliding down and icy vapor pouring out in a condensing plume of fog.

"The system should be warming her up now." Stephen seldom sounded excited, and he was hardly vibrating with enthusiasm now, but he *did* sound interested: for him, that was the equivalent of jumping up and down with glee. "These cryogenic procedures are barbaric – they're on par with bloodletting and trepanation, medically speaking – but from what I've read, after she's returned to a reasonable temperature, her heart will be jumpstarted with electricity or adrenaline or both. Apparently the initial reaction can be quite dramatic–"

The sleeper screamed and jolted upright, clouds of vapor eddying around her. Some collection of straps and restraints around her waist and legs kept her from floating up out of the pod, but her upper body was free. She stared around, eyes wide, then reached out, grasping Callie's gloved hands in her bare ones, and pulled the captain close.

"First contact!" she shouted, loud enough to make Callie turn her head away. "We made *first contact!* I had to come back, to tell everyone, to warn you, humanity is *not alone*–" She stopped talking, her mouth snapping shut, and then her eyes rolled up and her body sagged.

Callie squeezed the woman's unresponsive hands. "Is she dead?"

Stephen floated closer, removed his gloves, and touched the woman's throat. "No, there's a pulse. The jolt that started her heart shocked her into consciousness, but it wasn't enough to keep her awake. There are a lot of drugs in her system. Some were keeping her healthy while she was in hibernation, and some are trying to bring her metabolism and other systems back up to baseline. She's going to be sluggish for a while. I'll examine her more thoroughly back on the *White Raven*, but I don't see any immediate cause for concern." He paused. "For someone born in the twenty-second century, she's doing quite well."

Callie let go of the woman's hands and pushed herself away from the pod to float near the center of the room, considering.

"So." Stephen peeled back the sleeper's lids and shone a light into her eyes. "After she wakes up, do *you* want to tell her we've known about the aliens for three hundred years, and her first contact bombshell is old news?"

Liked what you read? Good news! You can enjoy the whole Axiom series…

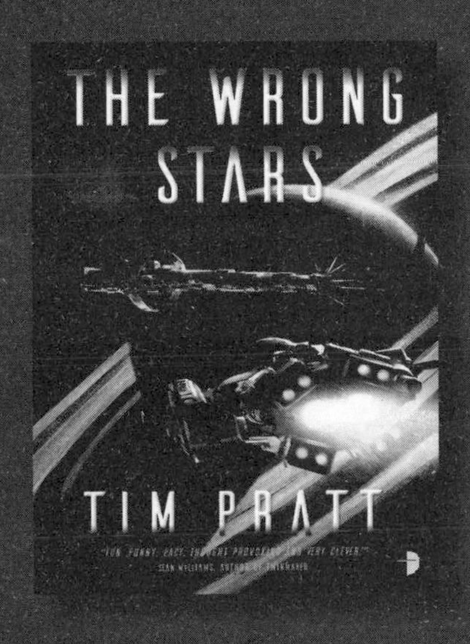

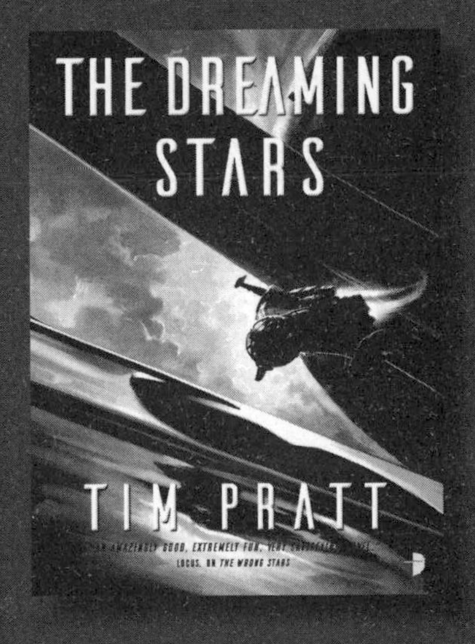

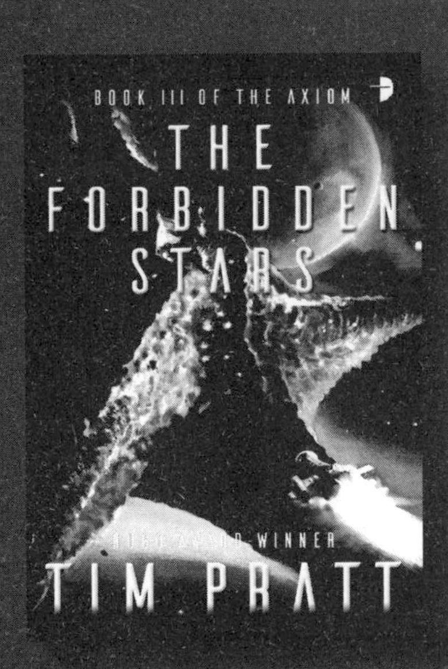

Out now from Angry Robot Books

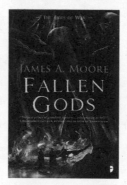

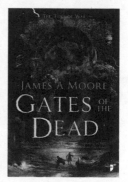

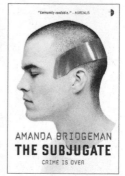

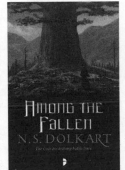

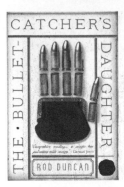

We are Angry Robot

angryrobotbooks.com

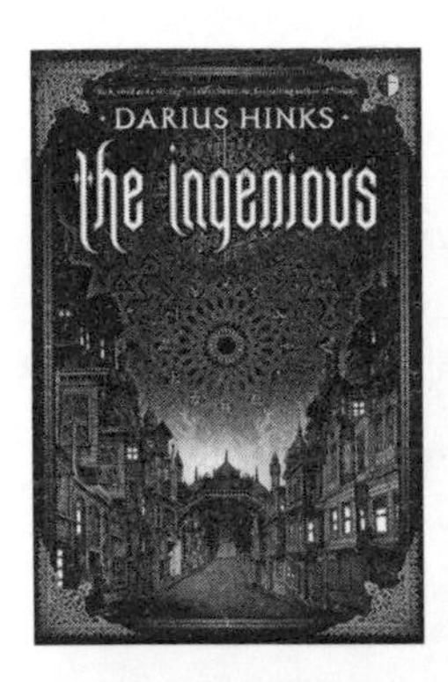
DARIUS HINKS
the ingenious

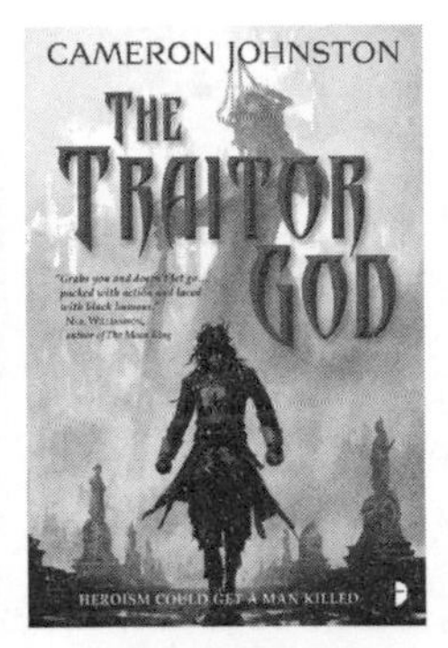
CAMERON JOHNSTON
THE TRAITOR GOD
HEROISM COULD GET A MAN KILLED

CAMERON JOHNSTON
GOD OF BROKEN THINGS

The INSTITUTE for SINGULAR ANTIQUITIES
S.A. SIDOR

The INSTITUTE for SINGULAR ANTIQUITIES
THE BEAST OF NIGHTFALL LODGE
S.A. SIDOR

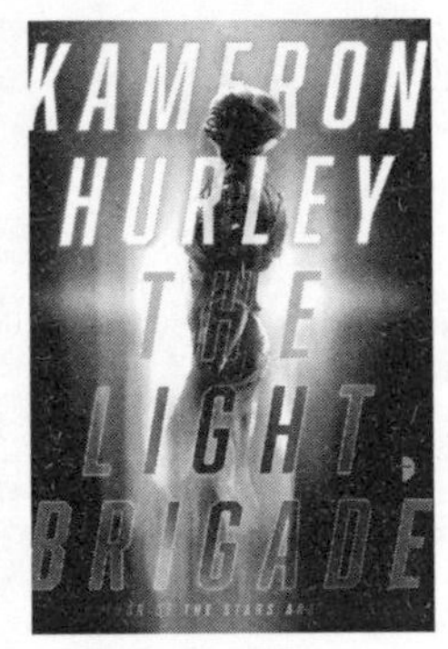
KAMERON HURLEY
THE LIGHT BRIGADE

JAINE FENN
HIDDEN SUN
SHADOWLANDS BOOK I

JAINE FENN
BROKEN SHADOW

SHADOWBLADE
ANNA KASHINA